Three

GIFTS

A Novel

AVIVA
PUBLISHING
New York

Mary Flinn

Three Gifts

©2011 by Mary Flinn

All Rights Reserved. No part of this book may be used or reproduced in any manner whatsoever without the expressed written permission of the author. The characters and events portrayed in this book are fictitious. Any similarity to real persons, living or dead, is coincidental and not intended by the author.

Address all inquiries to:

Mary Flinn

mflinn@triad.rr.com

www.TheOneNovel.com

ISBN: 978-1-935586-48-7

Library of Congress Control Number: 2011938992

Editor & Proofreader: Tyler R. Tichelaar, Ph.D.

Cover & Author Photo: Mimi Skerrett Williams

Cabin Photo: Terry Murphy

Cover Design/Interior Layout: Fusion Creative Works, www.fusioncw.com

Printed in the United States of America

For additional copies, visit: www.TheOneNovel.com

DEDICATION

For Leslie and Terry:
Without your Thin Place, this trilogy would not exist.

There is a Celtic saying that heaven and earth are only three feet apart,
but in the thin places that distance is even smaller.

ACKNOWLEDGMENTS

As a self-published author, it is difficult to spread the word about one's books. Writers like me are often caught in a catch-22 in trying to promote our work. Big bookstores won't sell our books unless they are recognized by good advance reviews in the trade magazines, followed by articles/reviews in the usual consumer media. On the other hand, the people who might provide such a service would not consider reviewing a self-published book in the first place. Still, there are many who have helped me get the word out. Thanks to Brad Jones, morning news anchor at Fox 8 News, Suzy Dubel, editor of *Guilford Woman* magazine, the High Country Writers, and Tyler Tichelaar, president of Superior Book Promotions, for helping me promote my work to the public. It's not easy being Johnny Appleseed.

And it is my readers, most of whom I have the pleasure to know, and some whom I have never met, who continue to encourage and inspire me along my way. We share a common bond in the love of the characters who have come to life in the pages of *The One*, *Second Time's a Charm*, and now in *Three Gifts*. It always makes me as sad when good books end and the characters leave us as it does when good friends suddenly move away, leaving us missing them, but hopefully, also leaving us as better people for having known them.

I wish to thank several people for their technical and expert advice in the crafting of *Three Gifts*. Thanks to Wayne Simpson, president of Wayne Simpson Architect, Inc. of Kennett Square, Pennsylvania for answering my questions about the day-to-day life of an architect, Dr. Robert Koehler of Greensboro, North Carolina for his knowledge about my medical questions, and Griffin Jones of the Guilford County Sherriff's Department for his take on being a deputy, as well as his loan of a couple of jokes for Glen to use. My husband, Mike Flinn of Summerfield, NC was helpful in providing his knowledge of the "jaws of life" operation. Thanks to Carmen Paisley for supplying Kyle and Yolanda's Spanish vocabulary!

Dick Wolfe and his staff at the Banner Elk Winery have taught me a great deal about growing grapes in the North Carolina mountains. Ken and Wendy Gordon at the Gamekeeper Restaurant between Boone and Blowing Rock are open for your business; it's well worth the drive down twisty Shulls Mill Road—just limit your alcohol consumption if you visit because you'll have to take that twisty road back! Megan Hayworth, of M.C. Adams Clothiers will also be glad to see you if you stop in her shop on King Street in Boone. If anyone reading this is considering an excellent college to attend, you cannot go wrong with Appalachian State University. Go Mountaineers!

Thanks to my family, Mike, Jessica, and Shelby, for their endless support and love; to Shelby Flinn for her author photographs, and to my niece, Kristen Flinn, for capturing on digital photography all of our precious moments at book launch parties. Mimi Skerrett Williams graciously contributed her breathtaking photography for the cover shot of *Three Gifts*, and she gave me some great photography tips while she took my latest author photo.

Friends Terry and Leslie Murphy have been so kind as to share their "A Thin Place" with all of my readers. Without their cabin and all it represents, this trilogy would not have had the spark I had in mind, when initially searching for an appropriate setting.

Thanks to my publishing coach, Patrick Snow for his knowledge and guidance. Shiloh Schroeder at Fusion Creative Works continues to awe me with her work in putting together a beautiful book. And a special thank you to my editor and proofreader, Tyler R. Tichelaar, Ph.D., who continues to teach, inspire, and advise me with his everlasting knowledge, grace, and humor, into becoming the writer that I strive to be. Living the dream never felt so good!

CONTENTS

Chapter 1

....

THE BIG DAY

....

She practically ran to her car in the garage, breathlessly anticipating the next phase of her day, the next stage in the rest of her life. "Chelsea Davenport! Is that you?" the familiar, crisp voice echoed from the parking deck at Appalachian State University. Even after two years, she recognized Anthony English's voice before she thought to turn around. She blinked in surprise as his large form loped toward her in a blue dress shirt and *tie*, his memorable pulled-back braids and coffee-colored skin accentuated by a large smile.

"Oh, my gosh, Anthony! I'm so glad to see you! How are you?" she exclaimed, eyes popping at the sight of her high school friend in a tie, feeling her feet leaving the ground momentarily as he swept her into a hug and set her gently back onto the earth. T-shirts and baggy jeans were what he always wore back then.

His large almond eyes cut away, as they did sometimes when he talked to people, still shy after all these years. "I was wondering when I'd run into you around here," he said. "I saw your mother last week and she filled me in on all the news. Have you started your new job yet?" He was noticing the leotard and skirt she wore, attire from the dance class she had just finished.

"Sort of. I've only been back in town for two weeks, living at home for the time being. I've been hanging around here for the last week, taking a class, just getting to know the faculty, and settling into my 'office,'" she said, scrunching two fingers of each hand as quotation marks.

"Huh! Wonder if your cubicle is any bigger than mine. It would have to be!" he laughed, scratching his chin. She had heard from her mother, his former high school art teacher, that he worked in the university's graphic arts department, after starring as the quarterback there all four years of his college career. He would have had a chance to go pro, if not for the back injury that revealed he had depleted spinal fluid and should never have played football in the first place. He had dodged a huge bullet, all those years, even back in high school when he had played football with Kyle.

"I don't even think I *have* a cubicle. It's just a desk next to Carmen De Silva's in the dance department office. There are three of us crammed in there now. Luckily, I won't be in there much. I'll be teaching summer school when I get back from the honeymoon," she said, unable to stop herself from smiling, raking stray strands of her long auburn hair away from her face in the warm May breeze as they stood at the garage's entrance.

"So, tomorrow's the big day for you and Kyle?" Anthony grinned again, his small teeth, a striking contrast to his full lips, always making her smile at him in return.

"Yes! You're going to be there, right?"

"Of course. I wouldn't miss it!" he said, shifting a package under his arm. "Who else from high school is coming?"

"You'll see Abby and Glen, of course. They're in the wedding party. Meredith is flying in tonight from Colorado Springs. I ran into her mother last night when I was out shopping for a few last-minute things. She's so excited. She hasn't seen Mer since Christmas."

"Mer's still writing for that magazine out there?" he asked somewhat bashfully, fingering his car keys. He'd had a huge crush on Meredith back in high school. She'd liked him too.

"Yeah, don't you guys keep up anymore?" Chelsea asked tentatively.

"Nah, not so much…" he said and looked away. Apart from their small group of friends, the small mountain community had not embraced the mixed-race couple back in their high school days, even though they were just close friends, from what Chelsea remembered.

"And Willie said he'd try to make it, but I'm not holding my breath," she said, a hint of disappointment in her voice. They'd all drifted so far apart over the years.

"Yeah, I guess it's hard, him being a celebrity and all," he said. Willie Morrison had been her dance partner in high school and had gone on to be a successful dancer in New York, as she knew he would.

"It's hard for him to have a life at all, you know? Ailey Two owns him. They have understudies, but he might not have earned that privilege just yet. I never did," she said, referring to her time dancing with the Carolina Ballet before she took the job at the University to be closer to her family, and ultimately, with Kyle Davis.

"Well, I'm glad for both of you. Plus, it will be really good to see our old friends again!"

"I know. It's great to see you again, and thank you!" she said, squeezing him on the shoulder. "So where are you headed?"

"Post office; getting ready to mail a package, and you?"

"I'm done for the day. I'm going to Kyle's to drop off my suitcase before the rehearsal tonight," she replied, feeling goose bumps rise on her arms at the thought of seeing him in just a few minutes.

"Okay, well, it was good seeing you. Tell Kyle I said hello. I'll see you both tomorrow. And break a leg, I guess!" he said, winking at her and heading across the street toward the post office.

She laughed. "Right! I'll see you tomorrow!" she called after him. He waved as she walked to her ancient Subaru; she unlocked the door with the key and settled herself behind the wheel, wrapping her colorful skirt around her legs. Starting the engine, she smiled to herself; it still purred like new after twelve years. Handed down first from her sister, Charley, to her brother, Jay, and then to her, this car had carried them all through the worst mountain weather, and then some. Living in Raleigh had been a piece of cake compared to the winters they had here.

She pulled the car into the street, waiting for a few students to scurry past in front of her while she checked her cell phone. Three-thirty was the time they'd planned to meet at Kyle's cabin, and she had exactly thirty minutes to be on time. He was always punctual. Normally on a Friday, he would still be working at the architectural firm he'd been with for a few months, but today was a special day. As her car wound around the mountain curves and switchbacks, she felt herself escaping further and further into the other world they'd made for themselves. It wasn't real, what they had. She wondered whether one day she would wake up and it would just be her life, but with Kyle, she felt surreal, suspended from the rest of the world somehow. However glad she was to be back at home and with her parents, she was so ready to be tied to this man she had loved for so many years, someone she thought she would never really have—until now.

Her car crunched up the driveway to the cabin, picturesque with its cedar log exterior and red tin roof pitched long and low over the front porch. Kyle's white Range Rover was parked in front. She climbed out of her seat and went around to the back to pull her suitcase out of the tailgate. Surely if he had heard her, he would be there, at her service. She left the suitcase at the foot of the stairs and walked up to the porch, peering through the window of the front door. No sign of Kyle. Maybe he was in the bathroom or downstairs, doing some laundry and last-minute packing, but most likely he was outside. Her sandals made little sound on the wraparound porch as she walked around to the side, following it around to the back deck that overlooked the river amidst dense green trees and birdsongs at the moment. He was there, looking out over the river, hands shoved deep into the pockets of his slacks, oblivious to any sign of her. So as not to startle him, she cleared her throat, making him turn suddenly.

His intense blue eyes lit up decidedly when he saw her; the smile she loved was building slowly across his handsome face. "Hey!" he said, obviously caught off guard. He stroked a hand across his strong jaw. "I'm sorry; I didn't hear you drive up," he said, going to her and taking her in an eager embrace, kissing her mouth gently. His light brown hair, streaked gold with sun from days outdoors on the building site, was as windblown as usual.

"You looked deep in thought. Is everything okay? You're not getting cold feet, are you?"

"No way," he whispered, characteristically, into her hair. "No, things are more than okay. It's just…ever since I've been back here, staying here alone, it's like I'm somehow reconnecting with my father. It's like he's…I don't know, *here*!"

The chill bumps rose again on her arms and she thought about it for a moment. His father had taken his own life here in this place seven years ago. After that tragic and unsettling experience, his mother had sold the cabin, and unbeknownst to Kyle, had invested the money from that property over the years, along with other funds, to help him buy into an architectural business and get on his feet when the time was right. Two years after college, Kyle had come back, found the owners, and convinced them to sell it back to him. Chelsea had often wondered how he really felt about being back here, dealing with those memories and the accompanying emotions. She had watched the feelings he kept about his father evolve over the years. The feelings of anger, doubt, and abandonment would come

15

pouring forth at times. There had been so many years that he had been angry with his father, even though she knew he loved him and missed him. She recognized his need for support and reassurance.

"Well, maybe it's his way of giving you his blessing. This *is* the day before you get married, and all."

He nodded, taking her hands in his and threading his fingers between hers. "Yeah, I kind of thought that too. If he's here at all, he's got to know how much I love you. Love is everything," he said quietly, looking into her eyes with the familiar smolder that sent her head swimming at any given moment, adding to the surreal feeling that had built up on the drive over.

"Yes, it is. And maybe your father wants you to know that he loves you, too," she said, more certainly than she felt.

"*Chelsea*...I love you more than I love God," he said, softly but intensely, shocking her. There had been a time when that statement coming from him wouldn't have meant much. He'd been mad at God, too. But after they had met and fallen in love, he had been grateful to God for sending her his way. He had called her his angel, and in a way, she almost believed it herself.

Still, she gasped at the heresy he'd let loose from his lips. He looked genuinely worried. She searched his eyes, trying to find the right words to put him at ease. His grip tightened on her hands.

"I know it's wrong to say that," he said seriously but then lightened the mood. "I'll probably get struck by lightning. You should probably stand away. But it's the way I feel," he said, the brief smile from his attempt at humor disappearing, his eyes narrowing in his sincerity.

She had to laugh and then apologized. "I'm sorry. Maybe it's the same thing. Maybe you love me the *same way* you love God."

"Not possible," he said, eyes full of desire flicking over her, and pulling her close again.

"Well, for me, it's the same thing, the way I feel. I love you *as much* as I love God. It's all one and the same. Like the Trinity, without…something else, I don't know quite what. But it's the same intensity of feelings."

He looked deeper into her eyes. "I just feel like finally, we deserve this. I *deserve* you. I always just thought I was really lucky, but now, it's different. I feel as if it's okay for me to be happy, that God wants me to have you. This is the way it's supposed to be…for both of us."

She blinked back hot tears, hearing these words from him, after all the years of self-effacement, doubt, and humility she'd seen from him. He wiped a tear from her cheek with his thumb.

"I think we just got married!" she whispered, melting into his arms.

Chelsea was flushed and overwhelmed on the day of her wedding. After a soaking morning rain, the weather had cleared into a balmy spring day, the breeze buffeting new blossoms around, stirring a kind of hope in her heart. So many people were in town. Their relatives and friends were all there for the occasion. Sleep did not come easily due to her excitement the night before in the violet bedroom of her family's farmhouse, the cool night air through the open window wafting over her comfortingly. Even for a dancer, she did not relish being the center of attention. As a dancer, it was different. It was art. She was someone else when she took the stage, but today she was Chelsea Davenport, vowing to be with Kyle forever, in front of them all.

A crowd was on hand for the event. Charley, her older sister, was finally here from Wilmington with her husband Steve and little Kitty, named for their grandmother, who had been Chelsea's favorite person in the whole world. Jay and Lauren and their two boys, Thomas, named after their father, and little Ethan would be there, along with her Aunt Becky and Uncle Wayne and her college-aged cousins, Bri and Brett. Kyle's mother, Shelly, her sister Stacie, and Stacie's husband Tyson with their daughter, Abigail, had arrived from the Outer Banks the previous day as well. Kyle's grandparents from Charlotte and her grandmother on her mother's side were also in town for the event. It all made for a full house—and a dry mouth at the thought of so many eyes focused on her every move. She could only hope that she wouldn't mess up her vows or fall down, or that it wouldn't pour down rain again as they were to make the brief walk from the library to the sanctuary for the ceremony.

She recalled Charley's wedding in the same church just six years earlier when she had done a lousy job of being the maid of honor. Chelsea had been so much more interested in Kyle than in the wedding, or paying attention to Charley on her special day. Now it was her turn, and Charley had shown her up badly already. Charley had kept her on track with all the plans, helping her choose the dresses, the flowers, the invitations, the cake, and had even thrown her a lingerie shower at Easter when people were in town and she could get away from the company. It was fortunate that so much of the planning could be done via email and on the Internet, and they had pulled it off in five months to the amazement and relief of their mother, Liz.

The rehearsal the night before had gone off without a hitch and Kyle's friends had taken him out for a night on the town, a baseball game, and bar-hopping, which had been event-free, as far as she knew. So there was nothing to worry about, except how to stop worrying. The bridesmaid brunch had been held earlier at the lovely Mast Farm Inn nearby, where her best friend, Abby, worked. Feeling the day whiz by, Chelsea was presently struggling to relax, seated in a chair in her bedroom, her hair under the competent hands of her sister. Abby was up next, and they chatted companionably as Charley turned strands of her hair around and around on the hot curling wand. Chelsea focused on her breathing and the conversation, concentrating on the comforting violet wallpaper, faded from generations ago.

"You are going to look absolutely *stunning!*" Charley exclaimed as she examined her work thus far. "Your hair has gotten so long. We're going to have a gorgeous cascade of curls when I get through with you!" She smiled calmly at Chelsea in the mirror, as Chelsea exhaled slowly and deliberately, avoiding hyperventilation.

"Ah! And I can't wait to see you in that dress!" moaned Abby, who had been with them when they had chosen the narrow ivory lace gown with the flared train and twisted strapless bodice with a scallop of lace at the center. Abby held up one of her pearl drop earrings at Chelsea's earlobe, *something borrowed*, studying the effect with the hairstyle. "You're going to look very sophisticated. And the guys in those black tuxes are going to be *so hot!*" she said, making them laugh.

"Really! Chelsea, you never told me how hot Tyson is!" exclaimed Charley, who had met Tyson, Stacie's husband, just the night before.

"Mmm, I guess he is," murmured Chelsea, and Abby wholeheartedly agreed. Ten years younger than the beautiful Stacie, he was indeed a hot number with his dark curly hair and quiet persona. He would stand up for Kyle today as his best man. That particular couple was about as pretty as two people could ever get. Most of the time, however, Chelsea forgot their good looks, appreciating more the inner beauty of them both, and the support they'd given Kyle over the years. It was odd the way those three had formed a bond, considering the difference in all of their ages. But her grandmother had taught her what little difference age makes concerning matters of the heart.

"We're all going to look pretty good," Charley murmured, wrapping more hair around the curling iron.

Chelsea breathed out again, glancing at the sea of deep pink dresses hanging on the back of the door, imagining the girls with their bouquets of stargazer lilies. It promised to be a beautiful ceremony. Her sister-in-law, Lauren, would sing and a harpist would be in the little sanctuary that would be filled to the gills. They had decided to have the reception at the Country Club just in case of bad weather. Charley's wedding reception had been here, in the backyard garden of the farmhouse, which had been lovely, but without Kitty there anymore, it wouldn't be the same. The land on which the development and the adjoining golf course sat used to belong to the Davenport family. Kyle's father had built the clubhouse and her father had done the landscaping so many years ago when they were a team. It seemed right to hold their celebration there.

"There! Now let's fasten these orchids in place and you're good to go," said Charley, reaching for three creamy flowers and pinning them around the right side of the cascade of curls she'd fashioned.

"Oh, sweetheart, that looks lovely!" cried Liz, as she peeked through the bedroom door. She smiled radiantly at both of her daughters and then winked at Chelsea. "Kyle is just going to *fall over* when he sees you!"

"I, for one, will be watching for his reaction!" grinned Abby, who had valiantly done her best to keep the two of them together during more turbulent times in the college years of their relationship. She and Glen had never wavered in their commitment to each other, but Kyle had waited patiently to see whether Chelsea would fall for the guy who was smitten with her at the University of North Carolina School of the Arts. Kyle had never had anything to worry about from Chelsea's end of the relationship, but he had waited and kept her at a distance, just to see what would happen. As much as his withdrawal had scared her and hurt her at the time, Chelsea had forgotten all of that now. After reuniting at Abby and Glen's wedding, they'd tried to stay committed to one another, but the long distance relationship they'd had after college had made it difficult. After a couple of lonely years spent following her passion, performing in a professional ballet company, Kyle had swept her off her feet at Christmas, surprising her with Kitty's engagement ring that had been left to her in Kitty's will. Tom and Liz had kept the ring in hopes that Kyle would eventually come to them to ask for their daughter's hand in marriage. He finally did, proposing to her two nights before Christmas during a snowstorm at the cabin. It had only been then that the future she really wanted had fallen into place. Following her heart had made for a long journey.

Abby sat in the hair chair next while Chelsea worked on her makeup in a different mirror as they chatted. Liz had disappeared to make her own preparations and to see about her mother while Charley styled Abby's silky dark hair into a large, loose bun at the nape of her neck.

"Charley, how long did you and Steve have to try for Kitty?" Abby asked. Abby had talked more and more about wanting to have a baby, realizing now that getting pregnant probably wouldn't happen on the first try, the way they'd all feared at some point in their youth.

"Well," Charley began, a faraway look in her eyes, recalling how it had happened for them. "I guess by the time we were really serious about it, it probably took us about six months. Are you and Glen ready to start trying?"

"We haven't been trying to stop it. We've been trying for a while," she said, her voice trailing off. They'd been married for over two years. Like so many hometown girls Chelsea knew, having a family quickly was the way things were done in Abby's view, a position Chelsea quietly did not share.

"I'm sure it will happen when the time is right," Charley smiled at her, tucking a last pin in place, and reaching for pink orchids for Abby's hair.

"All right, where *is* that flower girl?" Charley called out, causing four year-old Kitty to giggle as she ran into the room.

"Ready for me, Mama?" she giggled again while Abby lifted her into the chair.

"Okay, Pumpkin, you're going to have to hold really still! This curling iron is *very hot* and it will burn you if it touches your skin. I don't want you getting hurt."

Kitty's eyes grew wide and she nodded, placing her hands in her lap as her mother began winding her already curly dark hair around the wand. If there were ever the spitting image of Steve Jamieson, with his Cheshire Cat grin and black button eyes, it was indeed Kitty. "Do I get hairspray?" she asked eagerly, smiling his contagious smile.

"Yes," said Charley. "You'll have to close your eyes for that. And then it will be time for me to do my hair and then I guess we're heading to the church!"

Chelsea's heart thumped loudly in her chest at the thought of heading to the church, as she slid rosy lip gloss over her full lips.

"You look like a *princess*, Aunt Chelsea," said Kitty, black button eyes wide with wonder.

"Oh, thank you, Kitty! So do you! You could be the bride yourself!" Chelsea said, making her grin again.

"Can I have lip gloss too, Mama?"

"After you put on your dress at the church, you can. Right before you take us down the aisle."

"I get to go *first!*" Kitty told Abby proudly.

"Oh, I want a *girl!*" said Abby decisively. "We'd have so much fun!"

After kisses and hugs, the grandmothers were escorted down the aisle as Lauren's voice resonated sweetly with the harp throughout the small stone sanctuary. Then Liz, wearing deep rose, and Shelly, dressed in periwinkle, embraced Chelsea as well and waited for their escorts. Liz winked at Tom, handing Chelsea one of Kitty's handkerchiefs, embroidered with little blue forget-me-nots, before she went down the aisle on Jay's arm. *Something blue.* Charley held little Kitty's hand as a safeguard to keep her in the starting gate until the time was right. She did indeed look like a little princess in her ivory dress with the deep pink sash that matched the others' dresses. Chelsea stood beside her towering father, who was doing his best to entertain her and calm her nerves before they went in. Tom held up her hand and gazed down at her ring. He was so handsome in the black tux, his hair an equal mix of blonde and silver to match his mustache.

"Your hand is going to look different in a few minutes!" he said, referring to his mother's ring that had been passed down through the Davenport family for generations. *Something old.*

She smiled and nodded. "Dad, why didn't Kitty leave this ring for Jay? Shouldn't it have gone to the oldest Davenport boy upon his engagement?"

He pursed his lips, thinking about his answer. "Well, Mama knew you loved this ring, and she knew you loved the house, and the story about your great-great-great-aunt etching her initial in the window. She wanted you to have it. I guess she always imagined you'd be the lady of her house one day. She wasn't one to stay inside the box, you know. I think she made the right call, don't you?"

Chelsea nodded again. "I miss her so much," she said, "and Granddaddy."

"They're right here," Tom said to her, covering his heart with the palm of his free hand.

She made the same gesture, smiling back at him, suddenly looking away. He hugged her shoulders.

"You look gorgeous right now!" he whispered to her and she thought he might start crying along with her. "Kitty would be as proud of you as Mom and I are. You and Kyle are going to have a great life!" he said and kissed her on the forehead. As if to calm herself, she inhaled deeply of her bouquet of white lilies, more remembrances of her grandmother, and set her shoulders for the walk down the aisle.

Just then, a dark imposing figure appeared to her right as they stood lined up to go into the church. It was Willie! He looked dashing in a dark suit, his shirt open at the collar with a striped tie knotted loosely at the neck. He still had the multitudes of little braids on his head, but his face was stronger and more mature. Like the famous dancer he was becoming, he carried himself with an air of self-assurance, tightening his tie as he went directly to Chelsea, taking her hand, grinning, exposing the endearing gap in his front teeth. Beads of perspiration glistened on his forehead; he had booked it to get here.

"Girl, get out! You look *amazing*!"

"Oh, Willie, you made it! I can't believe you're here! How did you get away?" she asked hugging him around the neck.

"I pulled a string or two. I got on the first flight out this morning, and I'm leaving on the first flight out tomorrow.…It could be *me*, you know!" Willie said with a twinkle in his eye.

"Oh, don't tell me this *now*!" she said, feigning disappointment and swatting his chest. Her father and the bridesmaids laughed with her.

He looked shocked, saying, "You mean there was a chance? I would have been back sooner!"

Daisy Frazier touched him on the arm, advising him to find a seat quickly as the music changed. Daisy had been Kitty's lifelong friend and had directed most of the weddings in this church for as long as Chelsea could remember. Willie winked at her and walked elegantly into the sanctuary, slipping in beside Anthony and Meredith, who both greeted him enthusiastically.

Lovely harp music, Pachelbel's Canon in D began as Chelsea's heartbeat pumped in double time along with it. Charley, Bri, Abby, and she exchanged nervous smiles as they waited for Daisy to motion Kitty toward the aisle with her little basket of pink rose petals. Chelsea craned her neck to get a glimpse of Kyle, but she could not see around the pink dresses in front of her. She could tell that Kitty was doing a fine job of scattering rose petals along the aisle, veering this way and that as the onlookers tittered gently. The smell and swoosh of fine fabrics made her head spin as the wedding party positioned themselves, poised for the sanctuary door. Her palm felt moist on the warm sleeve of her father's arm. The other girls took deep breaths, preparing to go down the aisle, Daisy motioning to each of them in turn. She was at once severe but delicate in her purple dress and string of old pearls, as if a small gust of wind could knock her over at any given moment. She stood at the church entrance, blocking the view of the altar, as yet another picture was snapped of Chelsea and Tom while they stood waiting. Daisy motioned to them as the two of them stepped forward, watching Charley place a single pink rose on the seat that would have been for Kitty, then whisk around to the left of the altar. The music changed, transitioning to a contemporary song, "Hallelujah," one of Chelsea's favorites, ethereal-sounding, playing on the harp. People seemed confused at first and quietly awed by the unique music, but then they followed her mother's lead as she stood at the front pew of the church. They heard a rustle of clothing and feet as people stood up for them, making it that much harder for Chelsea to see inside. She stepped into the aisle with Tom as he looked at her one last time, patting her hand on his arm. "Ready, Sweet Pea?" he asked and she nodded, trembling slightly, inhaling her flowers once again. She saw the lovely altar flowers, and Father Michael, beaming, front and center at them. Chelsea wanted to remember all of this, the lilies and roses, the music, the faces of her friends, extraordinary in their finery, after listening to Stacie explain how she'd been so absorbed in Tyson's face on the day of their wedding that she never took in the details. She looked to the right and then she saw Kyle. Her heart stopped.

Kyle looked up after Charley had taken her place at the left side of the altar, in front of the other bridesmaids and cute little Kitty, with whom he'd been swapping funny faces to entertain her while she waited nervously for the rest of it to happen. Finally, that purple dress was out of the doorway and he could see! And there she came, the woman of his dreams, the woman who at this moment was the most gorgeous creature on the face of the earth. Damn! Did he say it out loud? He wasn't sure. He looked at her and gulped audibly. He cut his eyes to Tyson. "I know. Steady, dude," he heard Tyson chuckle discreetly. Shelly, Stacie, and his grandparents were grinning at his reaction, but the rest of the crowd had their eyes on Chelsea. He was definitely about to lose his balance just at the sight of his angel floating down the aisle to him. She was the one who had saved him. She was the only one who knew him, inviting him into a place in her soul where he was able to find his. She was the one who had waited patiently over and over for him to open himself up to her and fall deeply into her heart. She was the one who had given herself completely and without reservation to him forever. And he was the one she had chosen. He had never thought he deserved her, or deserved this much happiness until now. Whatever he had done, whatever lucky star he had wished upon, she was going to be his. This moment was really happening, and she was suddenly in front of him, smiling that serene smile only at him. But today her smile was so flushed with anticipation and joy that he could not help but return it the same way. This was so right! After the harp music concluded, Father Michael began greeting the dearly beloved who had gathered with them for this incredible thing they were about to do. That was what she was, *his beloved*!

Kyle felt his entire body shiver as Chelsea approached him, her hand laid across Tom's arm. She smiled at him again, as if to calm him, as if she understood exactly what he felt. He riveted his eyes to hers in an attempt to steady himself. Her father kissed her cheek and passed her hand to Kyle's and he closed his eyes briefly, absorbing the moment. Unknowingly, she left him thunderstruck at so many inopportune times, this being one of them. He prayed that he would not keel over right now, embarrassing her. He took her hand, aware that his was shaking, and damp. He rubbed his thumb along the back of her hand as Father Michael began describing the importance of the bonds of holy matrimony between a man and a woman. How could she look so focused? It was as if she were trying to remember every detail, looking at him and then to the others, smiling at their expressions. But all he could do at the moment was to try to hold himself up and look conscious…and remember to breathe. His beloved was looking at him again. He had been asked a question.

"I will," he said a bit loudly and the onlookers twittered again. She gave the same answer to the same question. Then Father Michael made them turn around to take a look at everyone who was there, everyone who would support them in their covenant with each other from this day forward. They were not in this alone. But it wouldn't matter to him if they were the only people on the planet. Right now, all that mattered was making her his wife and making her happy forever. He could do that. He wanted to be that man for her. He had to talk again, to repeat the vows. She held his hand as he stroked hers fervently, and she encouraged him with her eyes and her smile, as he tried to take in her lacey, sophisticated dress, her hair, and her flowers, all the details upon which she'd been so focused in the last few months, but all he cared about was seeing her face and wanting to give himself to her completely. He repeated the vows without error somehow. She repeated her vows, entrancing him by the sound of her voice, declaring these promises to him, for better or worse, in sickness and in health. This was everything. She would be his helper for the rest of their lives. God, he needed her! There was no separating them now, or ever again. The idea of their marriage lifted him as if a wave had surged under them. He had waited so long to be happy. A sense of calm overtook him. There were prayers and candle lighting, and then Father Michael was asking for the rings. He looked at Tyson, who patted his pockets, and then looked at Jay. Jay, looking like a deer in headlights, patted his pockets, shrugged and looked at Glen, as Kyle's heart pounded in his chest. Shit.

They were goofing on him! Glen patted himself all over, finally producing the ring, and passing it forward to Kyle, as the onlookers laughed loudly. Hilarious. He would address this later. So much for feeling calm!

After exchanging the rings, they sat down, waiting for the communion to begin. Lauren and another young man sang "The Prayer" so poignantly it gave him chills. Chelsea and he glanced at each other and sat close, holding hands, as their guests took their bread and wine. Everyone smiled at them and some made encouraging gestures as they went by on their return to the pews in the small stone church.

He watched her expressions, imagining her going to church there when she was younger, and wondering whether they would continue to sit in this pew together on Sundays, wondering whether it was proper to hold hands and touch as they were. His family had not been churchgoers much, other than Christmas and Easter. Chelsea had called them "C and E's." He did remember those unbearable childhood days of Sunday school in hot and uncomfortable clothing. Now in the sanctuary, he could not sit beside her without touching her. She smelled amazing and his thoughts raced ahead to the time when they would be alone together later, forcing him to concentrate on other things to eliminate those inappropriate thoughts for now. He glanced the other way, at Tyson, sleek and sharp-looking in his matching black tux with his dark curly hair fingered in place…the diversion was working. He felt calm again. He looked around at his mother and his friend, strawberry-haired Mark, her new guy, in the pew behind them, and then at his beautiful aunt, Stacie, and six year old Abigail behind them. And then he fell back into the spell of Chelsea's gaze as she smiled radiantly at him, sending a flame through him again. He felt his eyes sear into hers, grounding him once more.

They stood back up at the altar where Father Michael pronounced them husband and wife, and Kyle finally circled his arm around her waist and kissed her, twice. There was much applause as they smiled at each other and made their way back down the aisle as man and wife. *She was his wife!*

⚜

There were so many pictures! Chelsea found it easy to smile, and in fact, she could not stop smiling, knowing that they were finally married. They held hands through all the photography with the different family members and members of the wedding party. Finally, they headed to the country club for the reception and Chelsea was able to be alone with her new husband. She said, "My husband," over and over to herself, liking the sound of it. He helped her into the passenger seat of the Range Rover, which looked freshly waxed and vacuumed for the occasion. She took his face in her hands, immersing herself in his blue eyes, and they laughed together. "I can't believe this!" she said excitedly into his mouth, kissing him.

"I know! We're married!" he laughed, returning the kiss, squeezing her hand before darting around to his side and climbing in.

"Hi, I'm *Chelsea Davis!*" she practiced on him delightedly and they laughed again.

"I'd like you to meet my *wife*, Chelsea Davis," he tried out the words, one-upping her. They were at the club house in no time where the crowd was trickling in ahead of them. Abby and Glen, in their finery, stopped to wait for them and walk in together.

"Ready for the dance?" Glen queried, clapping a hand on Kyle's massive shoulder, referring to the first dance Chelsea and Kyle had been rehearsing. "What is it, huh, the tango?"

"Hardly! It's a waltz," Chelsea corrected him.

"Don't laugh, okay? I'm giving it my best shot," Kyle replied in his usual self-effacing way. Chelsea smiled at him. Dancing was something he enjoyed but was not nearly as comfortable doing as she. She knew he wanted to perform up to her standards, and she had taught him well, she thought.

"Leave him alone!" Abby said, narrowing her large doe's eyes and smacking Glen on the arm. They were so like Fred and Ethel, still, Chelsea thought with a laugh. "It's going to be sooo sexy!" Abby continued. "You both look really great, by the way. That was a beautiful ceremony."

"That's because we were in it!" said Glen.

"Yeah, and that was some show you put on looking for the ring!" Kyle retorted, giving Glen a smack of his own.

"You gotta love it!" Glen said shrugging, the constant look of mischief in his eyes.

"I've *never* seen Kyle smile this much!" Abby said into Chelsea's ear as the men held the door for them.

It was a heady feeling, entering the large candlelit room filled with people. Some were people Chelsea scarcely recognized; others, friends she was glad to see. She and Kyle clung to each other, reluctant to be separated; after all, it was their evening. Introductions were made by their parents, and then by them to their parents, of friends from college or work. Kyle played at re-introducing Chelsea to Mark Hargett, a solid and flushed, friendly-looking man with blonde eyelashes, who had been dating his mother over the past couple of years and seemed to be quite taken with her. Chelsea had actually met Mark the night before at the rehearsal, but this was fun for all of them.

"Mark, I'd like you to meet my *wife*, Chelsea!" he said, grinning and winking at her.

"*Mrs. Davis*, it's truly my pleasure!" he said with a warm smile and a handshake, playing along happily with their new fun.

"Hello again, Mark!" she laughed, still enjoying her new title. "I still want to hear your version of that mission trip in Costa Rica."

"Well, this guy can swing a hammer! He never, *ever* got tired! He made the rest of us look like old farts." Shelly joined them, congratulating them and giving Chelsea a hug and a kiss on the cheek, smiling happily at her son, squeezing his arm.

In Costa Rica, the men had spent a week out of the summer after Kyle graduated from college, helping to build a hospital wing, before he had begun his job at an architectural firm in Alexandria, Virginia. It was a church mission, associated with the church on the Outer Banks, where Tyson and Stacie had married. After their wedding, Shelly and Kyle had gone there a few times, and he had been invited to go on the trip when they discovered he was an architect and could build. Mark, the owner of a local sporting goods store, had been a member of that church and had forged a friendship with Kyle on the trip. He had met Shelly when the group departed, asking Kyle all kinds of questions about her on the trip. Encouraging Kyle to bring her along to a reunion dinner, he reconnected with Shelly, and the two had been an item ever since.

After dinner, the toasts began. Kyle glanced at Chelsea and took her hand under the table as Tom stood first. He extended his hand to Liz, who nodded at him as he smiled at Chelsea, and then at Kyle. "Where to start with you two?" he began, his voice breaking, causing him to pause and look around. Stroking his silver mustache thoughtfully, he took his glass and continued. "When the two of you met again on the terrace of our farmhouse all those years ago, it was like fireworks going off between you. We both saw it. Shelly saw it. You were in love before you knew it yourselves. Kyle, you had a lot to deal with, but the two of you found a way to get above it and find the best of life there is in the process—each other. You're both such driven people, and you've wanted everything life has to offer, and unbelievably, you've found the right balance. You're both a blessing to this family. Kyle, you've made Chelsea so happy. With the work you've chosen, your dad would be so proud of you! Liz and I welcome you into our family. You've already been a part of it for us, but now it's official. Welcome, son!" he said, and raised his glass. "To Chelsea and

Kyle!" Chelsea wiped a tear from her eye and Kyle blinked as well as they touched their champagne flutes together. He rubbed her hand again and leaned over to kiss her tenderly.

Shelly stood up next, perfect and poised in her diamonds and periwinkle silk, collecting herself and sniffing, giving Liz and Tom a wink. She held her glass, took a deep breath, and looked directly at Kyle as if seeing him for the first time. "You combed your hair!" she laughed good-naturedly and glanced at him with a twinkle in her eye. Others joined her laughter. Then she continued. "My son," she began, her voice thick with emotion as Chelsea watched Kyle look away; she knew his eyes were welling with unwanted tears. *The only one left*, Chelsea imagined her thinking. Shelly continued, "There was a time when you didn't like me. You didn't smile. You didn't talk to me. I thought I'd lost you forever. And then you met this precious young woman beside you today—who changed your life. And now you smile all the time! I'm so grateful to you, Chelsea, for giving me back my son! We're a family again, the two of you, me, Stacie, Tyson, and Abigail, and Mom and Dad. I feel so blessed to have all of you in my life," she said, Chelsea watching her glance at Mark. "And it's largely due to you, Chelsea. You saved us. You deserve to be in this family and we're all glad you're a part of it. Here's to Kyle and Chelsea!" she exclaimed, beaming at them and raising her glass to the "Cheers!" of the other guests.

Tears rolled down Chelsea's face as Kyle swiped at the space under his eye as well. They laughed, as she wiped her eyes openly, wondering how much more they could take. It was Charley's turn next, and Chelsea hoped her toast would be less intense. Charley grinned at her sister. She tossed her mahogany hair, smiling, and lifted her eyebrows playfully at her. "Okay, guys! We're going to lighten this up! Chelsea…you *apologized* to me today for not being a good maid of honor at my wedding! That could not be further from the truth. You were an excellent maid of honor…even though you couldn't keep your eyes off *Kyle*! Can any of you ladies *blame* her?" she laughed and the women in the large room joined her. "I guess I was a little slower to see how you guys connected because I wasn't really around much, but when I did, I knew Kyle was the love of your life. It was like you grew up over night. You loved him so much you considered him first in everything you did. I've seen how happy you are when you're together, and how lost you felt when you were so far apart. I'm so happy it's worked out for the two of you. Welcome to our family, bro!" she laughed and raised her glass with them.

They smiled at each other and sighed, relieved at her sense of humor. Then Tyson rose, adjusting his tux jacket and reaching for his glass as Kyle settled back and breathed deeply, making wary eye contact with his friend. Tyson smiled at him, reassuringly, lifting his glass just slightly. "Don't worry, dude; I'm not gonna make you cry," he said smiling, deep dimples appearing on either side of his suntanned face. His eyes met Chelsea's and then settled on Kyle's. "Man, when I first met you at seventeen, you reminded me so much of myself. You were going through a lot of the same stuff I went through, and you reacted the same way I did. Thank God you had Chelsea to get your head out of that dark hole you were in. Stacie and I couldn't pull you out of it. But she did. She's always been the one for you. I watched you pull yourself together, stand up, and take charge of your life. You became the master of your own destiny, which was something I was still just playing at. And I was thirty years old. You made me get off my butt and do it too. If I hadn't met you, I probably wouldn't have had the guts to go after this beautiful woman I can proudly call my wife," he said, smiling again and gesturing elegantly with his glass to Stacie beside him, stunning in her silky sapphire dress, blonde hair turned into an elegant chignon. She smiled serenely back at him. "You know all about how to love someone selflessly and completely. That's what it will take for the two of you to be happy and to make it work. You're already doing it, and inspiring the rest of us. Chelsea, welcome to the family! To Kyle and Chelsea!"

Kyle relaxed again, but only for a moment, realizing that the dancing was yet to come. He took a deep breath and thought through the music, the moves they had practiced in the dance studio under the direction of Carmen De Silva, Chelsea's new colleague and mentor in the dance department at the university. She was there, of course, and it made him nervous to know his new skills would be judged. He watched Chelsea, chatting happily with her mother and Father Michael at the table to her left. She seemed so relaxed, and he was glad. He was sure she was not dreading the dance to come. Looking around, she caught his eye and he felt his eyes lock onto hers, needing her attention and assurance. As always, she knew what he was thinking, reaching out to touch his face. He kissed the palm of her hand. The DJ was calling them to the dance floor as the photographer moved into position. Kyle drew in a breath, raised his eyebrows a notch, and she laughed, patting his arm.

"You're going to be *great!*" she murmured cheerfully in his ear, helping him calm down. They walked to the center of the spotlight and the music started. Slow, sultry Latin guitar music began and Bryan Adams' raspy voice was asking, "*Have you ever really loved a woman?*" Kyle took her in his arms, mindful of the carriage of his shoulders and arms. She fit perfectly in place as they moved their hips in synchrony to the music, to the *oohs* and *aahs* of the crowd. It was suddenly as if they were alone, swirling across the floor together. She held him together with her eyes, never looking away, always touching him with purpose, sensually, the movement between them becoming one liquid piece of art. He remembered what she'd told him when they started: "*Dance is love in motion.*" It was a song they had adopted in college after they had become lovers, realizing what they had been missing from one another. The words said it all: "*when you see your unborn children in her eyes.*" He twirled her and dipped her so easily, as if she were a dream in his arms. How lucky he was to have this experience with her, an artist in her own element. She was flawless, making it look effortless, making him look good. The dance was over, but surprisingly, he didn't want it to end. He took her in his arms, kissing her longingly to more sighs of approval and applause from the onlookers. She smiled at him and they took a brief bow before she joined her father on the dance floor for an easy spin to Louis Armstrong's version of "What a Wonderful World."

At eleven-thirty that evening, Kyle pulled into the driveway of his grandparents' empty home in Charlotte as they had arranged. In the morning, a taxi would whisk them to the airport for their flight to Punta Cana in the Dominican Republic. They could leave their car in the garage and have the house to themselves for their honeymoon night. It would be nicer than any hotel they could afford, certainly. They had spent the two-hour trip there talking incessantly about all the details of their wedding so they would remember it all. Suddenly, as he pulled their suitcases out of the tailgate of the Range Rover, he felt exhausted—not a good thing for the impending evening he had imagined with her. He looked at her and smiled, knowing he would soon get his second wind. He lifted her effortlessly and carried her across the threshold—into his grandmother's kitchen. "Really romantic, I know," he quipped as they looked around at the red roosters everywhere, and Elaine Edmonds' red gardening crocs at their feet. "The Tiffany box room is better. I'll carry you across that threshold too," he laughed, setting her down gently.

"What's the Tiffany box room?" she asked curiously.

"It's Stacie's old room, actually. When Tyson proposed to her, he gave her a Tiffany ring so my mother and Gran redecorated Stacie's bedroom in an aqua and white color scheme—you know, like the box?" he said, rolling his eyes as if it would be of little interest to her. "I was told to make sure you knew all this," he added.

"Awe! That is so sweet! What a nice thing for them to do!" she crooned.

His mood improved with her enthusiasm as he spotted a glass covered dish with Danishes, plates and cloth napkins set out for their breakfast, complete with a note about fruit in the fridge and how to activate the coffeemaker. "Well, tonight it's the *honeymoon suite*," he said, smiling at her again, bringing their bags in behind them. "Hang on just a minute and I'll be right back."

"No problem," she said, placing their care package of appetizers and wedding cake into the refrigerator. She took the moment to go to the powder room as he carried the bags upstairs in the spacious and elegant house. He remembered her awed reaction when she had first visited him at Dr. Dan and Elaine's on a Christmas break in college when he'd met her there from his home in Southern Shores on the Outer Banks.

After he had deposited their luggage, used the bathroom, and lit a couple of candles, he met her at the foot of the steps. She looked expectantly up at him in the lamplight, with eyes shining, melting him instantly. He went to her and took her hand, leading her up the stairs, sweeping her up in his arms and carrying her through the doorway of the beautiful room, lit only by the candles that had been left for them. He set her lightly on the floor in front of him and immediately embraced her, taking her face in his hands, sliding his fingers into her hair, kissing her passionately. Finally, they were able to be themselves and let their guard down. They made their way to the bed and collapsed in a kiss, snuggling into each other.

"God, I'm so tired!" she said, breaking away from his mouth and yawning.

"I know. I am too. I don't want to be tired, not now. Not when I finally have you all to myself."

"I know." She smiled at him and stroked his face, her fingers ending in his hair. "Why don't you get comfortable and I'll change." He helped her with her bag and she made him turn around while she picked out her choice of lingerie. He chuckled as she slipped into the bathroom to change. Like whatever it was would stay on more than two seconds!

He removed his clothes, dropping them into a pile on the floor, pulling back the covers, and sliding into the comfortable queen-sized bed. He sighed deeply and yawned, stretching out on his back. What an amazing day! He heard her brushing her teeth and regretted not doing the same, but it was too late. Her silhouette appeared in the bathroom doorway; he rolled onto his side as she stopped beside the bed, meeting his eyes and hesitating. He was on fire for her in that moment and forgot being tired. She wore a satiny little slip of a thing that appeared to be the color of peaches and cream, although it was hard to tell in the candlelight. It was cut low in the front, so he could clearly see the shadows and curves of her breasts. He swallowed and propped himself up on his elbow, pulling away the sheets to invite her into the bed beside him. She looked at him beneath the covers.

"No fair. You're already naked."

"I'm sorry. You said get comfortable."

"Well, yeah, but if I can't undress you, then you don't get to undress *me*," she said, her eyes sparkling at him, a smile playing around her mouth. As the actress within her appeared before him, his eyes grew wide; otherwise he remained motionless as she slipped her finger under one of the straps of the gown and it fell off her shoulder, exposing the full roundness of her breast and its taut pink nipple. He felt his eyes burning into her as he glanced at her sultry face, watching intently as she let the other strap fall and the gown slide down to her hips, revealing the rest of her, the hint of lace panties he was now seeing disappeared with the little gown onto the floor. He admired her dancer's body, not anorexic, but firm, toned and healthy, a woman's body. She placed one knee on the high bed, holding out her hand for assistance, which he offered wordlessly. She slipped under the covers beside him, her cool skin touching his warm body. He felt enormous beside her, taking her into his arms and kissing her deeply, feeling all the tension leaving his body and pulling her into him as close as he could hold her.

She moved her hands over his face, caressing him, kissing his throat and pressing herself into him. Her arms went above her head as she offered herself to him. He was floating in this spell with her, getting lost in her. "Suddenly the word '*wife*' is the sexiest word in the English language!" he whispered into her hair, kissing her again and again.

"I love you, Kyle," she whispered, returning his kisses. "*Love is everything*," she murmured, holding his face away and looking at him, her eyes filled with desire. And then there was no more talking.

Chapter 2

LUNA DE MIEL

Chelsea knew immediately upon their approach to the Punta Cana airport that this was like no other place she had ever seen. The thatched roof of the building loomed large amidst the canopy of palm trees on the coast of the Dominican Republic. After descending the stairs of the small plane, they hiked across the hot tarmac to the airport itself, crowded with lovely ladies dressed in colorful flouncy skirts, greeting them with cries of "Hola, hola!" Grinning, Kyle accepted several leis and Chelsea got a couple as well from the enthusiastic greeters as they were ushered quickly into the customs gate. Chelsea noticed there was no glass in any of the windows. The whole place was open to the air. Kyle conversed easily in Spanish with the men in uniform, producing the required blue entrance papers and their passports. Chelsea looked around at the other passengers, noticing that some appeared nervous, not knowing what to do or what was being asked of them. Kyle looked over and helped the family behind them, explaining what to write on the papers, and then repeated it to another couple, carrying their small airline bags like Kyle and Chelsea were. They retrieved the rest of their baggage and found the bus that proclaimed the name of their resort. Finally, sinking down in the soft seats of the bus, they relaxed, fanning themselves, letting the feeble air conditioning cool their damp skin.

This was definitely a Third World country, they realized along the somber bus trip to the resort, past the dirt yards and tiny block houses with no glass windows, and repeated warnings from their tour guide not to drink the water. He sat behind them after his speech and shook hands with Kyle, chatting amiably with them.

The resort was elegant and airy, with colorful flowers and lush green plants everywhere. The sea breeze blew across the wide tiled terraces, keeping everything cool and pleasant. Chelsea smiled and relaxed in the presence of the friendliest people she had ever met. Their dark skin, bright smiles, and rolling Spanish made her feel welcome and strangely at home. A porter disappeared with their luggage, and they found seats on one of the trams that took them to their villa. Although there seemed to be many people in the resort, it was not evident, due to the layout of the buildings on the meandering walkways, and the tropical greenery everywhere, creating lush privacy.

Their villa was stucco with narrow dark wooden doors and a high tile roof. Inside was thankfully air-conditioned and spacious with a large, comfortable white bed. A tiny white ghost crab crawled sideways across the doorway; Kyle picked it up swiftly, tossing it into the sandy bushes beyond the villa. Then he took Chelsea's bag and insisted upon carrying her across yet another threshold. They had almost made it to the bed when a small tinkling voice chimed behind them, "Hola, hola!"

A tiny smiling woman in the local ruffled white dress greeted them happily, introducing herself to them in Spanish as Yolanda, their daily maid. After setting Chelsea down, Kyle conversed with Yolanda in Spanish and they chatted as he introduced Chelsea, explaining that they had just gotten married and were on their honeymoon. She smiled knowingly and supplied the Spanish word he did not know, *luna de miel*. Yolanda went to the door and took off the "Do Not Disturb" sign written in both languages and handed it to Kyle with raised eyebrows. "*Me imagino el tiempo que estaran de cama!*" she said, meaning, 'I imagine you will be spending a lot of time in bed.' She was apparently explaining that they should be sure to use the sign as often as they liked and he laughed boldly, promising her she would see it often. Chelsea struggled to keep up with the Spanish banter but Kyle seemed practiced and comfortable with the language…and the topic.

After Yolanda bid them a good afternoon and departed, they sank down on the divine bed, absorbing the heavy dark furnishings, the bright red hibiscus blossom on the pillow along with chocolate mints. Chelsea folded herself into Kyle's arms, breathing in his delicious manly scent. This was heaven! They could vegetate and swim and eat and stay in this bed all they wanted with no one to answer to and no one to please for a change. The wedding had been exciting and fun, but exhausting, so they were both glad to be out of the spotlight and alone together.

A ceiling fan ticked above them and they lay still, holding each other, cherishing this time, this beautiful place, and this opportunity to learn even more about each other. After a few moments and a few sweet kisses, he spoke quietly, "What are you thinking about?"

"So much…and so little at the same time," she mused, sinking her fingers into his fine thick hair, taking in his presence and feeling a surge of contentment. "I was just thinking about the wedding and about how Father Michael told us that one of us would always be more in love than the other…."

"Hmm. I guess today it's me."

"More in love? You're wrong—for once. It's me today."

Kyle went up on his elbow and gazed at her, narrowing his eyes just slightly. "What if he's wrong altogether? What if we're both just as much in love all the time? How will we ever be able to know?"

A small wave of sadness washed over her, imagining that he might not always feel this way about her. She couldn't imagine that she would be the one to love him less. "I'm sure it happens. It's normal to feel that way. I don't want to think about it, but I don't think it's happening on this honeymoon of ours," she suggested with a smile.

"Yep, I guess that's when you know the honeymoon's over, when somebody slips…" he murmured, covering her open mouth with his.

⚶⚶⚶

The next time he awoke, the sun was shining brightly through the window. Remembering where he was, he smiled and stretched, aware of his *wife* beside him in the king-sized bed. He raised his head to glance at the clock. 5:23 a.m.! He was surprised at the brightness of the sun through the sheers at the window, and then remembered that the sun had been setting here at seven-thirty the night before, when they had walked up to the Dominican restaurant for dinner. They would definitely be readjusting their thinking about time while they were here. He watched her sleeping, her hair swept in a tousle across her pillow, the graceful curve of her back uncovered beside him. Gently, he touched her arm, still feeling her hands all over his body from earlier before dawn when they had made love again. She hardly stirred and he sighed, closing his eyes again. He should let her sleep. They would need rest if this was what the week was going to be like. He'd never expected the passion they shared would deepen for each other with marriage. If this was what the bonds of holy matrimony were all about, then bring it on! All the words were taking on a new dimension with her in this place, and he thought the ritual of the honeymoon, or the *luna de miel*, was a brilliant tradition! A gift from God was what she was, in so many ways. God had given her to him six years ago, and she had given him God. Marriage had been inevitable since he had reconnected with her back in high school.

And to think he had been dumb enough to have almost lost her! That senior year in college after he'd injured his knee, when he'd visited her at school and met her friend, Conner, had about done them in. Conner had been a stud, and obviously in love with her. Either she hadn't seen it, or she had refused to let herself be taken away from Kyle. It was a stupid, masochistic move for him to step away and watch it all play out. He had taken a huge risk…more than huge, he realized later. But she had not fallen for Conner and had stayed true to him. All that time he'd wasted, the hurt he'd caused…so many regrets, he thought, running a hand through his hair, and sighing. She stirred again at the sound, this time reaching for him, eyelids fluttering, touching him, kissing his shoulder, and snuggling into his warmth. Every touch, every kiss, every look from her was an expression of love. How far would he lose himself in her today? It was him today, the one more in love.

After brunch at the open air pavilion, they left their table skirting the beach and walked over to the water sports hut to book a snorkeling trip to the coral reef. Before they had left their room, they made their dinner reservations and had also made an appointment for a long-awaited couples' massage for that evening. They would have a late dinner and go back to their villa for yet another bottle of champagne that had been delivered to them already. Chelsea wondered already whether she would ever be able to set her feet back on earth after all this pampering.

The beach was magical. Lush palm trees were plentiful at the edge of the fine white sand, and the water was a magnificent shade of turquoise, so clear she could see her toes while standing waist-deep in it. That particular color was etched into her heart. She saw it in his eyes when he looked at her and smiled, as they strolled aimlessly back to their spot on the beach. Rows and rows of bright blue lounge chairs were arranged under the canopy of trees, some under thatched umbrellas to assure guests of shade and cool breezes. They passed an array of people on the beach, settling on a place further away from the crowd. Many of the women they passed chose to sunbathe topless, but it was not a very pleasant sight in most cases.

They had selected two chairs, one under the umbrella for her, and one in the sun for him. With her fair skin, she couldn't take the sun the way he could and had to use sunscreen regularly to keep from getting burned.

After one day, Kyle was as brown as a coconut, his hair becoming more sun-streaked than usual. She watched as he sat back in his chair, pushing his feet into the hot sand, the broad expanse of his shoulders noticeably relaxed. *He was beautiful,* she thought, regarding him from under the forearm she'd draped across her brow to shield her eyes from the sun. He was beautiful and *hers,* all six feet and one hundred and ninety well-developed pounds of him. At least, that's what the University of Virginia Cavaliers football brochure had proclaimed about him years ago. He'd worked hard to develop his strength, speed, and bulk back then. Strength training had been essential for protection against injury, which hadn't made any difference in the long run since he'd hurt his knee in his senior year. Still, she was glad her weight had never been published in the Carolina Ballet dance programs! But that was the difference between men and women, she supposed. Before the injury, he had played wide receiver at UVA three of his four years on a scholarship while he studied architecture. Then, after college, working for two years at a firm in northern Virginia had kept him so busy they'd hardly seen each other, not to mention her schedule with the ballet every weekend. Now, here they were together, and she still could not take it in.

⚜⚜⚜⚜⚜

He let his eyes drift to the variety of topless women they passed on the way to their chairs. It was like wandering through the pages of *National Geographic,* as opposed to what he thought would be *Playboy.* He had seen his share of all of that, and today he wasn't really interested in any of it. Chelsea was stirring enough when she stepped out of her beach cover-up in her red bikini. Who needed to look at any of those other women when she was with him? They drowsed in the chairs for a while, and then waded into the warm water to cool off and get wet. She wrapped her legs around him and he held her close in the water, kissing her, enjoying the closeness. He reached up, unhooked her top, and pulled it away playfully. She gasped, grinning at him. He folded it and tucked it into the back of his swim trunks and held her closer.

"I hope you're planning on giving that back later," she said into the side of his head.

"Later…meaning, how much later?"

"Surely you don't expect me to join the ranks of those tribal women out here do you?" she laughed, arching her back in the water and letting her arms fan out beside her.

"You've been walking around me all morning in the villa, wearing nothing but a smile; why not here?" he replied, smiling devilishly, regarding her lovely posture in the water.

"It's different when it's just us."

"Chelsea…" he began indulgently. "*Chica*…you're the most beautiful woman on this beach. You should flaunt your body," he said, swaying her back and forth in the water.

"I know you wouldn't be saying this to me in Boone!"

"Well…no, but this is different. What happens in the DR stays in the DR. Nobody knows us here. Nobody cares."

"Maybe *I* do," she said, but he couldn't tell whether she was serious. There was one way to find out.

"Maybe you *don't*," he said setting her away from him, backing away and walking out of the water. He heard her sigh, exasperated, behind him, and he laughed silently, going to sit on his chair, drying his face with a thick white towel from their villa. She watched him for a few moments and then swam around some more in the water, floating on her back, diving under, and then looking out at the view away from him, the back of her head slick and wet like a seal. Then she turned and folded her arms across her chest and walked out of the water toward him, regarding him seriously. She was sexy as hell…but she wasn't smiling. This wasn't good;

he had overstepped his bounds and had really pissed her off. He rose suddenly and carried a towel toward her, draped it around her shoulders, pulling her close, handing her back her top. "I'm sorry," he whispered, touching his forehead to hers.

They walked back up to the chairs and she took the towel off, to his surprise, spreading it across another chair next to his, lying down, and positioning herself to catch some sun. She glanced at him, her arm draped over her eyes in the sun. "Satisfied?" she asked haughtily.

You think you know a woman, he thought, and then she does something that blows your mind.

He looked amused for a second but then shook his head. "No, actually, I think you need sunscreen," he said seriously, taking the tube from their bag and slapping it across the palm of his hand. She broke into laughter.

They met Joe and Sarah from New Jersey on their snorkeling adventure to the coral reef. The two had been dating for seven years, making Chelsea at first wonder what they were waiting for. They talked about the scarcity of jobs in their town and how both of them had been forced to move back in with their parents until they could get their feet on the ground. Marriage at this point wasn't an option, but they wanted to be together in the worst way. It had taken Kyle and her six years to reconcile their situation so she could easily relate to their predicament.

Life under the sea was as spectacular as Chelsea had imagined from what she had seen in movies and in books. It was amazing to be in the midst of a school of fish, reach out to touch them, and have them quickly disappear, untouchable and elusive. The shining new ring on her finger seemed to attract the fish as they darted toward her hand more than once. They swam among fish of every color imaginable, of different shapes and sizes. The yellow and purple ones were her favorites, along with the orange, black, and white clownfish they saw. Large gray stingrays flopped along below them, one as long as Chelsea's entire body. Kyle coaxed her out of the water just in time for the boat to leave. Her fingers were pruned from the water and she rode back in the boat with him, curled into his arm, both of them lulled into the silence of another surreal world.

The massage later capped the perfect day. Monica and Sasha took them outside to a cabana by the beach where the tables were set up, candles were lit, and soft Latin music played to relax them further. When the heavenly kneading was over, they lay together on the bed until they were ready to get dressed and return to the villa for showers before dinner at the Japanese restaurant. Joe and Sarah were leaving as they arrived, and they laughed at the dazed expressions on the two of them.

Kyle had never been this relaxed in his life; nor had Chelsea, he imagined. As they sauntered back to their place after too much conversation at the dessert table with people they didn't know, he watched the other men checking out his wife. She turned heads all the time, but she didn't know it. He knew what they were looking at. First they noticed her hair, her figure, her face, the sensual way she carried herself. Then if they were lucky, they got to see her smile, and their looks changed from mere interest to something like respect. She was unusual in her love of people, and it radiated from her in a genuine way that people noticed immediately. Everyone who knew her was her friend. It was exactly what had lured him to her from the depths of his sadness.

He looked at her then, as if he were another man, seeing her for the first time. He'd never thought of sex with her as anything other than making love. The other guys he knew talked about women and sex in a much different way and used a different language about it. He was no stranger to that kind of talk, but he wanted none of it for her. Eddie Baxter, his freshman roommate from Fredericksburg, had been the worst. He talked about women, particularly his girlfriend, all the time, leaving nothing to the imagination. His girlfriend, and sometimes other girls, had frequently spent the night in their dorm room, and whoever it would be would go at it all night with Eddie in the squeaky metal bed just feet away from him. More than once Kyle had lobbed his pillow at them, imploring them to give him a break. He couldn't wait for the year to end, and from then on, he'd lived with Rishon Taylor, a fullback from Richmond. They got along fine. Rishon was quiet, respectful, and kept his side of the room neat.

It was dark on the walk back to the villa, as they held hands, clinging to one another, cicadas singing to them as they walked. He felt as if he were made of butter, after the snorkeling and that awesome massage on the beach. He couldn't wait to get back to their room and be alone with her again.

She looked at him in the darkness, tanned and windblown, feeling him turn to her and breathe in her perfume, nuzzling her cheek as they walked along. She had never been with another man and could never imagine it happening. Kyle Davis was all she had ever wanted. He was smart and sensitive, protective and gentle at the same time, but most of all, she knew he loved her deeply. How she had held onto him all this time she had no idea, but she figured it had to do with all the praying and wishing she had done over the years. They had been married for three days, and they had been the best three days of her life. Each day was a gift, a treasure with him. That she could have this every day, this feeling of complete satisfaction and love, was more than she could process. Being with him and looking into the bedroom eyes he was giving her made her want nothing more than to touch him and kiss him, loving him until sleep overtook them both.

He unlocked their door and kicked it closed after they entered the room, not bothering to turn on the lights. She could see him well enough in the moonlight. Their clothes could not come off fast enough. They had barely made it to the bed before his hands were on her skin, her breasts, sending her, gasping, to another place. She felt every inch of her body lighting up under his touch, as she closed her eyes, letting him take her to the height of pleasure over and over.

Tonight it was her; the one more in love.

⋘⋙

Every day was filled with snorkeling, sailing, playing with dolphins, or lounging in the meandering pool. The pool wove through the resort, appearing to have no end. They drank banana mudslides at the swim-up bar, or mojitos in the open air bar in the evenings. Every evening it rained, and they sat around in the open-aired atriums in the lobby where the ceilings were open in the middle, allowing the showers to fall freely, hypnotically onto the gardens below.

At times, they sat entranced with the scenery around them, or talked for hours, discussing the advice people had given them, or the wisdom the priest had shared during their pre-nuptial visits with him.

"I liked what Father Michael told us about children," Kyle began, one day, lazing at the beach as they faced each other on beach chairs under their thatched umbrella. "About how we should wait a while and get to know each other first. We're young enough; there's no rush to have children. I want them, like you do, but not for a while."

He stroked a stray strand of wet hair out of her eyes as she smiled and nodded her agreement. "We just found each other again," she said. "I don't feel like sharing you right now. We have a lot of catching up to do and a lot to accomplish before we start a family. I don't even want a *dog* right now."

He looked shocked and then laughed. "I know. I'd want another lab if we ever got a dog and there's not a good place to keep a dog in the cabin. If he were anything like Bono, he'd chew up the whole house. Keeping it outside would be out of the question with the cold weather and the bears around the cabin." Her eyebrows rose at the word "bears."

"So…it's just me and you for now…" she commented tentatively, taking his warm hand in hers, feeling her skin dry and tighten in the sun.

"Woman, you're all I can handle at this moment!" he said, leaning in to kiss her lightly on the lips. "It's me…today," he said softly.

"No, it's me," she murmured, *the one more in love* hanging between them.

⚜

On the fifth day of their honeymoon, they had returned from parasailing and found their usual spot on the beach, settling in for the afternoon. Chelsea looked extremely tan now in contrast to the print bikini she wore. The effect was stunning. She gazed at him from her chair and asked him, shielding her face from the sun with her hand, "What was the best advice you were given about marriage?"

He thought a moment. "My grandfather told me never to get into debt and to live within our means. And the other thing was Tyson's."

"What'd he say?"

"He said, 'Never think you know her because she'll always surprise you.' I'm thinking he was right. I know Stacie's rocked his world from time to time, but in a good way. When you walked out of the water that day without your top on, that blew me away," he said, smiling.

She smiled and settled back into her chair, topless again at the moment, closing her eyes to the sun. "I want to know everything about you. Don't ever hold back," she said, looking at him directly again, "even if you think it will hurt my feelings. I want to know it all. You can't be mine, really, if I don't know it all."

He studied her with serious eyes for a moment. "But what if it were something hurtful? I'm not hurting you on purpose," he said making it sound like a promise.

"Maybe I'm tougher than you think."

"Oh, I don't doubt that for a minute." He thought about the word *knowing*, about *knowing* her in the biblical sense. That word had taken on a new and interesting dimension for him as well. The *knowing* she was talking about ran even deeper and he wanted that too. He wanted to know everything about her. He had known her most of his life, but did he really *know her*? Did she know him? Did he know himself?

He swallowed the old anger before it got the best of him, ruining his buzz. If his mother had really *known* his father and *known* that he was ripping off his clients, then maybe their relationship would have been better, even salvageable, or maybe not, but maybe she could have made informed decisions. Maybe she would have left him. Maybe she would have still stayed with him. At least knowing those things, she would have had some remnant of control. Maybe she could have helped him atone for what he had done. His mother had not deserved the pain and the shame Stuart Davis had dumped on her after he had taken his life. How she'd endured it, Kyle couldn't imagine. There had been a time when he was younger that he had been so angry at her for letting her husband spiral out of control. Now he understood that she'd had no idea of the turmoil he'd plunged into. He looked back at his wife, sitting up now, sensual in her half-nudity, and gazing at the water. He decided then and there that he wanted to know *everything*.

He watched Chelsea fasten her top before they waded out into the cool, clear water, almost feeling their skin hiss on contact. It had been hotter here than they had expected, but water was always close by. He held her hands as she floated out from him, the gentle waves doing nothing more than lapping at them from time to time. Suddenly, she jumped and raked her hand down her leg, a surprised expression on her face.

"What is it?"

"Something's on my leg! It's burning my leg!" she cried, grabbing his shoulder and jumping away from the spot where she had just been. He took her hand and pulled her toward the beach, stomping through the water as fast as they could. When they got out of the water, they looked down, inspecting her right leg. Her knee was bent and she sucked in breaths through her teeth and he felt her tremble. A large angry-looking welt appeared above her knee and striped down her leg.

"Damn! You just got a hell of a jellyfish sting!" he said, holding her arm because she could hardly support herself from the pain. He helped her limp to their chairs and she fell onto hers, gasping and flapping her hands.

"*Oh…it hurts!*" she said breathlessly, sucking in more air.

The welt was large and round, as if the animal had sat down square-ly above her knee. Kyle could see where the long tentacles had wrapped around her calf below it. He panicked, wondering what to do. They had Benadryl in the bathroom in their package of medicines they'd been ad-vised to bring. It was a start anyway. He reached into the pocket of the beach bag and fished out the key to their villa. Quickly, he lifted her in his arms and carried her off the beach. She wiped tears off her face and he shook his head in sympathy. "Don't try to be brave. I'd probably cry, too," he said and she sobbed for a moment into his shoulder.

They met Yolanda, finishing up in their villa as he opened the door and laid Chelsea on the bed. Yolanda's face registered instant concern as she and Kyle discussed what had happened in Spanish while he rummaged through their medicines, coming back with two of the pills. Yolanda nod-ded and told them, "I have something. Better. I come back."

While they waited for her to return, Kyle poured water from their water bottles on a washcloth and laid it gently across her leg. "Any bet-ter?" he asked, watching the pain distort her face as she took the bottle and swallowed her pills. She nodded, although he didn't believe her. The chill from the air conditioning made her shiver in her wet bathing suit, so he handed her one of the large towels to cover up with. Several moments later, Yolanda was back, supplies in hand. She went to the table and took a coffee cup, dumping in baking soda from a yellow box; then she poured in vinegar and stirred it until it was a smooth paste. She showed it to Kyle, dipping the spoon up and down in it to demonstrate the consistency.

"Take out sting," she said, removing the wet cloth from Chelsea's leg. Then Yolanda dropped a blob of the wet paste on the welt, spreading it gently, adding more to cover the wound.

Chelsea smiled weakly and propped herself up on her elbows. "It's working! It's so much better. You're amazing, Yolanda."

"Old medicine," she replied, smiling.

"*Gracias!*" Chelsea breathed.

Chelsea slept most of the way home on the plane, mostly from the effects of the antihistamine. Her head lolled on Kyle's shoulder as he wrapped his arm around her. She'd worn shorts, which were more comfortable than anything, keeping any fabric from touching her jellyfish sting. He looked down at her leg, noticing how red and tight the wound was looking. This wasn't good. It was probably infected. He would take her to the first urgent care clinic he could find. His grandfather was a doctor. He'd probably write her a prescription right there in the airport! It had been an unfortunate ending to an otherwise perfect trip. At least they'd slept more, instead of staying up half the last couple of nights, entertaining themselves otherwise.

He tried to prepare himself for re-entry into the real world. Chelsea had another week before summer classes started, but he'd be back at work tomorrow with Frank Maynard, the architect who'd hired him for the historic renovation project on the old inn in Blowing Rock. The large project was coming along nicely, and he wondered what would be the next job they'd take on. Frank had been his mentor in high school when he needed a building project to meet his graduation requirements. After helping

Kyle's mother, Shelly, with her husband's disintegrating business following his suicide, Frank had shown a particular interest in Kyle's future. Shelly had explained that Stuart Davis's dream had been for Kyle to take over his business one day, but that had not played out for him, after a myriad of bad business practices on Stuart's part had driven the business to ruin. Kyle had kept in touch with Frank over the years, as they had continued their mentor-protégé relationship throughout college and later, when he worked doing renovations on historic properties in Virginia. When Frank had won the bid for the inn project, he needed help and knew Kyle was just the person for the job.

The pilot announced their descent to Charlotte-Douglas International, and Kyle shook Chelsea's shoulder gently. With the medicine in her system it would take her a few minutes to wake up. He put away his iPod and turned on his cell phone, ready to call his grandparents as soon as they landed. The plan was for them to have Kyle's car at the airport so they could head home without delay. They were probably pulling into the airport just at this moment.

Chelsea woke and stretched, then snuggled back into his arm, laying her head on his shoulder. He looked at her leg again. "That's a gnarly-looking wound you've got there, Sunshine," he said softly into her hair.

She stretched her arm across his chest. "Today…it's me," she murmured contentedly into his neck.

Chapter 3

FEATHERING THE NEST

Monday morning was mourning in and of itself. Reluctantly, Kyle had to get up and pry himself away from her early, before Chelsea was ready to release him to the rest of the world. She had prepared his lunch and a bagel for breakfast with his coffee while he showered and dressed. They shared coffee-flavored kisses at the door of the cabin before he left her for the day. He was dressed for the work site in a pair of jeans and steel-toed boots. She imagined him wearing a hard hat and safety glasses, pouring over plans with Frank. The project at the old inn would be taking all of his time and Frank would be there as well, supervising the work through lunch every day until it was finished.

Her mother had left a pot of vegetable soup, a loaf of homemade bread, to Kyle's delight, her Aunt Becky's bread and butter pickles, and a bottle of wine on the porch when they'd arrived at home the evening before. It was a sweet and respectful gesture, accompanied by a note that read, *Welcome home! Call me for lunch tomorrow. I know you'll be lonely! Love, Mom.* How right she was! Home…this cabin was her home now. After her shower, Chelsea put on a pair of shorts and a tank top, twisting her wet hair into a bun, ready to get down to the business of making the cabin her home. Being here felt good, as opposed to the remark she'd heard a woman saying at the reception about how it was a man's place and wouldn't suit Chelsea, but what did she know? Chelsea had been appalled at the comments people made about them anyway; another woman mentioned that strange music at the wedding and their provocative dance; she'd not even worn a veil! But Kyle's cabin was special. It was the very place where they'd declared their love for each other back in high school when she'd realized Kyle was floundering in his beliefs about love, about God, and the pain he'd felt over losing his father, and ultimately and mistakenly, thinking he'd lost the love of his mother. Here was the place he'd found Chelsea, found God, and realized that the possibility of having his mother's love was still within his grasp. It was the only place Chelsea had ever wanted to be with him, the place his father had built for his family, his piece of heaven. Sadly, with the turn of events in his father's life, the piece of heaven had turned into hell for Stuart Davis, so it was here that Kyle had returned to rediscover his life and come to terms with what his father had done. But Kyle was feeling a connection of sorts with his father after all this time, and it seemed right to be here in the midst of it all. She got the feeling his remembrances were not altogether pleasant, but he did not share it all with her…yet.

She shivered briefly and sipped her cup of coffee, sitting on the sofa, collecting her thoughts for the day. Her eyes found the spot in the corner of the window directly in front of her, the Christmas card window. She had etched her initial in the corner of that window on December the twenty-third, the evening Kyle had proposed. That gesture was one more page in a long-standing family tradition which she and Charley had kept alive upon engagement. The story went that their great-great-great-aunt Annette Davenport had etched her initial in the family's farmhouse window to assure herself that her diamond was in fact real. Chelsea's ring was the very same one, passed down to her from her grandmother, Kitty Davenport, and it had seemed only natural to christen the cabin with the same tradition. She slipped on a light hooded jacket, opening the door and stepping onto the deck in the trees. The mountain air was exhilarating.

She felt so alive! Breathing in the morning air, still chilly and foggy, she listened to the familiar birdsongs she found so comforting. She was beginning to recognize their melodies, like the conversation of friends greeting each other each morning. She smiled, feeling loose and tender. She could still feel the astonishing sensations he created within her, just thinking about it. A giddy laugh escaped her lips at the memory of the passion they'd shared earlier, at the break of dawn, before he'd had to get up for work. It was fortunate for her that she didn't have to appear anywhere respectable for another few days. She would have to practice the control it would take to keep the flames of that passion from creeping across her face at each thought of making love with him. She couldn't stop thinking about it! He was her addiction. There could be worse things to be addicted to, she decided. She would start with her mother today and see how she did. Oh, it would be so difficult to control her emotions concerning her *husband*, especially in front of her mother!

The plan for the day was to haul her remaining clothes and the wedding gifts over to the cabin and go through each item, deciding where to place each gift of love their family and friends had bestowed upon them. She and Kyle had agreed that she would have full discretion on where each item would be placed and what it could possibly replace. The guests had gotten creative with their gifts, knowing that the cabin was already put together and that Chelsea had inherited her grandmother's china and crystal, as if there were anywhere in the rustic little home for any of that luxury. Kyle was being a good sport about all of it, trusting her to take command of the household.

First on her agenda was to call her mother, and then Abby, arranging lunch dates respectively. Then, she knew she would be expected to call Charley and Stacie with a full report on the honeymoon. She laughed again, remembering the advice from Stacie: "*Be a slut in bed so he won't go looking for it anywhere else!*" That task had come so naturally that she giggled again, putting down the phone and escaping a moment before attempting to key in her home phone number.

She looked down at the wound on her leg, above her right knee, less red and itchy today, thanks to the prescription she'd started on the previous day. Kyle's grandfather had taken one look at that leg in the airport and written her a prescription for a high-powered antibiotic on the spot. He'd cautioned her about something; what was it? She'd been so dazed from the Benadryl and the flight that she'd forgotten. Her phone was buzzing; her mother had beat her to it and was calling her.

"*Hey, Mom*!" she gushed into her cell phone. They talked for a few minutes and arranged for her mother to arrive in half an hour with the clothes and gifts she and Tom had already loaded into the Tahoe, both looking forward to spending the day together and catching up on everything.

Her mother arrived with a load of gifts so Chelsea poured her a fresh cup of coffee before they unloaded everything from the SUV in the driveway.

"*Holy Cow*! Look at your leg!" her mother shrieked, upon first inspection of her married daughter. They collapsed upon each other in a hug that felt wonderful between them.

"Oh, Mom, it's so much better than it was!" Chelsea reassured her, which did nothing to reassure her mother.

"Oh, *sweetheart*! Well, other than that leg you look like the picture of health. That's quite a tan you've developed. My goodness! I know that must have hurt! Are you taking something for it?"

"Kyle's grandfather wrote me a prescription for Keflex, and it's *seriously* so much better today. I was wondering how in the world I was going to get into a pair of tights for the ballet class I'm teaching next Monday."

"Ooh, *ballet*? I thought you were hoping to get away from ballet here?" Liz asked in a commiserating fashion.

"I know....Well, it seems I'm the *expert*, now. Monday, Wednesday, and Friday at 8 a.m." she said and shrugged.

"Oh well, I guess you have to pay your dues when you're the newbie."

"Exactly what I thought. Hopefully, it won't be like this for long. They might not like the kind of ballet I'm going to offer!" she said playfully.

"That's one way to skin a cat," her mother smiled conspiratorially at her. Chelsea was suddenly so glad to see her mother.

Liz had come inside and was now looking around the place, breathing in the smell of pine, as most people did for the first time. She looked back at Chelsea and smiled. "I always forget what a special place this is. Stuart was a very talented builder," she said, remembering their friend, a sad expression on her face. She had wandered to the open door at the porch and stepped out on it, looking back toward the river, listening to the birds and the soft swooshing of water. Chelsea followed her out.

"I remember when Tom used to meet Stu up here and they'd take Jay and Kyle fly-fishing when they were just little boys. It used to scare me, but they were always safe with the boys here. Sometimes when it was just the two of them, they'd get to drinking…and that wasn't so safe. But he was a good friend. I'm so sorry about how it all turned out. Has it been difficult for Kyle, being back here?"

"It was at first, but I think it's been getting better." Chelsea paused, remembering what Kyle had told her the day before the wedding. "It's like his dad's still here, somehow."

Her mother thought about her comment and pressed her lips together, nodding.

"So, how was the honeymoon?" Liz asked, eyes sparkling.

Chelsea thought she was ready for her flippant answer, but instead, her voice caught in her throat and her face flamed in spite of her best efforts. "Incredible," she said almost soundlessly. "*He's so incredible, Mom.*"

Her mother smiled knowingly, stroking her hand across her daughter's hair. "I know, darling. I'm so glad. Enough said. But I want to hear about

Punta Cana when you're ready to talk about it," Liz laughed, reddening Chelsea's face further.

She took a breath and tried to refocus. "Well, the *place* was fabulous! The beach was beautiful. We snorkeled everyday and we ate and drank like pigs. I know I've gained at least five pounds!" They laughed, going companionably to unload the gifts from the back of the Tahoe.

"You have some real treasures here," her mother said, carefully extricating a giant potted geranium and a large, rough branch that she thrust down into the plant inside it, and setting it on the gravel beside the truck.

"What *is* that?" Chelsea asked, laughing.

Liz laughed as well, pushing her dark hair out of her face with the back of her hand.

"Do you remember the ladies from the beach, from Duck—Murph, and Karen, Stacie's doctor?"

"Of course! They were all so nice and so much fun."

"They're into making these. It's called a bottle tree. They put it together and added these beads and this little plaque, but Stacie was instructed to place this empty bottle from the wine we drank at your wedding on the branch," Liz explained with a flourish of her hand to indicate the special starfish bottle like the one Chelsea had dropped in December, on the grocery store floor, upon running into Kyle unexpectedly. That had been the night he had proposed to her, and everyone loved hearing the story. She had caught him just as much by surprise, arriving a day early, to no one's knowledge, to seal the deal on her new job. It was destiny, and the bottle tree made the perfect gift. What thoughtful ladies they were! Chelsea fingered the little wooden plaque lovingly. *"Don't wish for a star, reach for one,"* it read.

"Oh, you're right; this is a treasure!" she murmured. "I know just the place for this," she said, inspired, carrying the little tree up the steps and around the corner to the back of the porch. She set it carefully under the eaves near the door.

"Stacie said they went tromping around in the woods behind Shelly's house one day and found the branch, so Shelly is in on it too!"

"Kyle will just love this! These are the things that will make this *our home*."

They spent some time bringing in other gifts and her clothes, finding space for them in other closets until she could rearrange things later. The cabin was not built to be a permanent residence, so the sharing of closet space would be determined by what they required for each season. There were piles of gifts and Chelsea assigned them to a place in the sun room for placement later as well. There would soon be a pile for goods to be switched out and given to charity, a pile for gifts to be placed somewhere in their home, and a pile of things to be figured out later.

Exhausted, Chelsea and Liz heated bowls of soup, made cheese toast, and had their lunch in the kitchen with glasses of iced tea, laced with mint the previous owners had planted outside the front porch. It made excellent ground cover as well as a refreshing glass of tea. The day was warming up quickly, and they were glad the weather had finally turned.

"Your dad is dying to see you!" Liz said, wiping her mouth on a cloth napkin. "We got used to having you in the house again, so we really missed you while you were away."

"I can't wait to see him too. We should get together and look at the wedding pictures. I saw they were on the website already for us to see."

"We'll do it. Maybe you and Kyle can come up for dinner one night. Dad's been working himself to death here lately."

"It's good that you're so busy. Have you been working in the store too?" Chelsea asked, referring to White Horse Nurseries, her family's landscaping and nursery business.

Her mother looked troubled, taking a bite of her cheese toast. "I've been there a lot. Your dad's been worrying about Jay."

"Why?" She couldn't imagine what her brother was doing now. Of the three siblings, he was usually the one who kept things interesting.

"He and Lauren are talking about moving to France next spring—March maybe."

"*France?* Why?" Chelsea cried, eyebrows raised in surprise.

"He wants to learn how to grow grapes and start a vineyard on our property."

"Isn't it too cold here for that?"

"Well, maybe not. Jay says there are hybrids that can be grown in this climate. Tom is so torn. He wants Jay to follow his heart, but he doesn't want him to go over there and then not come home. Or what if it doesn't work out? He stays up at night, losing sleep over the whole thing," Liz said, shaking her head.

"How long are they planning on staying?"

"You know, Lauren has friends over there from when she lived there. They've assured her that they can find housing, so they're planning on staying a couple of years."

"Thomas will be in school by then."

"Her friends have told them there will be good schooling for him."

"Who would take Jay's place in the business?" Chelsea found herself perplexed at the whole notion of this move, so she could imagine her father's distress. He tended to be a worrier inside, despite his usual laid-back demeanor.

"There are droves of people looking for jobs, but Randy Winkler would probably take over Jay's position. He has a family to feed and works hard.

He'd probably welcome the promotion. If Jay ever came back, he would be devoting himself completely to the winery."

"If he ever came back...*Mom*! This is so weird! Jay loves the farm as much as I do."

"I know; it's a lot to take in. Jay waited until after the wedding to spring the news on us," she smiled.

Chelsea sat in silence a moment before she shook her head, tossing her napkin on the table.

"By the way, I don't know if I ever thanked you for our wedding. It was amazing and we enjoyed every minute of it. We talked about it all the time on our honeymoon."

"You did thank us...and you're welcome. I've never seen two people more right for each other than the two of you. I'm so glad you're happy," her mother said, smiling at her, reaching across the table to pat her hand.

"Was it like this...with you and Dad?" she asked her mother, this time without the flushed cheeks or embarrassment.

Her mother thought, looking off for a moment. "It was at first, and then it kind of came and went. Oh boy, when I met him, he was larger than life! I'll never forget the way he and Stuart hung around my group of friends when we came up here to ski back in college. He called me every day after that. I was head over heels for him, but you know, I played hard to get!" She winked at Chelsea, then continued, clearing her throat. "Then after we started raising all of you, it changed...but not in a bad way. We were both working. You all were so much busier than I ever remember being when I was a kid. It was a lot to keep up with! You can get awfully caught up in the trappings of your life. Someone once said, 'Am I the sculptor, or the chisel in my life?' I don't ever want you to be the chisel, sweetheart," she said to Chelsea. "Actually it's the wrong question altogether. You're the *clay*...and God made you to do marvelous things. He doesn't want you hiding under a bushel. Don't ever allow yourself to get locked up inside yourself. As long as you and Kyle focus on your happiness and your love, you'll be fine. It seems so simple…but it can get so hard." Liz stopped, taking a sip of her tea, then spread the napkin carefully across her lap as Chelsea nodded, waiting for her to continue. "After Kitty died and you went away to college, your dad and I had another chance to get to know each other all over again. It's been wonderful! Things are great with the two of you now, and I hope they always will be, but sometimes it changes. I want you to remember to hang in there, for better or worse, because there's always hope that no matter how bad things get, they can change again. Your love will carry you through a lot of hard things. You've already shown Kyle that. I know that because of all the things you've gone through together; he's as committed to you as a man could ever be. I have no doubt you'll have a wonderful life, no matter the ups and downs you'll have."

Chelsea felt hot tears rolling down her cheeks and wiped them away with the tips of her fingers. "Thanks, Mom. I love you."

"I love you too, sweetheart," she said and they stood, clearing the table.

❦❦❦❦

At five-thirty, he walked up the steps and through the door to a wonderful aroma. A cheery wreath of sunflowers on the door greeted him as he pushed it open and stepped inside. Instantly, he felt at home. It was an odd feeling because it *was* his home, but there was a different feel to it altogether. Maybe it was that awesome smell of dinner he was getting! His eyes adjusted to the dim light inside, and then he saw her, sitting on the sofa in a pair of shorts and a scoop-necked shirt, hair falling in soft waves over her shoulders as she cleared away the last of the gift wrapping from the coffee table. She smiled, watching him walk in the front door.

"Finally!" she said, rising and going to him, putting her arms around his neck and kissing him there. He found her lips and kissed her enthusiastically.

"Hey! You look so happy. And I'm *really* happy to see you!" he hugged her again. She felt curvy and sexy in his arms and he smiled in spite of himself. He'd thought about this all day and couldn't let her go. "I've missed you since I left."

He looked around as she took his arms away from her waist, going to the refrigerator. She took out a bottle of beer and opened it, pushing in a wedge of lime, handing it to him. "Welcome home! How was your day?" she asked. They both laughed at the cliché she was now entitled to use as his wife. Her eyes sparkled at him, her cheeks flushed with happiness. She could not have been more beautiful, he thought.

"It was great, when I could get my mind on my job!" he laughed back at her. "I have to say I was a little distracted at first, but Frank was pretty understanding about it all. He laughed at me all day. I see you've been busy, too," he commented, looking around at the changes she'd made. "I knew this place needed a woman's touch!"

"I'll give you the tour when you're ready."

"I should probably shower before you touch me any further," he smiled warily, watching her react to the comment about touching. She was as bad as he was! "Dinner smells fabulous. Do I have time?"

"Absolutely. There's a chicken pie in the oven. There's no rush."

"Mmm-mm! I could get used to this!" he said, going toward the bedroom.

"At least until I'm back at work. Let me show you what I did in here," she said, motioning to the new comforter, a dark earth-tone and purple paisley print. She turned the covers down and showed him the new sheets. "Feel these," she said, tempting him, guiding his hand over the softness of the new creamy sheets on the bed. "I washed them before I put them on," she added.

"That was probably a waste of effort. We'll just have to wash them again," he said softly into her hair before he pressed his mouth into her cheek.

"Where is Yolanda when you need her?" she moaned and turned her mouth to meet his.

"You got that right!" he said, making himself drop her hand, going to the shower, noticing the new deep purple towels she'd hung earlier. "Wow, this is all so nice. Is this my house?" He heard her laugh as she left him in the bathroom.

He dressed in khaki shorts and a threadbare chambray shirt he'd had since high school. Thankfully, it was starting to get cooler outside, and he noticed she'd set the table on the porch. He found her out there, lighting a ceramic pot in the center of the table.

"What's that?" he asked, rolling up his sleeves and shaking his damp hair back away from his eyes.

"It's a firepot. You fill this little cup with fuel and it burns like a lantern. Remember? It's a gift from Anthony."

"Cool. There have been so many gifts, I'm glad you're keeping track of it all," he said, shaking his head, watching the blue flame lick the edges of the green and yellow pot, reminding him of autumn leaves.

"Want to sit a minute? The pie is cooling."

They relaxed in Adirondack chairs in a corner of the deck, and he motioned to her to let him examine her leg. She slipped off a flip flop and propped her foot on his knee. His hand went behind her calf and he stroked the back of her leg gently, taking in her deep pink toenails. It was so cool having a girl around! The simple touch of the sole of her foot on his leg was so erotic he felt his breath catch. He tried to collect himself. It took so little for him to get into her. He remembered why he was looking at her leg. The wound was indeed better and starting to look less angry.

"It looks so much better. Not as itchy today?"

"No. It is much better," she said, gathering her hair in her hands and moving it to one side, around her shoulder. That particular gesture always made him crazy too. He realized that if they didn't eat dinner soon, he was going to be carrying her back into the bedroom before he could stop himself. She grinned at him, seeing all of this in his eyes. Was he really that transparent? They were definitely on the same wavelength! She extended her hand and they returned to the kitchen to serve their plates.

"I'm having lunch with Abby tomorrow," she said after he'd said the blessing. "We're eating at the inn around noon."

"Good. I talked to Glen today, too. He wants us all to get together. We should have them over as soon as we get settled."

"Yes, she said they'd like to see the place. I think I'll be finished settling in by tomorrow. Does it look okay?" she seemed to ask him apprehensively.

"It's great! It's homey and comfortable. Seriously, you've done a great job putting it all together. It's not nearly as full and cluttered as I thought it would be." She knew he didn't like clutter. It was the designer in him she figured, but she didn't want to disrupt his home too much.

She grinned. "Look behind you," she said, referring to a large branch in a pot with a wine bottle and beads on it with a plaque.

He squinted at the little tree, liking it but not understanding it. "What is it?"

She explained about the bottle tree. "Murph and Karen Walters made it from a stick behind your mom's house. That's the bottle of wine we drank at our wedding. Stacie brought it up here in the back of their Jeep and she and Mom put it together. So it's kind of a group effort by all those women who love us!"

"Don't wish for a star. Reach for one," he said, reading the quote on the plaque. "That's definitely what we did. I like it, especially that starfish bottle," he commented, nodding and smiling at her, remembering their engagement night.

"This is fun isn't it, having dinner together, just us, in our house?" she asked after a quiet moment; he nodded again, then looked a little disappointed.

"I have to go out for dinner on Thursday," he said quietly, gazing at her for her reaction. She looked up, interested.

"Why?"

"It's a business thing. These investors from Florida are going to be here and they're taking Frank and me to dinner." He thought about the Floridians his father had worked for, absentee clients, mostly, and people he'd taken advantage of because they weren't hovering and paying attention to what he was doing. He'd known they'd had money and when the prices he'd promised changed from time to time, they didn't bat an eye. It was the perfect situation.

"No wives allowed?"

"I guess not this time. It would ordinarily be done at lunch, but since we've been working through lunches, they offered to take us to dinner somewhere."

"You don't sound too excited about it."

"Well," he pondered, chewing. "This is really good, by the way," he said, referring to her dinner. "They want to build some high-end condos and they want us to design them. They've been researching builders and they like Frank's work. But the thing is, they want to blow up the side of the mountain…that ridge right there," he said, pointing past her head at the ridge just beyond theirs. "Can you imagine looking out there at night and seeing a bunch of lights and crap?"

She looked concerned. "Is it a done deal?"

"No, but Frank is dying to take the project. See, after the inn is done, there's nothing else in the works. I could be out of a job in several months if we don't land this."

She looked more concerned. "Really? What about other renovations?"

"There's nothing on the books right now, not after the inn."

She nodded slowly, processing what he had told her. He could tell she had never thought about him not having work. But that was the way the economy was right now. They were both lucky to have jobs, and jobs they liked. They'd discussed their budget over the honeymoon, and how they should try to live simply. She'd had the idea of making a pot of soup every week, and one night a week would be pinto beans and cornbread. Then they would allow themselves a night of comfort food, another night could be stir-fried vegetables, and one night would be pasta. They could get by with so little. They had their entertainment down as well—and it was free, he thought with a smile. They were undoubtedly too tired to go out, at least for a while.

"What?" she asked, eyes shining in the twilight, again his angel.

"I was just thinking of ways we can entertain ourselves and not spend money," he said suggestively.

She cleared her throat. "Yes, well there's reading—we both like to read…and TV," she said. He could tell she was trying not to smile, deliberately steering away from his thoughts.

"*Or*, there's messing up those nice, clean sheets in there as soon as we throw these dishes in the dishwasher," he said, sending her an unmistakable message with his eyes that she got immediately. She made that helpless little look with her eyes and her entire face gave in. That was all it took for him. He leaned across the table and cupped her chin in his hand, kissing her, then blew out the firepot. "Tonight, it's me," he murmured.

Chapter 4

TO HELL AND BACK

The week went by too fast for Chelsea's liking. By Thursday, they were both exhausted. Tuesday evening was spent on the phone with all the relatives they hadn't seen since the wedding, giving a report about the honeymoon. It had been a little emotional to say the least, as everyone was so happy for them. Chelsea had talked to Jay to get his side of the story about his plans to move to France. They had visited Chelsea's parents on Wednesday night, looking at wedding pictures on the photographer's website and eating dinner. They unwrapped more wedding gifts and Chelsea spent time each day writing thank you notes, taking her dance class, and making mental preparations to start teaching her classes on the following Monday.

By Thursday, she was almost glad Kyle was going out. She planned to eat something from the freezer and watch a movie in her pajamas on the couch while he was gone. She would miss him, but it would be nice to be off-stage for a while, so to speak. He, also, was totally beat when he arrived at five-thirty, ready for a shower, a beer, and some snuggling with her on their newly decorated queen-sized bed.

"I wish you could come with me," he murmured into her hair, breathing in her scent and stroking her hair away from her face as she curled into him, fresh and damp from his shower.

"So who are these people and where are they taking you?"

"Have you ever been to the Gamekeeper Restaurant?"

"That's the place that serves the wild game?"

"Yeah, I went there with my dad once. They know that Frank hunts and that he likes that kind of food, so they're meeting us there."

"Are they hunters, like Frank?"

"Hardly," he said, reluctantly pulling away from her to dress. She watched him walk to the closet in his boxers, putting on a pair of slacks and looking through his shirts. "They're two women from Florida…Miami, I think. They have a lot of money and they're looking for an investment. One of them has a house up here."

She pondered this information. "Two women? That sounds odd. How old are they? They must be older to have all that money."

"I don't know," he replied, holding up the dark blue shirt with the white stripes that was her favorite. She shook her head.

"Don't wear that. I don't want them all over you," she said, giving him her best pout.

He smiled lopsidedly and hung it back on the rack, selecting a royal blue dress shirt next and sliding his arms into it. That one looked even better on him and made his eyes look bluer than usual.

"Are you kidding me?" she said, slipping off the bed and pushing him aside, rifling through the hangers. Her husband knew how to dress, that was for sure, but tonight she just didn't feel like showing him off. She felt an old pang of jealousy, oddly, after the total immersion she had been in with him for the last twelve days. She selected a tan shirt and a patterned necktie that would look nice with his navy blazer and the slacks he'd wear. Next she proceeded to slide her hands under the blue shirt, feeling his chest in the process, causing him to breathe deeply and roll his eyes.

"Why are you doing this?" he asked impatiently, but enjoying her attention just the same.

"I don't want you to look too appealing."

"They're probably gay," he said, and she threw him an admonishing look. He never joked about people's sexual orientation. He was just trying to assuage her worries. "You know you have nothing to worry about, right? We're still on our honeymoon, aren't we?"

"Until someone slips," she whispered coyly, planting a passionate kiss on his mouth. He raised his hand to wipe off her lip gloss, but she said, "Leave it," giving him the same smoldering look he was so good at giving her.

He shook his head and laughed, slipping on the tan shirt and tucking his shirttail into his pants. He took her into his arms and she smiled, pressing her lips into his throat. "Tonight, it's me, the one more in love," he said. She smiled into his neck, grateful for the reassurance.

At seven o'clock on the nose, he pulled into the drive leading to the old woodsy lodge that used to be the dining hall at a camp for girls. The Gamekeeper was probably a definite improvement, he thought, upon seeing the twinkly lights through the woods. The whole effect was rustic and charming and he remembered liking it, and feeling special when his father had taken his mother and him there. That had been at the end of the summer before his junior year at prep school, the same year his father had taken his life. He remembered that evening as one of the better times, even though his dad had downed a few drinks and he had driven them home. The road was just as curvy now as it had been then.

He parked beside Frank's dark green Suburban and climbed out, taking a deep breath and hoping for a light evening. He was whipped, so he hoped it would be an early one, too. Frank was in the bar, dressed similarly in a tie and sport coat, beside a short slim lady, laughing and chatting easily. As Kyle approached, Frank looked up and smiled, extending his hand to Kyle's shoulder.

"Hey! Kyle, I'd like you to meet Lynn Schiffman. Lynn this is Kyle Davis," he said warmly, and Lynn smiled at Kyle the same way. She was tiny, dark wavy hair framing her pretty face. She wore minimal makeup and had that athlete's build about her. He guessed she was a runner. The small lines around her eyes and mouth, and the strands of silver around her face made him think she was in her late fifties, but well-preserved, certainly. She wore a soft pant suit of neutral color and an interesting beaded necklace. They were designer clothes, the kind his mother used to wear. Lynn had a great handshake and he liked her instantly. She studied him with recognition under her smile as she held his hand.

"You must be Stuart Davis's son," she said, oddly discerning his face. He felt the air being sucked out from within him. This could be really bad. He couldn't read her expression. Was she shocked, surprised, troubled? There was something there, and he was sure it wasn't good. She was from Florida, the place many of his father's clients had come from to build their summer homes, and ultimately, to be taken advantage of. She must know the connection, and the implications. "You look just like him, except for the eyes." Of course, he had his mother's eyes. He felt all the color drain from his face at this point. The bartender inquired about what they would like to drink as Frank looked on, apparently concerned.

"Yes, ma'am, he was my father," Kyle said, trying for bold and proud, and hoping he'd mastered it. He wondered why she didn't already know that, if she had known his father.

"Lynn, what'll you have?" Frank asked, touching her slightly on the elbow.

"Oh, uh…Maker's Mark, neat, please," she said to the bartender and then glanced back at Kyle. She even drank his dad's poison. How well had she known him? "And…maybe one for my new friend here?" she asked, good-naturedly toward Kyle.

He cleared his throat, struggling for composure. "No, thanks, just a beer," he said, glancing at Frank, who looked innocent enough.

"Same for me," said Frank. "Make it a Yeungling," he added, and Kyle nodded at the bartender. He wondered where the other woman was. Lynn was still looking at his eyes. No doubt she would make some comment about them as most women did; he cut them away subtly, straightening his tie.

Instead, she filled in the gaps, supplying answers to his questions. "I knew your father. He built my house," she said kindly, trying to make him feel at ease. But he still didn't know how it had gone, how his dad had treated her, or even still, how she had treated him. He was getting such a weird vibe from this woman! He nodded, prepared to ask another question, but Lynn looked beyond him just then, ending such conversation.

"Oh, here's Pam!" said Lynn, looking past him at the imposing and attractive woman who was undulating toward them on a pair of black heels that surely added three inches to her more than six feet. She wore a knit dress so tight and low-cut it hid no secrets from the viewer, secrets she probably should have been keeping, but she seemed like the kind of woman who wouldn't care. Her long dark hair and dark eyes were set off by an unnaturally white smile and a deep leathery tan. She stopped in front of Kyle, extending her hand, and saying in a throaty voice, "Hi, I'm Pamela Van Dervere, the silent partner!" She giggled heartily, as if "silent" were a large joke. She took his hand in an intimate grasp, hardly a professional gesture, which seemed to go along with the outfit—and the *perfume*! He recognized it immediately. It was a Chanel fragrance that his grandfather kept Shelly and Stacie swimming in every Christmas. He knew this after having watched them open the same boxes year after year.

Kyle introduced himself, head swimming as Frank was then introduced. Pam looked back at Kyle, taking in his eyes, which he tried to avert from her ample and artificial chest. She ordered a dirty martini and they stepped out onto the deck to have their drinks while waiting for their table. "You have the most *amazing* blue eyes!" she said to him. He glanced sideways at Frank, who seemed to be enjoying his discomfort immensely. Frank's deep set brown eyes were laughing at him. She was flirting. So what? Everybody flirted. He knew how to play this game, or more importantly, how not to play this game.

"Thanks," he replied pleasantly, fingering the knot of his tie, wondering how much worse this evening could possibly get. They were called to their table where they seated themselves boy-girl around the four-top, making it look like a double date as opposed to the business dinner he'd anticipated. He was ready to talk business, but the others were clearly enjoying themselves, ordering a second round of drinks, looking over the menu and commenting on the food. Frank favored the buffalo steak and the ladies discussed the duck, while he thought about the mountain trout like his dad and he used to catch in the river behind the cabin. He knew he should get back down there and do some fly-fishing. Chelsea's dad would enjoy that, and maybe Jay and Glen. Maybe he could start a river fishing guide service if he ended up getting fired tonight! Surely, he had been aware somewhere in the back of his mind that he would eventually run into one of his father's former clients, and it wouldn't be good.

A server in black started toward their table, then stopped abruptly, turning on her heel and heading the other way, apparently forgetting something. Something about her was vaguely familiar, the blonde hair piled on top of her head, the dangling bronze earrings. He pondered the quail and felt Pamela's hand resting on his arm.

"So tell us about you, Kyle!" she gushed warmly, giving him her best smile and adjusting the neckline of her dress, keeping the girls inside the playground. Not bad, but not real either.

Frank was grinning at him again. Had he not told them *anything* about him? He was beginning to feel like the green kid, the grunt, who wouldn't be taken seriously. He glared at Frank.

"Well, I graduated from architecture school at UVA," he started, and Frank interjected.

"Top of his class!" He was proud, great, but he could have done a better job of advertising.

"Oh, we *know* all that. What do you like to do? Are you dating?" Pamela laughed as Lynn gave her an admonishing look.

"Actually, I just got married twelve days ago," he said happily, thinking it would throw her out of her chair, but it seemed to have the opposite effect.

"Oh, did you just return from your honeymoon?" she crooned, and when he nodded, she dug in further. "How sweet! Tell us about your wife. What's she like?"

"Chelsea's amazing. She's a dancer. She danced for the—"

"I was a dancer once…thirty years and thirty pounds ago," she interrupted him wistfully. He imagined her sliding around a pole in some smoke-filled bar.

Even Frank's eyebrows had cranked up a notch. Kyle took a deep breath, wondering how much longer he could stand this. Her perfume was knocking him out. How old *was* she?

"I was a swimsuit model," Pam went on as the server approached again, and this time, he recognized her. It was Elle McClarin from high school, twenty pounds heavier and needing a root touch-up. She had been obsessed with Kyle in school, even slipping him some Rohypnol at a party once. She later got arrested and charged with a felony. He almost choked on his beer. She looked straight at him.

"Hello, Kyle. Congratulations," she said, filling Pam's water glass and then Lynn's, moving on to his and Frank's.

"Hi, Elle. Thanks." He would be watching his back tonight; kitchens had knives.

"I'm Elle, and I'll be taking care of you tonight. Would you all like to order another round, or would you care for a bottle of wine with your dinner?" she asked professionally. She must have seen him and run back into the kitchen to collect herself. That's what that was all about, pretending to forget something.

Lynn answered. "Let's have the Franciscan Cabernet and four glasses."

"Excellent choice," Elle commented. "I'll be back with that while you look over the menu. Any questions while I'm still here?" They shook their heads and she disappeared toward the bar.

"Friend of yours?" asked Lynn.

He cleared his throat again and smiled. "A classmate from high school."

Frank looked somber, wondering, probably. He had probably heard the roofie story from Kyle's mother back in high school. How much worse could the night get? Elle returned with the wine and filled their glasses. Kyle excused himself to go to the restroom where he met Elle full on while coming down the narrow hall on his return. She was headed for the ladies' room, and there was no room to avoid her.

She pealed into laughter, hardly able to contain herself. "Good *God!* Who is that woman you're with? Oh, you're in big trouble with Chelsea. That *babe* is all over you!"

"Shut up, Elle. It's business and that *babe* is older than my mother," he said, reddening, struggling for the upper hand.

Her laugh burst from between her lips. "Well, *I* wanna be in *your* business! It looks a whole lot more interesting than what *I'm* doing!" she laughed, brushing past him and heading into the restroom. It had been over six years since he'd seen her and this was how it went down. Elle was still as hard and cynical as ever. Time had not softened her one bit. Some things never change, he thought irritably.

As he returned to the table, replacing his napkin in his lap, he looked at Lynn, who seemed ready to talk to him. He might as well find out the answers to his questions, and he wanted to divert his attention to her instead of the all-consuming Amazon to his right.

"So my father built your house up here?"

"Yes," she said pleasantly, propping her elbows on the table and resting her chin on her hands. "Eight years ago. It's a beautiful place. Maybe you've seen it? I wanted something Frank Lloyd Wrightish since my property was on the side of a hill. He certainly achieved that. It's a real masterpiece. I wonder if you're as talented as he was," she mused wanly, no innuendo intended, he thought from her tone.

"I can hope," he said modestly. So far she seemed innocent enough about Stuart Davis's business practices. Kyle wanted to know so much more.

"We could run by there and let you see it, if you think we'd have the time this evening," she suggested, glancing at Frank. Suddenly, Kyle wanted nothing more than to see what his father had done, to see why it pleased her. He wanted to know something good about the man he still did not understand.

"We might be able to swing that," Frank offered, questioning Kyle with his eyes until Kyle nodded.

"I was so sorry to hear that he'd passed away. It must have been very sudden?" Lynn continued, making him realize she had no idea what had happened. That had been the way his mother had wanted it. No one was supposed to know their dirty little secrets. That had been hard on him at seventeen, when he'd found his dad, cold and lifeless in the cabin, the empty bottle of Maker's Mark and pills on the table, and no one was supposed to know. His mother had said he'd died of a heart attack. Now, hearing Lynn's question, he detected more than mere curiosity in her tone; angst maybe? Her eyes held the same message, but this was neither the time nor the place to address it.

"Yes, it was," he said, unable to continue his mother's lie, averting his eyes yet again, wondering what to look at this time. Then he remembered how to fade away, to become a stone, so that no one would talk to him. Nobody messed with the brooding dark fellow at school. He slipped easily back into the persona and became quiet. Elle returned to take their order. Later when she delivered their appetizers, he did not look at her, but remained stone-faced at the table. The whole table was quiet and they ate in silence. He felt guilty for spoiling the party, but he struggled to handle the situation. He obviously had not learned. He ached with the memories this conversation had unearthed in him.

Frank started talking business and the details of Lynn's plans for the condos spilled forth. She wanted something generic and boring, Kyle thought dismally—something with lots of concrete and lighting. Lots of lighting that would be visible all over the night sky and ruin the area's beautiful darkness and solitude. How could he possibly design that for her? It would be his project, Frank had said. He drank more wine and then the entrées came. Pamela prattled on about the restaurants in South Beach, and her divorce, but he ignored her as much as possible, being distant without being rude. He enjoyed the trout and listened to the good-natured conversation between Frank and Lynn. He liked her more and more.

Another bottle of wine was presented to the table as the conversation changed to the naming of the property, helping to dispel some of the unpleasant thoughts Kyle was having. Frank wasn't keen on Lynn's choice. He ran a hand over his prematurely white hair and looked across the room. "I don't think you ought to call it Raven's Ridge," he said as Lynn's face fell. He looked to Kyle for support and continued. "It's a good name for an overlook or a trail, but not for somewhere people will live. It's kind of a bad omen." Lynn looked confused.

Pam said, "We both like the way it rolls off the tongue...*Raven's Ridge*, you know?"

Kyle stepped in. "Well, traditionally the folk legends imply that ravens are a sign of impending death; the more ravens there are, the closer death might be. So, the name might not sit too well with the locals, if you see what I mean."

Both women's eyes grew large. "I had no idea, being from Florida I hadn't heard about that. But now that you mention it, I'm not so hot on Raven's Ridge anymore," said Lynn, and Pam looked at Kyle with renewed interest. She stroked back her hair and took another sip of wine. He did the same.

"What do you suggest?" Pam asked Kyle, ignoring Frank.

Kyle thought a moment. "Well, you picked a beautiful property. I've been hiking up there plenty of times and there's a great view. You should probably incorporate some hiking trails in your plan...but when it snows there, like many mountain ridges, it's gorgeous. When the sunlight hits the snow, it sparkles just like sugar," he said as Pam rested her chin in her hand, gazing at him, imagining the sight, or maybe something else.

"Well, there you go," said Lynn. "Why don't we call it Sugar Ridge?"

Frank pondered it a moment. "I like it."

"It rolls off the tongue nicely, too," Pam said, glancing at Kyle again. "To *Sugar Ridge*," she said, raising her glass.

Eventually, after the plates were removed and the third bottle of wine was emptied, Elle was tempting them with the owner's homemade bread pudding.

"I have an idea. Why don't we get a couple of those for the road and go take a look at the house your dad built?" asked Lynn, looking to the men for a consensus. Frank and Kyle nodded their approval. Kyle's head swam with the wine that had slid as easily across his tongue as velvet. Pamela decided it was a fine idea and the four of them took to their cars for the short trip up the mountain to what Lynn described as her paradise.

Frank offered to drive, so Kyle flopped into the passenger seat. Frank followed the red tail lights of Lynn's Lexus, her "mountain car," down the winding road and up the next mountain toward Blowing Rock.

"You didn't tell me we were going to hell tonight," Kyle said wryly, giving his boss a sidelong glance.

Frank chortled, adjusting the seatbelt over his stocky frame due to the large dinner they'd just consumed. "Well, you've had an interesting night, to say the least," he commented.

"I can't work with Pam, ever!" he said loosely.

"You won't have to. She's just along for the ride. Besides, she wasn't—"

"Oh, yes, she was!" Kyle corrected him, making Frank laugh again.

"It's those '*amazing* blue eyes' of yours!" Frank mimicked her.

"Jeez!" Kyle muttered under his breath.

In a short time, they were at the house. It was indeed a masterpiece, set into the very side of the rocky ridge. Its landscape lighting was so subtle it seemed to become part of the sky itself, more so than any lighting he'd ever seen.

Lynn led them inside the rugged structure and into a large open foyer that led to a magnificent rustic and woodsy great room, decorated in warm rich tones. Pam teetered toward the kitchen in search of dessert plates and coffee. The staircase was angular and squared off, the way he had pictured the work of Frank Lloyd Wright.

"She wasn't kidding!" Frank commented under his breath.

"Kyle, I know you want to go home to your wife, but let me give you the quick tour," Lynn said, leading him up the stairs as the others followed.

He had to know, and he'd had just enough wine to ask, with imploring eyes, "Did my dad...treat you fairly during the building?"

"Yes, why would you ask?" she replied without hesitation, a puzzled look in her eyes. She didn't think anything was amiss, so he felt relieved that Stuart Davis had not screwed her over. Maybe none of it was true at all. Who could build something like this and be that crooked? He sighed with relief. Maybe it was because she was so nice. They were standing in a bedroom and the others had moved on, commenting about the design of the large windows, allowing breathtaking views in the daytime. "What happened to Stuart...if you don't mind my asking?" Lynn asked apprehensively, touching her fingers together.

Kyle hesitated. He had told only a handful of people about his father's suicide—the police and his headmaster from school, his mother, and Chelsea. He sighed and met her questioning look. "He committed suicide...over the business, and some other things...my sister's death being one of them." He felt that familiar rush of heat ascend to his face at the mention of his sister. He could almost hear Desiree's wild laughter and feel the exuberance of her presence, as if she were just in the next room.

Lynn looked at him, shocked, then sighed, and shook her head. "Oh, Kyle! I'm so sorry. I didn't know. I *did* know about your sister, and I'm sorry about that, too. Your dad was so good at what he did. *Look at this place!*" she whispered incredulously. "I knew your father very well. I just can't believe he would have done that," she continued, raising those same questions again.

He nodded, an idea suddenly coming to him. "Why not build your condos to look something like this? Build them into the landscape instead of buzzing the ridge. Keep as many trees as you can. Use the understated landscape lighting. Build fewer of them, but *better*," he said, letting it pour out of him. "It could be incredible. You have the money to make them extraordinary. That's the kind of thing people want up here."

She looked at him, blinking. "Can you do that?" she asked him earnestly.

He nodded. "I'll have to take a good look at the landscape, but from the pictures you've shown us tonight, I think it's possible. It'll be the challenge of my career so far, but with the right vision, I think it can be done," he said and she held his gaze with her wide hazel eyes.

She put out her hand and he took it, feeling that firm handshake again.

Later as they left the amazing house, Lynn gave him a motherly sideways hug. "I know this has been a tough night for you, Kyle. But I'm really looking forward to working with you, and Frank," she said, including Frank in her warm smile.

Pamela stepped in for her hug as well. It was not so motherly, and he felt her hand behind his head, mashing his face into her neck. Never again would she touch him, he thought, nodding at her politely, stepping aside to let Frank have a turn.

⚜

As he wove down the mountain from back at the restaurant, Kyle was aware of bright lights in his rearview mirror. Some idiot was all over him. "Get your own speeding ticket," he muttered, concentrating on the road and trying to focus all his energy on his driving. He realized he'd had far too much wine to be driving, and especially on this road. Suddenly blue lights flashed around in the mirror, sending his stomach plummeting to the ground. "Shit!" he said, pulling over, putting the Range Rover in park, and fishing around his glove compartment for his registration. He hadn't been five hundred feet out of the parking lot! This night was getting worse and worse!

He put down his window, resting his elbow on the door of the car, holding his license and registration between his fingers. His heart pounded. This was just great! He imagined having to call Chelsea from the police station to come and drag his sorry ass out of jail. He remembered this scenario all too well from when he was seventeen and getting an under-aged DUI, getting arrested and handcuffed on the way back from a party in prep school after his father's death. Losing his sister and being banished to the boys' school had been bad enough, but dealing with his father had about broken him. He'd been pissed off and arrogant enough to go looking for whatever mind-numbing substances he could find. But that night the handcuffs and the jail time with the cast from *Deliverance* had humbled him, shaming him into living his life to a certain self-determined and rigid code. Yet, here he was, circling the drain once more. Shit. A bright flashlight shone directly in his face and a hand slapped his arm, startling him.

"*Hey, Buddy roe!* How ya doin'? How was the honeymoon?"

Kyle looked up at the cop.

"God! Glen, you are such an *asshole!*"

Glen Dunham's impish face grinned at him openly as he crouched in the Range Rover's window, obviously glad to see his best friend. He laughed at the trick he'd played on Kyle, and eventually, Kyle laughed too.

"Where've you been, man?" Glen laughed again.

"Hell," said Kyle morosely, and Glen hooted with laughter.

"I thought that was you, pulling out of the Gamekeeper."

"Am I under arrest? If not, I'm keeping a really pretty lady waiting," he said, hearing his cell phone buzz, signaling a text from Chelsea on the screen, probably wondering what was keeping him.

"Well, you don't sound like you should be driving. I just got off duty myself. Why don't you pedal this thing back to the parking lot and I'll give you a ride home. I doubt you're in any shape for those curves and switchbacks coming up."

"Probably not. Hey, thanks, man." Kyle managed to pull back into the road and park the Range Rover in the parking lot, a discreet distance from the street.

"Better me stopping you now than my colleague down the road," Glen remarked as Kyle pocketed his keys and buckled in. "This was your business dinner?"

"Yup. Frank and I are going to build condos for some women out of Florida after the inn is done."

"Very cool. Business must be good."

"I hope it'll stay that way, at least." Kyle thought a moment and remembered one of his bombshells of the evening. "You'll never guess who waited on us tonight."

"*Elle McClarin!*"

Kyle nodded. "How'd you know?"

"I see Aiden Caffey from time to time. He told me she worked there. You know they have a kid together, right?"

"No way!" Aiden had played football with them in high school and had taken to hanging out with Elle after she was arrested and shunned from her crowd at school.

"Oh, yeah. He's about six years old now. She was pregnant when we all graduated, but Aiden wouldn't marry her. He figured she was tryin' to trap him into it."

"Smart dude. So she had the baby while she was paying her debt to society? How did I not know this?" he asked, trying to articulate his thoughts intelligibly. He remembered that Elle had served a few months in jail after her sentencing.

"Probably. I didn't know about it for a long time either. You moved to the beach and then went off to college. No reason for you to have known. Funny how the wrong people end up pregnant and the ones who really want to be can't get knocked up for anything, you know?" he said vacantly, which seemed an odd admission for Glen.

Kyle's head swung over to look at him. He should have more control with that move. He really was trashed. This wouldn't go over well at home. But Glen didn't notice.

"You and Abby still trying?" he asked, carefully pronouncing his words.

"Always. If there's anybody in this town getting laid as much as you right now, it's me, bro. Not that I'm complaining!"

"Practice makes perfect!" Kyle said hopefully to his friend as they pulled up in front of the cabin. "All right, man, thanks for the ride. I owe you one. We should all get together, okay?"

"Sure! Hope you're not in too much trouble! Give Chels a squeeze for me. Take care now," Glen clasped Kyle's hand before he swung out of the squad car and made his way up the steps, concentrating on each step.

At eleven-thirty, Chelsea placed the stack of thank you notes in its rubber band on the kitchen table to remind herself to mail them in the morning. *Breakfast at Tiffany's* had been over for an hour and she had thought

Kyle would be home by now for sure. He had texted her when he left, but that had been forty-five minutes ago. She was getting worried when lights flooded the driveway. She expected to hear his Range Rover stop, the door shut, and him bound up the steps, sport coat slung over his arm. Instead, she heard an engine continue to run, voices in the yard, and a door shut. Footsteps crunched slowly in the driveway. She peeked out the window to see Kyle walking rather fluidly up the steps, his necktie loosened, and a *police car* backing down the drive! She flung open the door.

"*What happened?* Are you okay? Where's your car?"

He fell into her arms, seeming to be at a loss for words. "I'm so glad to be home! God, I love you!" he breathed into the side of her neck. She smelled the distinct scent of *Mademoiselle* on him and instinctively pulled away. "What have you been doing? I've been so worried," she cried, not believing this was happening. Whatever it was he had gotten into, it couldn't be good.

He regarded her, looking confused. "We were at dinner. And this woman, Lynn, my dad built her house so we went up there. You should see it. It's astounding." He stopped, realizing she didn't like what she was hearing.

She stared at him, taking in the sound of his voice, like toothpaste being squeezed slowly from a tube, the same way he had walked up the stairs. He was plowed! She watched him swaying slightly and he backed up to the sink, leaning there for support.

He raised his hands in defense. "Look, I know this doesn't look good. So much happened tonight. It was just too much, you know?" he said, taking off his blazer and pulling the tie from around his neck.

She didn't know what to say. Waves of hurt washed over her, thinking about how she'd worried about his safety while he had been out smooching with some woman named Lynn in one of his father's haunts. Then she wondered whether that's the way it had been with Stuart Davis. Was this the first sign of the alcoholism that had consumed him? After all, they were back in this cabin, and Kyle was essentially reliving his father's life. He even looked like Stuart right now. It was so disconcerting. She thought of what she'd said to him at the beach that day, *"I want to know everything."* She did and she didn't. Knowing everything might be more than she could take. Still she gaped at him, unable to speak. Whatever she said at the moment would be of little consequence anyway. He probably wouldn't remember it tomorrow. Sure, they drank, but she had never seen him like this. He probably wouldn't remember what he'd done anyway. And then it would just be her, stewing about it and never getting her answers. *"For better, for worse; in sickness and in health,"* she thought, distressed. Could she do this? This was the real thing. There had to be an explanation, but right now he was in no shape to deliver it.

"You should go to bed. It's late. Where's your car?" she said to him, trying to keep the emotion out of her voice. He took her hand and looked at her through bleary eyes.

"It's at the Gamekeeper. Chelsea…I'm sorry. You don't deserve this. It was awful. I'll tell you about it tomorrow. It's just…too much right now."

"So, I guess they're not *gay*," she couldn't help herself from muttering, and he laughed sharply.

"You got that right!" he chuckled, starting to the bedroom, veering to the right a bit and then shooting straight into the room.

She turned off all the lights, locked the door, set the security system, and followed after him. He was sprawled across the bed, fully dressed, snoring, when she came in, not three minutes later. There was no room on her side of the bed, so she reached for her pillow, pondering which room she'd sleep in tonight. "I need a dog," she muttered, turning out the light.

Chapter 5

....

SLIPPING

....

Kyle awoke to the sound of the shower running. He lay in place for a moment, trying to remember where he was. He squinted his eyes to decipher the time on the clock beside the bed. After refocusing his eyes a couple of times, it appeared to be six o'clock. Beside the clock, he began to make out a glass of water and three brown pills. At least he thought there were three. He had to refocus his eyes again to make sure. Whatever the case, it was not a good sign that his wife had left pain relief medication on the bedside table for him. He knew why when he tried to sit up. His head was spinning, causing him immediately to reach for the glass and down all three pills at once. It was slowly coming back to him. He took a deep breath and smelled coffee...and the perfume from the night before. He groaned ruefully and held his head in his hand as he sat on the side of the bed. He certainly had some explaining and some apologizing to do. Just then, Chelsea walked through the bedroom in her bathrobe, scrunching styling gel into the ends of her wet hair, giving him a tight smile on her way to the kitchen.

No good morning kiss? No greeting whatsoever. He knew what this was. He was in the doghouse! He was about to attempt to stand up when she was beside him, sitting on the bed, handing him a large cup of coffee.

"Oh, you're the best! Thank you," he managed to say groggily, smelling the sweetness of her beside him.

She sipped from her own cup. "What time do you have to be in? We need to get your car," she reminded him quietly, as he let this register.

"Yeah...I guess Frank can't be feeling any better than I am. Let's just get there when we get there. The subs can start without us. He set me up for all of this after all," he said, turning his head toward her slowly, so as not to throw his equilibrium. She returned the careful look, questions in her clear aquamarine eyes.

"I'm so sorry about last night. I know I worried you...and then you didn't sleep here. That's a first," he commented sadly, touching her hand.

"Not that you'd have known, but no, there was no room on the bed with you laid out across it in your clothes," she said frankly, noticing the pile of clothes he'd eventually gotten out of at some point during the night. "Why don't you have a shower and we'll talk about it," she offered, knowing he probably needed time for his memories to fall into place. She stood and walked back into the kitchen.

Still, no kiss, he thought glumly—not that he deserved one. He sighed and stood, making his way carefully to the bathroom. He didn't feel too bad, he thought, cranking on the warm water and letting it pour over his head, washing away the last remnants of the woman who had ruined the evening. Even Elle would have been tolerable compared to Pamela, but what was really eating at him was all the déjà-vu about his dad, hearing about him from Lynn, and the odd news that his dad had been a good guy, maybe. He thought it would be welcome news, but something about it didn't sit right with him—that and the sad and disappointed looks his beloved wife was giving him this morning. It was more than he could stand.

He sighed and dried himself off, going to the closet to get dressed, his head still swimming from all the wine. The coffee and the ibuprofen were taking their time coming to the rescue.

When he made it to the kitchen, she was dressed in her dancer's attire, ready for a class she would probably take somewhere after she helped him collect his car. A bag of hers and her laptop, no doubt with her lessons for the following week, stood ready by the door with her shopping bags for the grocery store. She stood by the sink, fixing his lunch. He noticed a slice of cheese toast and a banana set aside for his breakfast. Slowly, he went to stand near her and leaned his back against the place where the kitchen counter turned the corner. This little corner was where they'd shared their most intimate and profound discussions in the past. It was the place where they'd declared their love for each other in high school, when she'd dissolved his misery and he'd felt whole again for the first time in years. It was the same place where she had tried to seduce him while they prepared dinner, and almost foiled his plans for proposing to her the night of the December snowstorm. When he'd put her off to collect himself and accomplish his mission, she'd thought he was preparing to break up with her. God, she'd been so confused! He almost smiled at the misunderstanding and she looked up, the hurt crossing over her face again. He'd seen that before once, a couple of years ago and it made him ache, knowing he was the cause of it...again.

He searched for her eyes again, trying to connect with her, but she seemed determined to get his ham sandwich just right. He reached for her arm and said to her gently, "Baby...." Suddenly her eyes filled with tears. He rarely called her that; he could tell it moved her, just as her reaction moved him. She was in his arms in an instant and he held her desperately, kissing the curve of her cheek tenderly. "I'm so, so sorry!" he whispered into her hair, grateful for the scent of her, the way a woman was supposed to smell.

"I know!" she whispered back and drew away slightly, wiping her tears fiercely from her face. "It was just…seeing you so drunk last night. I couldn't help but think of your father here, like that, and wondering if…" she couldn't finish her thought.

"No, it's never going to be like that," he said, stroking her cheek and meeting her troubled gaze with determined eyes. "I promise you!"

"And then the *cops* drop you off?"

He raised his eyebrows and chuckled, surprising her. "No! That was Glen! I thought you saw him. He pulled out behind me on the way out of the restaurant parking lot and thought he would play with my head, turning on the blue lights in my mirror; scared the hell out of me. He gave me a ride home, which was probably for the best," he said, smiling at her, and she couldn't help but smile back.

She shook her head. "What a little shit!" she laughed.

"I know. He really had me going." The tension seemed to have eased a bit. She picked up their breakfast plates as they moved to the table, sitting across the corner from each other.

"I still don't understand how you had Lynn's perfume all over you," she began apprehensively.

He sighed and raised his eyebrows, setting their coffee cups down. "It wasn't hers. Lynn's really cool. It was Pamela's. They're about as opposite as day and night. Pam hugged me before we left Lynn's house. I know; it was so inappropriate. She's inappropriate in many ways. But she's just the silent partner, and Frank doesn't think we'll be seeing much more of her. Anyway, you should see the house my dad built for Lynn. It's…*unbelievable*! It's like something I've seen in Frank Lloyd Wright books. I never knew my father had done anything like that. It had to be his best work ever. I know she'd like to meet you, and show it to you as well. You'd like her. She didn't know what happened to Dad. She had a lot of respect for him, and I don't think he treated her badly," he said, his voice drifting off, and she waited for more.

"So it wasn't all that bad then, really?"

"I guess not, when I think back on it all. I just wasn't really prepared for any of it, and I guess I didn't handle it all that well," he conceded, then looked at her for the next bit of information he was about to reveal. "I guess it was a combination of all the stuff that happened that made me suck down all that wine."

"What else happened?" she asked, wide-eyed.

"Elle McClarin was our waitress," he said slowly for effect.

"No way!" She laughed at the idea of this on top of everything else he had explained so far. "I can imagine that was uncomfortable."

He smiled at her reaction. "You would hardly have recognized her," he commented.

"Abby told me she and Aiden have a six-year old son," she offered.

"That's what Glen said."

"Yeah, Abby thinks it's so unfair. She wants a baby so badly while someone like Elle gets to be a mom. It isn't right."

They gazed at each other for a moment, and then he said, "I'll bet I didn't even kiss you good night last night."

"No, you didn't."

"And then nothing this morning? Does this mean the honeymoon is over?" he asked, placing his hand on hers.

She looked at him tentatively. "Only if you're slipping."

"I'm not slipping. Today, it's me who's more in love."

She looked at him carefully, shaking her head, "No, you're not. It's me; believe me. I had to dig down deeper, and I know I love you more right now."

Feeling humbled but hardly redeemed, he pulled her out of her chair and onto his lap. He kissed her tenderly, and she returned the kiss the same way, pushing her fingers into his hair. He looked at her and said, "You're not cooking tonight, okay? I'm taking you out. I'd like to try and make this up to you."

"Ah, atonement for your sins?"

"Damn right," he said, kissing her again.

<center>~~~~~~</center>

In the evening, he made it home before she did. He showered, and he worried for a bit before he heard her car on the gravel in the drive. He realized the waiting and wondering was yet a small taste of what she'd gone through the night before. When he opened the door to greet her, she held a small unwrapped package in her hand.

"Hey," he said, taking her into a hug, noticing she did not hold her face close to be kissed. She returned the hug with a wistful smile and tentative eyes turned up at him.

"What do you have there, another gift?" he asked.

"Yes. This one is from Daisy Frazier."

She must have stopped by her parents' house on her way home. He knew this gift would be special. Daisy had been Kitty's best friend, and since she had directed their wedding, he thought the gift must have touched Chelsea. But Daisy had already given them towels, or something.

She removed a small stained-glass circle from the box, tissue paper crinkling, and held it by a silver cord to the light. "She told Mom this was an afterthought. She dropped it off today," said Chelsea, holding it to the fading light at the doorway. Inside the circle was a design of bottle green, resembling the outlines of three leaves joined at the center, in a clear, leaded glass background. "It's the Celtic symbol for the Trinity. She saw it today at that cool place called Art Walk in Boone and said she had to get it for us."

"Hmm...maybe she thinks we need a blessing," he said, trying for humor.

"I know we do. It can't hurt," she said, not returning his sentiment. "So, how was your day?" As she asked, he thought she noticed he was wearing the blue shirt with white stripes that he knew she liked, and he had worn in an attempt to please her.

"It was good. It took me until about lunchtime to feel right again. Frank had the same issues."

She nodded. "Did you hear any more about the project?"

"Yeah," he said, dragging a hand behind his neck. "They dropped the condos right in our laps. Frank was thrilled."

"Poor choice of words, Kyle," she said, and he felt himself returning to the doghouse. He looked at her with pleading eyes. She smiled, lightening the mood to his relief. "I'm just kidding."

He smiled back at her, afraid to push his luck. "When would you like to go to dinner?"

"Soon, I'm starving."

"Me too. How does Makoto's sound...for sushi?"

"That would be nice. I'll go change," she said, giving him a wan, backward glance as she disappeared into the bedroom.

Normally, they would have opened a beer or poured themselves a glass of wine, but it seemed the wrong thing to do and he did not mention it. He picked up the stained glass piece and walked out onto the deck, breathing in deeply the woodsy, clean air he had missed living outside of Washington. He had taken a big risk, leaving his successful job and coming back here, but he had done it to be with her. People had thought he was nuts, but somehow, he had known it would work out, and he had hoped desperately that she would have time to see him occasionally, but that she had ended up here was just too serendipitous. He gazed at the Trinity symbol and thought about her comments that afternoon before the wedding rehearsal, about how her love for him was like her love for God, one in the same, almost the Trinity. Maybe there was something to this gift from Daisy after all. He shook his head briefly and looked up to find her walking toward him.

She wore the soft summery dress in the shade of blue he liked, reminding him of spring rain clouds. Fluttery ruffles made a deep V at the neckline, allowing him to take in the little star necklace at her throat, pleased that she still wore it. The whole image of her took his breath away. Damn! She was trying as hard as he was!

He adjusted his gaze and spoke softly, "Wow, Mrs. Davis…you look… *perfect!*"

She smiled the smile he'd been waiting for, and he went to her slowly, wondering whether she would kiss him finally. Her arms went around his waist and she raised her lips to his, giving him the tenderest of open-mouthed kisses, leaving him floating in this thin place. He'd heard of this before, that thin place between earth and heaven, that place where one transcended the world. It could only be here, in this place, with this woman. This could be his life all the time if he didn't screw it up, and he felt suddenly washed with grace, humbled to be with her right now.

"I want to make this right with you," he murmured, his forehead pressed to hers.

"You already have. It's fine…we're fine," she answered, her eyes searching long into his. He pulled her into a strong embrace. Thunder rumbled just faintly from far away as he kissed her deeply, finally redeemed.

Chapter 6

FAMILY

Abby and Chelsea sat companionably on the soft creamy sofa together, sharing mugs of tea and covered in a blanket. It had gotten chilly after the rain that evening. Kyle and Glen had managed to cook steaks on the grill under an umbrella, and after the dishes had been put in the dishwasher and the trash taken out, the two men could be heard downstairs in the basement, playing a rowdy game of pool.

"Kyle is quite the attentive husband!" Abby commented, tossing her veil of silky black hair over her shoulder, blowing on her cinnamon tea.

Chelsea felt the glow return to her face that was usually there at the mention of him. Her eyes demurred into her own mug of tea. "Do you mean because he cooks, helps in the kitchen, and takes out the trash? It's all because he spent so much time in Stacie and Tyson's restaurant."

"I know; it's all that but he also can't take his eyes off of you! I haven't seen him swept away like this, ever. You're still on your honeymoon, aren't you?" she asked with a slight wink and a grin.

"Yes, we are, and it's still amazing," Chelsea murmured, almost glad to have someone in whom she could confide. She still wanted to pinch herself every day. He had given up his ritual of morning runs in exchange for activities with her until the last minute when they had to get out of bed every morning. On those mornings, it had been the sweetest way to wake up, especially with rain pouring on the roof, and they lay in each others' arms, nestled in their own cocoon of joy.

"That's great for you guys," Abby went on dreamily. "Just think what it will be like when we have our families together." She had given up drinking wine, thus the consumption of the tea, and Chelsea had joined her. She and Glen were still trying for their first child so she wanted to do everything right. "Of course, my child will be the oldest, but won't it be fun, taking them for hikes on trails along the parkway and picnics at the lake?"

"Yes, and fly-fishing with their dads in the river, when they're old enough."

"And don't forget skiing!" Abby said and they laughed. There were so many things Kyle and Glen liked to do together, and no matter whether these dream children turned out to be boys or girls, they would be doing it all. "But let's not forget the shopping and the girl stuff!" Abby reminded Chelsea, her doe's eyes large under her incredibly long eyelashes.

"Oh, of course!" Chelsea smiled, knowing if it weren't for Abby's passion for shopping, she would have zilch for a wardrobe.

"I have to take you to my friend Megan's boutique. It's called M.C. Adams Clothier. You know, it's on King Street. She has great clothes and even better sales!"

"Sounds like my kind of place! We're really sticking tight to our budget. It will be hard to know whether Kyle's business will continue to be this good. We're going to sock all our money away and try to stay out of trouble."

"It's nice that you don't have to worry about a mortgage," Abby remarked, casting her eyes over the cabin.

"Oh, there's a mortgage. Kyle played it safe and parked his money for a shot at buying into a business if he ever has a chance. Frank might eventually offer him a partnership, but I'm sure he'll have to prove himself first, and then earn his keep. But then, you never know with the economy if Frank will be able to offer him that, or even be able to keep him on."

"And how's all that going?"

"It seems to be good…for now. They just landed a deal on designing and building some condos on the ridge right over there," Chelsea said, inclining her head toward the windows in front of them.

"And he's still working on the inn in Blowing Rock?"

Chelsea nodded. "That will take a long time to finish. He's plenty busy for now, that's for sure."

"And you like your job, too?"

"I do. Teaching was a little intimidating at first, but I'm getting into it. I love choreographing again; however, I can do without the eight o'clock ballet classes. But I'll suck it up like a big girl."

"Aargh! The eight o'clock class! I never liked those. Don't you miss performing?"

Chelsea felt an old pang of loss for an instant. Of course, the performances would be missed, but she had realized over time that her true passion was choreography and teaching. Inspiring someone else to feel her own passion made her art even more worthwhile, so stepping out of the limelight had been a positive move. "Yeah, I really do. It's going to take some getting used to, but I'll have an opportunity to perform from time to time. And it's nice, not being so exhausted all the time, and not having to worry about what I should and shouldn't eat, you know? I'll never eat another grapefruit again!"

"Plus, you're with Kyle."

"That definitely makes it all worthwhile. I don't have to do this forever. Who knows what will happen in the future?"

"You could be fat and pregnant before you know it…but not before me, okay?"

"That's a *promise!*" Chelsea laughed as the men emerged from the basement.

⚜

Six days later, Chelsea joined the throng of people on King Street in Boone, making her way steadily through the crowd of people, taking in the colorful flowers on the street corners that added to the place's festive feel. There were business folks, college students in packs, some of them with their parents, and some ASU faculty members like herself out for lunch. She felt a twinge of pride that she was included in the latter group. So far, no one had treated her like the loser she thought they would, at the early departure she'd taken from the world of performance and into teaching, and she felt confident that after the summer sessions, she would feel at home on the dance faculty and into a routine.

She smoothed the short madras skirt she wore over her black leotard and pulled the short-sleeved cardigan tight across her chest. In the shade, it was still cool in the mountain breeze here, even for the first of June. She was excited to see her former dance teacher, Sonya McIntyre, again, and they were meeting for lunch at Boone Drug. Sonya had a project idea to share with her about joining forces to teach dance to handicapped students. She'd had experience with that kind of venture in college, and then with the Ballet. It was fortunate that she was early since she was on a mission. Anxiety tugged at her again and sent chill bumps down her arms once again like she'd had at ten-thirty this morning. She'd had the same bout of nausea she'd had around that time the day before. Yesterday, she'd chalked it up to something she'd eaten the night before. But how would pinto beans and corn bread make one sick to one's stomach? And then there was that comment from Kyle, when she'd run her hands over his slim torso in their bed and apologized for starving him with her cooking. "Don't be ridiculous," he'd said, caressing her breasts tenderly and laughing gently, "Now you, on the other hand are filling out nicely!" She had felt so sensitive where he had touched her, and now she was alarmed at how her body had changed.

Pushing her bag higher on her shoulder, she ran a hand through her hair, blowing loose in the breeze. She made out the sign for the drugstore and slipped quickly inside, scanning the old place for Sonya. Good, she had made it there first. She purchased the pregnancy test quickly and took the stairs up to the ladies room, which was thankfully empty at the moment. No way could she have mentioned this to Kyle. After all, they had decided to wait, and she couldn't believe she had been so careless! Her period was four days late and he had already questioned why she didn't want a glass of wine last night. Surely, he was bound to figure it out, and she had to know. It had finally dawned on her what Dr. Edmonds, Kyle's grandfather, had cautioned her about at the airport when he'd written her the prescription. He'd told her that the antibiotic would lessen the effects of her birth control pills and to use a backup method. But had she paid attention? Had Kyle? He'd been busy looking for their luggage on the carousel during that conversation.

She sighed deeply, sitting on the toilet, carefully holding the stick under the stream of urine; she closed her eyes, uttering a prayer, weeks too late. She adjusted her clothing and washed her hands, hearing someone knock at the door. "Just a minute," she called out, staring at the double pink lines in the box on the stick, indicating "pregnant." She felt suspended from herself for a moment and took deep breaths, wiping perspiration off of her forehead. What would Abby's reaction be? She felt waves of guilt fueling her betrayal. She had about thirty seconds to get it together, so she stuffed the test stick back in its wrapper and popped it in her purse, steeling herself and opening the door.

A minute, cheerful woman with dark sparrow-like eyes and wavy brown hair greeted her enthusiastically. "Chelsea!" Sonya squealed, throwing her arms around her former student, swinging back and forth with her in the doorway of the ladies' room.

The look of shock on Chelsea's face was suddenly so easy to explain, being caught off guard like this, and she laughed with Sonya at their meet-cute there in the tiny hallway.

"Hey, Sonya! It's so wonderful to see you! I guess you're next," she said, extending her hand into the doorway of the ladies' room. "I'll go on down and get us a table. Can I order you some tea?" she asked, thinking fast, trying desperately to appear normal.

"Sure, unsweet, please!" Sonya agreed, changing places with Chelsea.

"I remember," said Chelsea, already disappearing down the stairs, breathing deeply again, getting her bearings.

⸙⸙⸙⸙⸙

Kyle stood in the sunshine at the foot of the stairs, looking for the best angle. He raised the Canon, snapping a picture of the magnificent house his father had constructed for Lynn Schiffman. Gravel crunched under his feet as he walked a few feet over, finding another shot and taking it as well. She had invited him to come and collect the blueprints his father had drawn of the house that she had unearthed from a hall closet. He thought it would be helpful to have them as well, hopefully to glean some inspiration for the condos he was planning for her. He pushed up the sleeves of his Oxford shirt, walking around to the other side of the house to capture another few shots. He looked up at the deck, watching Lynn, unrolling the plans out on a table for his review, anchoring each corner with stone coasters. She had apologized for Pamela's behavior on the telephone earlier and assured him that she was not in town.

"I'd like to come back at night and get some shots of the landscape lighting if that's okay. It's so subtle. So who did your landscaping?" he asked, clicking off some shots of the rhododendrons in bloom around the base of the deck and the stairs.

"It was a friend of Stuart's. I still use his company for maintenance since I'm not up here as much as I'd like to be. It's Tom Davenport, with White Horse Farms Landscaping," she said, looking down at him.

A slow, incredulous smile grew across his face and she smiled back at him. "Do you know him?" she asked, brushing her hair out of her eyes in the easy breeze.

He slipped the lens cover back on the camera and climbed the stairs to sit with her at the table. "Yes. He's Chelsea's father."

It was her turn to make the incredulous face. "What a small world..." she commented.

He shook his head. "It doesn't surprise me, really. Tom does some really special work. But he and my dad had stopped working together a long time ago, or so I thought." At her questioning look, he continued. "He and my dad and mom were all in college at N.C. State together. Tom is from here, from an old mountain family. My parents moved up here from Charlotte when my sister was a baby and Dad and Tom went into business together...for a while."

"So I guess they did projects together from time to time?" she was trying to understand as he was.

"Well, I didn't think so after they split up, but I guess they did," he shrugged and sat up to the table to take a look at the plans. "I think Tom would be a great choice for a landscape architect to add to this scheme of yours," he suggested.

"It couldn't hurt your relationship a bit, either," Lynn said, grinning.

"Oh, Tom's been like a father to me since I moved back in high school and got to know Chelsea again. That was after Dad died," he said, sniffing and looking back at the plans. *He was more like a father to me than my own father was*, he thought, the dull pain returning for what he hoped would only be an instant.

"So, what was going on with Stuart's business that made him take his life?" she asked directly, dashing that hope. He studied the plans a moment longer to compose himself under her watchful eyes.

In a way, he was relieved to be talking about it. Maybe he would get more answers. He shrugged again and placed his palms together. "Price-gouging, fraud, stuff like that. He was cooking the books and ripping off clients when he worked with Tom. Tom found out and didn't like it so they parted ways. Then later on, the IRS got hold of his business records in an audit and it was all over from a business standpoint. He thought he'd be doing my mother and me a favor by checking out. There's something called 'spousal forgiveness' in a situation like that, where the business takes the hit, but the wife and family aren't held liable, so my mother got to keep his insurance money and the personal property. But she had to sort out all the business dealings he left her with, and liquidate everything. That was how she met Frank. He helped her go through it all and straighten it out. Then…Frank helped me with a high school project and we've kept in touch all this time."

Lynn looked at him somberly through wide hazel eyes, nodding silently. Then she said quietly, "And you wondered if he had ripped me off as well? During this project?"

He nodded.

Looking troubled, she cleared her throat and sat back, sighing and crossing her legs, smoothing her hand down the dark denim of her jeans. "I was pretty hands-on in the building of this house, Kyle. I was here all the time. I had a lot of input on the design. Your dad and I spent a lot of time together, pouring over these plans," she said, gesturing to the blueprints on the table. "We talked price all the time, and I have to say I rode him pretty hard about it, keeping him on budget."

Kyle nodded, sensing how shrewd she'd probably been. What else was she not telling him?

"But, you know, I never got a sense that he was trying to stick it to me. He seemed totally above board with the whole thing. I would never have suspected this at all, what you're telling me."

"So he gave you references? Surely…."

"Oh, yeah. I talked to people. Nobody I spoke to said anything that would have steered me away. He took me to the cabin he built, down near the river. He was so proud of that place. It was his haven."

How many times did he take her there? He couldn't help wondering the purpose for that visit; was it to showcase his work, or for personal reasons? He couldn't tell from her expression, her tone. Instead, he said, "I live there now. Chelsea and I do." She seemed surprised, so he told her the story about his mom giving him all the money when he decided to move back and how he'd bought the place back. "You've been there?" he asked, thinking she would give him more answers.

She looked at him tentatively, as if wondering how much to tell him. "Yes," she finally said. "We had a lot in common. My husband had died the previous year from a brain tumor and we had that bond that people share through loss. It was the best thing I ever did, coming up here and letting him build this beautiful place. It was very cleansing for me, and it's almost as if Ben is here….I don't know," she mused, shaking her head. "It probably makes no sense to you."

"Actually, it does. I have the same feeling about my dad when I'm at the cabin."

She nodded, regarding him carefully. "I thought it was just the mountains…" she said, smiling wistfully.

They were silent a moment before he spoke. "I'm sorry about your husband. I guess I thought you were divorced, like Pam."

She laughed, "Oh no. Pam's husband, Vince, and my husband and I were in business together. We owned two hotels in South Beach. That's how I know her. Suddenly, after Ben's death and her divorce, the two of us were left with some money and I came up here in the summer to build this house, while running the hotels with Vince. Pam is just enjoying the ride and likes the diversion. One night, she and I were up here and got the wild hair to do the condos. I bought that property and here we are." She smiled. "But, as you can imagine, Pam doesn't really like the mountains. There's not enough going on up here to keep her busy!" she said, laughing for his benefit, effectively deflecting the attention away from his father.

She had so far evaded the answer to his question, but he couldn't bring himself to ask her directly. It was none of his business. What good would it do to know whether they had ever had a thing or not? Opening a can of worms like that was not healthy, yet the question burned inside him... *Were you in love with my father?* He wanted to ask her, but at that moment, his cell phone buzzed in his pants' pocket. He pulled it out and glanced at the screen. It was Chelsea. She had never called him at work.

Her heart hammered in her chest as she waited for him to answer his phone, while Sonya looked on worriedly. This couldn't be happening! It couldn't be her father. He was her rock. How can the whole world turn upside down in just an hour?

"Hey, what's up?" Kyle greeted her guardedly on the phone, making her want to cry at the sound of his voice.

"It's my dad. He's in the hospital. Mom just called. He had a heart attack earlier today and they have him over there, running some tests. Can you meet us there?" The words poured out of her mouth; for now, all her other problems seemed inconsequential compared to this. Sonya looked questioningly at her.

"Oh, no! I mean, sure, I'll meet you. Where are you right now?" he asked, his voice edged with urgency.

"I'm sitting here with Sonya at Boone Drug. I can be at the hospital in fifteen or twenty minutes by the time I get to my car. Are you at the inn?"

"Uh, no, I'm at Lynn Schiffman's, looking at some blueprints. I can leave in five minutes. It'll take me longer than you to get over there. I wish I were at the office. I'd be right there and could drive you," he said regretfully. The Mountaineer Builders office was on King Street, just a few blocks down from where she sat with Sonya. She could hear the rattle of papers on the phone.

"Okay, I'll see you there. Call me when you get there, and I'll tell you where to find us."

"Okay…be careful. I love you!" he said into the phone.

"Do you want me to drive you?" asked Sonya, brows knit in concern.

"No, no thanks. I'll be okay. The drive will help me calm down."

"Well, all right. I'll be sending up prayers for your dad. You'll call me when you can?"

"Sure, thanks, Sonya. And I'll work on that project. It's a great idea. It will be wonderful to work with you and your students," she said and hugged her small, slender friend and colleague.

"Don't worry about that right now. You just go and be with your family. Want me to call Carmen to let her know what's going on?"

"Oh, God, yes, that would be great. I completely forgot I have a two o'clock class to teach."

"Don't worry. She'll take care of it."

After another hug, Chelsea bolted back up the street and up the hill to the parking lot, quickly finding her car. Traffic was always bad at this time of day so she zipped across to Rivers Street to avoid the worst of it. Every light she approached turned red; the cars in front of her crawled along at a snail's pace. She rapped her hands hard on the steering wheel. It was Friday, for God's sake! Why wasn't everyone zooming around as they normally were? Finally, she reached the hospital and read the signs, discerning where to park. After passing through the front door, a receptionist greeted her pleasantly, directing her to the cardiology unit where her mother had said they would be.

Breathlessly, she whirled into the room, where Jay and her mother stood beside her father's bed. Liz stroked Tom's blonde and silver hair away from his eyebrows. Her dad needed a haircut, she thought, trying to smile for him, but she was shocked to see the pallor of his usually robust face. The strange hammering began in her chest again, but his slow smile caused it to abate slightly.

"Hey, Sweet Pea," he said, his voice weaker than she had ever heard it, bringing hot tears popping to the surface of her eyes. He looked steadily at her, she thought, hoping to calm her.

She blinked, struggling for the strength she knew he would expect from her.

"Hey, Dad," she said with a quick glance to her mother while she bent to kiss his cool forehead. "What are you doing, scaring us like this?"

"Oh, just keepin' things *lively*," he said in the mountain twang she loved.

She looked at Jay, who was trying to smile at the moment, obviously stuck in his own struggle. "Hey, Chels," he said, taking her hand and giving it a squeeze.

She looked back at her mother for reassurance and found her mother's serene smile. Chelsea asked her, "So what happened, and what is the doctor saying?"

Liz cleared her throat, glancing at Jay. "Jay found him this morning when he didn't come back out of the office with instructions for the work crews. He's had some tests, and they found a blockage, which caused the heart attack. Dr. Pray wants to place a stent as soon as they can arrange the procedure. She has to have a surgical team on standby just in case they need backup."

Chelsea's eyes grew wide and Jay nodded, acknowledging her realization. Their dad could have open heart surgery if things didn't go well. Their dad could die, if things didn't go well. The hammering was back, and she felt Jay's arm around her. She would not cry. Her father needed her to be positive. He needed to hear something good come out of her mouth. She wanted to tell him something hopeful. He was about to be a grandfather again, and she wanted to shower him with this news that would ordinarily make him so happy, but she couldn't just yet. Kyle didn't even know. Tears were sliding down her cheeks and her mother was watching the nuances pass across her face, questioning her with her deep brown eyes. What could she say?

"Well, I like her name, at least! Dr. Pray sounds like the right person for the job!" she said and they all laughed. "When do they expect to get this going?"

"It could be any time now. We're just waiting to hear," her mother said.

"Kyle is on his way," she said, feeling her phone buzz in her pocket and reaching for it.

"Honey," said her mother, "you'll have to take your phone outside the nurses' station. They don't allow cell phones back here."

"Okay. I'm going to tell him where we are. He probably just got here. I'll be right back," she said, squeezing her dad's hand and finding a place to sit at the end of the corridor where she could place her call.

Within minutes, Kyle was striding down the hallway, the mere sight of him settling her heart, allowing her to breathe a little easier. Butterflies ensued though, as she thought of the news he would be hearing in just moments, and she wondered how he would take it. Would there be time? Would there be time to tell Kyle, and then to break the news to her family in the room down the hall, before her father was whisked away into the operating room?

Kyle, svelte in the gray shirt and black slacks, was almost there, and she stood, raking her fingers through her hair as he took her in his strong arms, kissing her forehead. She felt herself leave the floor for an instant in his embrace, and then she looked at him, his heart-stopping blue eyes wide with concern and questions. "What do you know?" he asked softly, stroking her face, and looking around.

She led him to the sofa where she'd been sitting and placed her hand on his fine, brown cheekbone, feeling his scruffy chin where he had not shaved this morning. He continued to look questioningly at her, watching her expressions change as she struggled with how to tell him everything.

"He collapsed in the office this morning and Jay found him. The tests show a single blockage and they want to put in a stent, but they have to get a surgical team in place as a backup in case it fails…" she said, her voice breaking. He held her hands and kissed her cheek, waiting for her to go on. "Dr. Pray is doing the procedure."

"Oh, yeah, Veronica Pray. She's the best. She was my mom's tennis partner years ago. She didn't make it to many matches. I heard all the stories about why she didn't make it here, or there. That's how I know she's good."

Chelsea smiled, relieved. He looked recharged. "Can we go in and see your dad?"

She cast her eyes beyond him, searching for words. "Yeah, in a minute; I need to tell you something."

"What is it, angel?" he asked, sensing her angst, as she kneaded his hands on her lap.

"I just found out about something. I want to tell Dad, too, to give him something really good to think about before he goes in there."

He waited; she sensed he was holding his breath in response to her mood.

She met his eyes with the joy that suddenly consumed her at seeing him, feeling him here beside her, this man whom she loved more than life itself. Her family was waiting inside for them, but suddenly, she felt an unusual sensation around her, as if God were there, holding hands with them—she knew this was right. This was the third part of her trinity, she thought at once, the third gift; God, Kyle, and now, this baby, the next generation of the family she loved so deeply. He was smiling at her, waiting.

"I'm *pregnant!*" she cried softly, pulling his hands to her lips and kissing them.

He looked at her for a moment and blinked, then stared at her. His hands were on her face and he looked astonished. "What? A baby...*us?* How did this happen?"

"I think it was the medicine I took for the infection. Remember? Dr. Dan said we should use backup and we didn't."

He shook his head imperceptibly, then glanced at her stomach. He leaned in and kissed her tenderly as a couple of nurses at the desk looked on with smiles of their own. "How long have you known?"

"I suspected it a few days ago. I've been sick a couple of times and my period is late."

"Oh, yeah," he said. "And you didn't drink wine with me last night. Did you take a test?"

"Yes, today, at the drug store before Sonya came in. She about knocked down the bathroom door while I was doing it! Are you…okay with this? I know it wasn't what we said…."

"More than okay. I love you so much right now. I just can't believe it." He laughed gently. "Wow!" was all he could say. "And I had so much to tell you, but it can all wait."

"Is it good?"

"Yes, and it's about your dad too, and some business coming his way," he started, as they saw Dr. Pray coming toward them on her way to her father's room. They stood and met her before she got to the door. To Chelsea, she seemed alarmingly young to be working on her dad's heart, and she looked to be in a hurry. She wore her dark hair in a lopsided ponytail, hurriedly made, without makeup or jewelry, but a large smile for them, and an air that radiated competence.

"Kyle?" she asked, extending her hand as he took it, greeting her and nodding. "It's been years! You've certainly changed! And you must be Chelsea? Hi, I'm Dr. Pray. Let's go see your dad. We're going to fix him up, as good as new," she said, standing aside for them to enter the room before her, reassuring wrinkles appearing at her eyes when she smiled again.

Kyle went to Liz and gave her a hug, clasping Jay's hand across the bed. He stood beside the bed and took Tom's hand in his, saying, "Hey, Tom. How're you feeling?"

"A little weak…hope to be better real soon. Good to see you, son," he said. The tears sprang back into Chelsea's eyes as she looked meaningfully at Liz, who winked at her.

Dr. Pray explained that they were ready for him in the O.R. as soon as the prep team came for him. She glanced over his chart, explaining the procedure, reassuring them it was a simple process that should not take too long. If all went well, the surgical team would be dismissed. Tom was in good health, otherwise, so she didn't expect any issues or surprises with his particular case. She answered their questions; then darted out to begin her preparations elsewhere.

When the family was alone, Chelsea glanced at Kyle and then at her family. He took her hand and spoke first.

"We have something to tell you. Tom, we hope this news will give you a little more strength to get you through what you're dealing with."

Chelsea stepped closer to her father's bed and rested her hand on his arm. "You have to know we didn't plan this, but...we're going to have a baby!"

A slow smile spread beneath Tom's mustache; he laughed weakly, joining with Liz's laughter. "Well, I'll be!" he said in a raspy voice, taking Chelsea's hand at the bedside.

"Oh, honey, that's wonderful news! Charley was a honeymoon baby, you know!" her mother laughed, dissolving Chelsea's worries that her family would be concerned about their timing.

Jay gave her a hug and clapped Kyle on the shoulder. "Way to go, dude. Congratulations!"

Liz was already around the foot of the bed, giving her daughter a warm hug and then doing the same to Kyle. Chelsea filled them in on the details as her father beamed and held her hand. A nurse came in moments later and bustled about, checking the I.V. and disconnecting his machines. Liz was instructed to gather Tom's personal belongings, so Chelsea helped her put everything in a plastic bag for the next leg of their journey.

Later that night, Kyle and Chelsea lay exhausted, snuggled together on the sofa on the cabin's sun porch, watching the full moon shine through the stained-glass Celtic Trinity symbol, which hung at the window. He breathed in the sweet scent of her, and held her close, kissing the top of her head. He was palpably aware of just how precious she was, and the life she was carrying inside her. It was amazing, this news, this new dimension into which they had suddenly stepped. Things were certainly changing fast around here! Worries were beginning to tug at him. She was going to need a new car. Maybe they should get a dog, so she would have extra protection when he wasn't there. He wondered whether she would want to continue working after the baby was born. The baby! He rubbed his stubbly chin across her hair and she raised her face to kiss him on his neck. She was sexier than ever to him now, more vulnerable somehow, and certainly so deliciously ripe!

"What are you thinking about?" she murmured into his skin, making incredible things happen to his body.

"How hot you are," he grinned into her hair.

"No, seriously."

"Seriously. How I'm so much more in love with you right now than I've ever been. How can that be possible?"

She smiled and then sighed. "I'm worried about what Abby and Glen are going to think."

He was quiet. He had thought the same thing and it felt awful. "I know. I can't even imagine how we're going to tell them."

"This has been such a roller coaster of a day. There's all that and I'm so relieved that Dad is okay, and I'm so blown away with all of this. I haven't even told you about Sonya, and our big new plans."

"And I need to tell you what I learned from Lynn today…but you go first," he said, stroking his fingers through her hair.

She turned toward him so she could see his face. "A lady brought her daughter into the studio last week and wanted to sign up for dance classes. They just moved here from Georgia. The girl is seven and she uses a walker and wears a bike helmet all the time. She has cerebral palsy and has fallen so many times she's had three plastic surgeries on her face. But she wants to be a ballerina. She begged Sonya to let her daughter take classes, and Sonya thought of me. She remembered the dance program we did with handicapped students at NCSA. It was really successful and we did something like it at the Carolina Ballet as well. Sonya said there have been other people who have asked her about teaching their handicapped children, so we're going to start a class. I'm going to talk to Carmen about it next week and see if I can get a grant to start a project with some of our students at ASU and teach with Sonya at her studio."

"That's impressive. You'd be perfect to coordinate the whole thing."

"It felt like something else big was falling into place as we were talking about it, but the whole time I was swimming in my new knowledge about being a mom!" she laughed.

"You'll be a great mom!" he said quietly, threading his fingers through hers. "I hope our kid will be fine, you know?"

"I know…I'd like to wait until I go to the doctor before we start telling people."

"Sure, I agree. Do your parents know?"

"I mentioned it to Mom and Jay before we left the hospital," she said. "Tell me about your conversation with Lynn."

"She said your dad did the landscaping on her house. They still do all her maintenance."

"So my dad probably knows her?"

"That's what I think. I'd like to get his take on how she and my father were," he murmured absently.

"Do you think they had something more than a professional relationship going?"

"I don't know. I get the feeling there's more to it than she wants to tell me, but she wasn't shy about asking me what happened to him."

"She didn't know about the suicide?"

"No, and it happened right after he must have finished her house, so if she says they knew each other as well as they supposedly did, then she should have known. She didn't know about any of the stuff he was doing."

"Then he must have treated her well."

"He must have. She was pretty involved in the process. She said she'd been at the cabin here. She drinks Maker's Mark, too. I don't know. It's just kind of weird."

"Maybe Dad will have some answers."

"I don't want any of this to upset him. If there was something to it, now isn't the right time to get into it, you know?"

"You'll find out in time, I'm sure. Let's go to bed," she said, sliding her hand into the neck of his shirt and kissing him softly on his mouth. He lifted her off the sofa and carried her into their bedroom.

Chapter 7

···

FATHER'S DAY

···

Father's Day fell on the warmest day of summer so far. The Davenports spent the day having a leisurely picnic at the lake on the family farm. Everyone was there, aside from Charley and her family; Tom, recovered and guardedly slow after his stent procedure, Liz, Jay and Lauren and their two boys, along with Wayne and Becky and their family, and Kyle and Chelsea. Fella, the old yellow lab, lazed under the immense oak tree near the picnic tables where Kyle and Tom sat now. The other fathers had taken their boys on a hike around the lake and the ladies were sunning themselves on the dock, exclaiming over Chelsea's lack of tan lines, and commenting that there was no wonder she was pregnant!

Kyle smiled at their banter and offered Tom another strawberry, which he took readily. His color had returned along with his appetite, although he was long and lanky, hardly the type one would expect would suffer a heart attack. He had the slight paunch that fifty-something men usually had, but who could blame him, living the good life of the empty-nester?

"You know, this heart attack was mostly the fault of my father's poor genes, but God, I miss bacon and eggs!" he sighed, tossing the cap of the berry onto the ground. Fella raised his head to look.

"You didn't eat that stuff all the time anyway, did you?" Kyle asked.

"I grew up eating it every day," Tom explained ruefully. "Then when I met Elizabeth, she tried to improve my eating habits, but she'd fix bacon and eggs about once a week. We learned a lot after Mama had her first stroke. I love Elizabeth's cooking too, but it's oatmeal and toast and grapefruit for me from now on. Have you ever had those egg substitutes? It's like eating cardboard! There's nothing like fresh hen's eggs when you've had them all your life," he sighed again. "And no more barbeque or fried chicken for me ever again. Hotdogs all the way, pecan pies, and banana pudding…oh, I'll miss all that good stuff. I'll tell you, son, it sucks getting old!"

Kyle chuckled as he bit into a strawberry himself. "That would suck. So, you're planning to ease back into work?"

"Oh, yeah. I hate being away. Jay's got things under control, but I really love being there and having my hands in the whole mess."

"Frank and I might have something for you if you're interested and feel like taking it on," Kyle offered, wiping his hands on a paper towel. Tom's eyes looked interested. "We've landed a condo project up on the ridge, just beyond the cabin," Kyle continued. "The client knows you, and she's going to need a top-notch landscape architect. Actually, you did the work on her house about eight years ago. Lynn Schiffman?" he added tentatively.

Tom took a deep breath and narrowed his eyes, focusing on a point past the lake as they heard the women howling with laughter about something they'd been discussing. Kyle almost regretted saying anything. Maybe he should have checked with Liz first. It had been over a week since the heart attack. He thought Tom seemed to be up for this.

"Yeah, I know Lynn," he said in an unreadable tone. "Your dad and I worked on her house together. It was like old times," he said, wiping his hand over his mustache absently. Then he looked squarely at Kyle. "It was some of the best work he and I did together. We still do all of her maintenance, but I haven't seen her in years. We talk on the phone occasionally, and the rest of it is handled through e-mails. It's a shame, really, the way we've all gotten away from exchanging a few friendly words from time to time. She's a nice gal. I appreciate the business. What made you think of me for the job?"

"I went and saw the house. I think your landscaping and lighting are perfect for the kind of places she wants to build. She'd like to create something a lot like what you and Dad did, sustainable of course, and on a smaller scale, less obtrusive to the landscape than some other models she was considering. The property is on the ridge just to the east of the cabin. Chelsea and I will have to look at it, you know," Kyle said wryly and Tom's laugh boomed forth, causing the women to turn and look at him with smiles.

"Oh, yes! We don't want a project like that messing up *your* landscape!" he said, pushing up his sleeves.

"Exactly!" Kyle nodded. "So do you think you'd be up for it?"

"That's probably exactly what I should be doing, sitting inside and drawing, instead of running around the place all day. I'll talk to you about it. It sounds like a good idea. Have you started on it yet?"

"Nope, but I will be soon. It's going to be a great project. I couldn't be more grateful to Frank for the opportunity. I just ordered the survey. We could ride up there and look at the property if you want. Maybe we could go up to Lynn's house too and look at it together. I want to take some outdoor pictures at night of what you did there."

"Well, you should probably look at the original plans. Stuart outdid himself on that one, all right."

"So did you. Actually, I have the plans. Lynn found them in a closet. Apparently, they worked on them a lot together."

Tom dropped his eyes, deep in thought. "You know...I think that house was Stu's swan song. It was the last house he ever built. He really wanted to do it right. He was so tired of messing things up. Something changed when he met Lynn," he said quietly. "That house was really something special."

"Do you think it was because she was...so involved with the planning?"

Tom nodded slowly. "I'm sure that had a lot to do with it. He had no wiggle room; that's for sure," he said, taking a sip of his iced tea. "That and the fact that he was dying to build something in that style. It was the greatest challenge I'm sure he ever had. He was certainly up to it. I'd never seen him so inspired. I really thought he was turning things around. That was about the time he got audited and it all fell apart." He looked at Kyle again. "How much of this do you know?"

"About the business?" Kyle asked, cautiously, meeting his look. Tom nodded. "I know what he was doing and how he got caught. I knew my mother didn't know how bad it was until it was too late."

Tom looked away again. "He didn't tell her much. It was the only way he could protect her. If she knew, she would have been liable as well. It was a good thing he never gave her any interest in the business. He knew what he was doing," he said frankly.

Kyle sighed. "I don't think Lynn knew anything about any of it."

"Like I said, he knew what he was doing. That's why he had so much on him. It got to the point where there was no one for him to talk to...."

Kyle let his statement hang for a moment, pondering it all. "I'm surprised Lynn didn't know what happened to him after they had worked together so closely." His observation was more like a question.

Tom pursed his lips and thought about his answer. "Well, I think that was the way it was supposed to go down, remember?" he asked gently.

"Yeah…I guess so."

"Well, onto brighter subjects," Tom said with a grin. "I know we were surprised by your news. I guess *you* were too! What's it feel like, knowing you're gonna be a father yourself?"

Kyle laughed gently. "Amazing. My mother called this morning and wished me a happy Father's Day. That was weird. She's happy for us, but not real thrilled about being a grandmother! It was something we were going to wait on for a while. I've known Chelsea for most of my life, but I feel as if we've just gotten to know each other again. We didn't want to rush into it, but it's good. I feel really…protective and responsible."

"Yeah, that's the gist of being a dad. You'll do just fine. I remember feeling like that when Liz got pregnant with Charley right out of the chute! But remember we're here if you need help, and you will." His cell phone rang and he pulled it out of his pocket, checking the caller ID on the screen. "Speaking of Charley…*Hello, Puddin*!" he said pleasantly into his phone as the other ladies came to join them, warmed from the summer sun.

Chelsea slid into the seat beside Kyle, laying her head on his shoulder. He leaned over and kissed her forehead, noticing the light new freckles that had bloomed across her nose. "It's your sister," he whispered, and she grinned, knowing she would get a turn to talk. Charley, a labor and delivery nurse, would want the full report about the pregnancy. It was nice, seeing how excited Chelsea was becoming over the expectation of their child; he was beginning to feel the same way. Their families were so happy about it, even though it was initially such a shock. He sighed, thinking he was glad that Glen and Abby were at the beach with Glen's family for the week. It gave them time for Chelsea to see her doctor and for them to think about how to tell them the news. Neither one of them was looking forward to that conversation. Chelsea looked into his eyes, seeming to think the same thing. It was odd the way they could do that, know what the other was thinking. It had always been that way with them. She was his touchstone, always on the same wavelength, so comforting.

She snagged his cup, taking a long drink of iced tea, and helped the ladies finish packing the baskets her mother had brought down for their picnic. As always, Liz had fixed heart-healthy food—turkey sandwiches with spinach, havarti cheese, and olive oil mayonnaise. On the side were fresh vegetables, mango salsa as well, with strawberries for dessert. Genetics aside, how could a tall, easy-going man who ate like this have a heart-attack? Maybe there was something to all this responsibility, Kyle wondered.

Running a hand through his hair, Kyle glanced down at Chelsea again, as she grinned at Tom, chatting happily about their upcoming vacation in Wilmington with his oldest child, the only one in the family who could not be there. It would do him good to get away with Liz. Charley had been so worried about him after the heart attack. But it was one of those things that solidified a family. Kyle imagined more holidays with all of them, and thought back to Christmas Eve just six months ago when they had all taken him in, giddy with their engagement news as well as the end of the yearly Christmas tree sales. Never before had he been a part of such a boisterous and jolly occasion, he had thought as he had sat around the large dining room table with them. The old table had been extended by several leaves to include all those over eighteen, while the children were relegated to the kitchen table that had been expanded for them as well. Chelsea had laughed and told him about making it to "The Big Table" her senior year in high school. There would be countless more celebrations just like this one, and their child would also be wrapped in the whole warm and loving family quilt.

What would he look like? Or would they have a girl with the same clear eyes and unusual auburn hair as that of his beloved? He knew their child would have a lot to smile about. How could he or she not, in this sea of love? So what if they weren't ready? Surely this was a gift, as Chelsea had said. He would be ready, glad there were still many months left to get used to the new life in which they found themselves.

She was speaking cheerfully to Charley on the phone now, reporting that she had a doctor appointment the next day and would fill her in on all the details as soon as she could; and yes, she was a bit green on some days, but on other days, she felt okay. He closed his eyes, remembering, and even smelled the turkey on the large platter that had come over from England or France, which he couldn't recall. He heard laughter, and the clinking of the fine silverware on the bone china that was chipped and worn from use over so many generations, and the scraping of antique chairs across the floor boards as a fire crackled in the cavernous fireplace. He imagined Chelsea, large with child, beside him at that table in six more months. They would travel to Charlotte to spend time with his family too, but they would have to figure out how to divide their time fairly among everyone. His family was not nearly as large or loud, but they had become just as joyful and just as devoted to each other over these last years, due to the additions of Tyson, Abigail, Chelsea, and now, possibly Mark, to the mix. He had never felt so alive. Knowing he would never be alone again filled him with thankfulness.

⚜︎

They left the doctor's office armed with a special diet, a prescription for prenatal vitamins, and a strange sense of being transformed into some other couple than they'd been upon entering the place. Kyle had hugged her close, laughing in her hair on their way out of the office.

"Can you believe we're going to be parents?" he exclaimed in his quiet way, eyes sparkling at her. She held his hand on her shoulder and leaned into him as they walked to the car. "Everything will be okay," he reassured, relaxing her.

She was three weeks pregnant. It had obviously been the result of their disregard of Dr. Dan Edmonds' instructions. "Your grandfather must be

125

so pissed at us!" she murmured into his shoulder, peppery and manly-smelling.

"No way. He's thrilled! He and Gran are going to be great-grandparents, so they think it's really cool. Now, my mom, on the other hand…no big surprise there. It's all about her, you know?"

"She's way too young-looking to be a grandmother."

"Keep telling her that and you'll be the favorite daughter-in-law."

"I'm the *only* daughter-in-law," she reminded him as he held her hand and opened the Range Rover's door for her. He was even more tender and considerate with her than usual these days, and it melted her heart every time he did something like that. When he laughed, she pressed the palm of her hand to the side of his face. "You're going to be a great father," she said, and he leaned in to take the kiss she offered freely, there in the parking lot. It had only been weeks since he had tucked her into this car and she had touched his face the same way, saying, "*Can you believe we're married?*"

"The middle of March," he said, grinning, restating the due date the doctor had predicted, as he backed the SUV out of the parking space and pulled out into the lot, driving carefully. "Maybe our baby will have the same birthday as Abigail," he suggested, eyebrows raised.

"That's fitting since she was a big surprise, too!" Chelsea said, smiling, remembering that Stacie and Tyson had conceived their daughter in a tropical storm named Abigail, and that they had been just as surprised as Kyle and she were at their predicament. She had come into the world on March seventeenth, almost six years ago.

"It's nice that with all these surprise pregnancy stories, no one's giving us any flack," he agreed with a sideways smile at her.

"Not yet, at least," she said tentatively, and he let the implication of her statement drift away. What was the use of discussing it? Abby and Glen were sure to be shell-shocked when they learned the news.

She sighed and placed her hand across the flatness of her belly, wondering what it would feel like to be large and swollen. He rested his hand on top of hers and smiled at her again. She tried to imagine feeling movement, hearing the heartbeat, already wondering whether the life inside her were a boy or a girl. Her conversation with Sonya came back to her, and she pondered how a mother would deal with having a handicapped child. Would she have the courage? There would be no choice; of course she would find it, and Kyle would take it in his usual stride as well. She thought of sleepless nights and school plays and possibly dance recitals or football games.

"What's on your mind?" Kyle asked softly, making her realize she had closed her eyes, picturing it all.

"Just that our kid is *never* going to play football," she blurted suddenly. He laughed out loud.

"That's probably smart," he muttered, looking ahead at the road. "No wonder I married you."

⚬⚬⚬⚬⚬

On Saturday night, they sat at the table on the deck together, dinner dishes pushed aside, listening to the quiet and never-ending swoosh of the river through the woods. A woodpecker hammered on a hollow tree near the river, adding an interesting cadence to the evening's music. Someone down the twisting road was enjoying a game of horseshoes; they could hear the faint "clink" of metal upon metal and the occasional shout of victory threading back up through the trees. It was unusual to hear even that here in the evening, but it was officially summer now, and outdoor family gatherings would be more frequent. As the green of the forest surrounding them wrapped them in a warm peacefulness, they did not talk or touch.

The flame from the firepot flickered, beckoning as a focal point for their gazes. Kyle imagined the following day when Tom and Jay would join him again for an afternoon of fly-fishing. It had been since before the wedding that they'd fished together, and he was looking forward to the easy talk and quiet camaraderie the three of them shared. Then later that evening, they would visit Lynn at her house for dessert, as a celebration of joining forces on the condominium project, while allowing Kyle the opportunity to take the night photographs of the landscaping he'd mentioned. Frank and Faith, Tom and Liz, and Pamela Van Dervere would all be there. Lynn had laughed easily, reassuring him that there was safety in numbers and that she and Chelsea could divert him from Pam! He sighed and his cell phone buzzed in his pocket. He frowned, flicking a look at Chelsea, wondering who would be disturbing their peace and quiet just now.

"Glen," he said with eyebrows raised, and she did the same. They were probably just hitting town after their vacation. "S'up, man?" Kyle said into the phone good-naturedly.

"Just getting back from the vacay, bro. You guys up for some company?" Glen's bright voice came from the other end.

Kyle glanced tentatively at Chelsea, who had heard and was nodding slowly. It was going to be sooner than later, he thought, resigned to the fact. "Sure, come on by, but we're not doing your laundry!" he joked, keeping it light as long as he could.

"Oh, right. I have a feeling that's going to be my job tomorrow. Or maybe Abby will do it while I mow the grass."

"Yep, you'll be doing that for sure. We've had rain while you were gone."

"All right, we'll be there in a few. We're bringing a little treat too."

"'Kay, then see you soon." They disconnected and Chelsea rose, lifting the plates and Kyle's empty beer bottle. As he stood to help her, they looked apprehensively at each other.

"He sounded pretty cheerful," Kyle said guardedly.

"Yeah, I hate to ruin it for them," she replied glumly.

"Maybe it won't be as bad as we think," he said, taking the dishes from her and placing them in the racks inside the dishwasher, as she cleaned the skillet from the chicken she'd cooked. He covered the salad bowl and pulled out a container for the leftover vegetables as she placed things back into the refrigerator. They heard Glen's car rolling over the gravel in the drive as they wiped the counter and checked the stove one more time. She refilled her glass of iced tea and seemed to set her shoulders in preparation for the meeting. He bumped her playfully as they went to the door to greet their best friends since high school. "It will be okay," he whispered into her hair, giving her a lingering kiss, a signal from him that there would be more of that later, and she responded in kind with that fiery look he loved.

Abby was the first to bound up the steps and wrap Chelsea in a large bear hug. "Hey! I've missed you!" she laughed, as Glen followed, carrying a brown bag, shaking hands with Kyle, and kissing Chelsea on the cheek.

After all the greetings were exchanged, Kyle invited them out to the deck. "So, what's in the bag?"

"Got a shot glass and a salt shaker?" Glen grinned. Kyle looked warily at Chelsea, who looked apprehensively at Abby.

"We just found out this morning that we're not pregnant, so this is a way of celebrating being without child one more time! We might as well enjoy ourselves," she laughed as Glen reached into the bag, producing a bottle of tequila.

"Holy moly," said Kyle. "This can only mean trouble. Tequila changes you into another person, man. Don't you know that?" he laughed, clapping Glen on the shoulder and meeting his mischievous look dead-on.

"Yeah, well, we were hoping it would be okay if we crashed here if it gets out of hand," Abby said, wide eyes sparkling at them both. "It's not as much fun doing this by ourselves anyway," she said, giving an impressive pout.

Kyle and Chelsea exchanged glances. He knew what she was thinking; maybe the tequila would soften the blow, and they laughed, both giving in. "It's a good thing you called now. Twenty more minutes and I'd have had this pretty young thing in the sack!" Kyle said uncharacteristically, and she seemed to know he was saying it for show, but meaning it just the same. She smiled appreciatively at him and went to the fridge for a lime and the salt shaker. They managed to find a couple of shot glasses and headed out to the deck. Chelsea grabbed a bag of chips and a jar of salsa from the cabinet. He nodded his approval at her thinking. Who knew what they'd had to eat? They would need something to absorb all the booze they would surely consume. Chelsea looked ready to pass out at the moment. He took her hand as she picked up her glass of iced tea, searching for her eyes to steady her.

"It will be okay," he whispered before they joined their guests outside.

She sliced the lime into small wedges as Glen described their week at the beach. They'd gone to Isle of Palms and rented a beautiful beach house with Glen's parents, his two sisters and their families. He was explaining more of their predicament. "We thought maybe I'd have a chance to celebrate Father's Day too, but not this year…" his voice trailed off and Abby shook back her hair, setting the shot glasses on the deck's railing. Chelsea placed the chips in a basket and opened the salsa, pouring it into a bowl and setting it out prominently.

"Have you guys eaten?" she asked, obviously deflecting from the subject.

"We stopped for barbeque about an hour ago," Glen said to their shared looks of relief. "Try this," he continued to Kyle, who gestured for Abby to take the first shot Glen had poured at the railing. She immediately reached for a lime and rimmed it across her hand from the base of her forefinger to the base of her thumb. She sprinkled it expertly with salt, licked it, and downed her shot. Then she sucked the lime and tossed it over the side as Kyle and Glen watched it fall.

"Bio-degradable," Kyle commented as if there were no worries, and taking the next shot, performing the same ritual along with Glen. They smacked their shot glasses back down on the rail and sucked limes, tossing them toward the destination of Abby's.

"Come on over here, honey! Sidle on up to the bar and let me set you up!" Glen said to Chelsea, causing her to laugh.

"Oh, no. I'm abstaining tonight. Somebody's got to take care of this motley crew!"

"Now, remember what Mark Twain said? *Be good and you will be lonesome,*" Glen reminded her with the usual laughter in his eyes, making her laugh too. She shook her head.

"Oh, c'mon, Chels; humor me! You abstained with me the last time and this is way more fun!" Abby encouraged her.

"Nah, I'm good, really," she insisted. Now it was Glen's turn to apply the peer pressure.

"Really? My drinking partner is wimping out on me tonight? What gives?" he asked, looking back and forth from Kyle and Chelsea's poker faces.

"I'm just not up for it tonight; leave me alone, okay?" she joked with him, but Abby was obviously sensing something in the shared looks.

"What's wrong, Chels?" Abby asked, cautiously.

"Yeah, did somebody die?" Glen said, looking at them, warily. "*Wait— the rabbit?*" he said heavily, ready to laugh, but didn't after seeing the looks on their faces.

"Oh, crap! I'll take 'dumb things to say for four hundred, Alex!'" He tried desperately to save the situation, but in an instant, they all knew the truth was out.

Kyle looked back and forth from Chelsea to Glen, and then to Abby, apology deep within his eyes.

"You're shitting me, right?" Abby asked, gruffly, tossing her second lime of the evening over the rail. "Don't tell me *you're pregnant!*" The pain of the betrayed crossed her face for a split second as she struggled to recover.

Chelsea met her friend's eyes, washed in the guilt she'd felt since they'd gotten the news. "Yes. I am. It was an accident. Remember, I told you about the jellyfish sting and taking the medicine? It happened while I was taking the antibiotics and it was…just an accident," she said softly, knowing it was not an acceptable explanation, knowing it was a crowning blow to the courage her friend had continued to muster, month after anguishing month of wanting what she had. "I'm *sorry*," she said. It came out as hardly a whisper, and hardly adequate for what Abby must be feeling.

Abby blinked at her and dropped her eyes. Kyle glanced at Glen, who was wiping his face with the palm of his hand and returning his look with incredible understanding.

"Hell, don't apologize! It's okay, guys. Congratulations! Planned or not, this is great news for you both, seriously!" he said enthusiastically, pulling Kyle into a powerful hug and then doing the same, only more gently, to Chelsea. "Congratulations, sweetheart!" he said and kissed her on the cheek, making eye contact with Abby, who hugged them too while murmuring her congratulations.

They resumed the shots as Glen continued the discussion. "Well, I guess Father's Day was good for you then. It takes on a whole new meaning, duddn't it? That's fantastic news!"

"So, when are you due?" Abby asked, warming a bit.

"The middle of March," Chelsea supplied, glancing at Kyle for support.

"That will be a good time. You'll still have the excuse to stay inside, and when the baby's just old enough, the weather will be better and you can start getting out and strolling," she said wistfully. "I'll bet your parents are thrilled!" Her eyes looked friendly again as they listened absently to Kyle and Glen's conversation.

"Man, you're a stud! Maybe you should come to my house!" Glen said, raising his eyebrows and throwing back another shot. Kyle shook his head, trying not to picture it.

"You mean, like a *Big Chill* kind of thing? I don't think so, dude. I like y'all but not *that* much," he laughed, licking salt off his hand, sending Chelsea a look that said it was his last shot.

"Well, it's got to be me, you know?" said Glen, "At least fifty percent me as far as we know yet," he laughed as Abby shot him a look of disdain.

⚜

Later as Chelsea tucked a wobbly Abby into the guest bed, they heard the guys on the deck talking boisterously and laughing. Chelsea smoothed her friend's soft dark hair away from her mouth and pulled the covers around her chin in the dim lamp light. She murmured yet another feeble apology.

"What's it like...always getting everything you want?" Abby slurred, eyes closed and breathing deeply, falling off to sleep, driving the night's largest pang of guilt through Chelsea's heart.

Chapter 8

BACK TO HELL

The wardrobe debate began again inside the small walk-in closet of Kyle and Chelsea's bedroom. He stood, bare-chested, in a pair of jeans yet to be buttoned, flipping through the shirts again, shooting her hopeful looks whenever he came across the possibility of a suitable selection. She stood, cross-armed in the doorway, dismissing this choice and that. He popped a sigh from the corner of his mouth and cranked up his eyebrows at her.

"Well, I could just go like this, if you don't like any of these shirts." He said it as a question, pointing his hands toward his torso.

"Ha! Right!" she said, pushing him aside, taking over his spot at the rack and looking through the selection herself. She pulled out a shirt from the back of his side of the closet and handed it to him. "I like this one. This is perfect!" she claimed triumphantly as he rolled his eyes.

"That's about a thousand years old," he said, referring to the loose weave white button-up shirt with the thin dark blue stripes. "That goes back to my high school days when Mom used to dress Dad and me alike. Hmm." He held it up to examine the tag inside. "You know, this is my dad's shirt, actually. I'm sure I outgrew mine years ago. I guess this got left in the closet somehow. It ought to fit me now."

"Then it's perfect," she said, finalizing the discussion. He slid his arms into it, buttoning it without further resistance.

She smiled smugly and thought to herself, *it's only a shirt; what's the big deal?* But it was a big deal when they were coming face-to-face with the formidable Pamela Van Dervere. At least, that's what she thought. Kyle had said so little about her, but that was usually his strategy when he hadn't wanted to worry her about other women's unwanted advances. In the past it was what he had done. They had been apart for so long she had forgotten being jealous of *real* people, only those she conjured up in her dreams of him. She wasn't sure which was worse! It was her turn to sigh, and he watched her as he rolled up his sleeves.

"So, do I get to pick out your outfit?" he asked coyly.

She shook her head and looked insulted, "Of course not! I've had this planned all day," she said, eyes playing mischievously with him. He looked on curiously as she pulled a slim, strapless aqua dress off the rack and held it up in front of her.

"Ah!" he said, recognizing her outfit from the rehearsal the night before their wedding. "*Me gusta*…but you're going to make me look like a bum. Remember, they said it was casual?"

"This can be casual," she said slowly, pulling her T-shirt over her head, slipping out of her shorts and unhooking her bra, letting it fall to the floor.

"Okay…" he said, a slow smile beginning across his face, watching her step into the dress.

She turned and caught her hair around one shoulder. "Will you zip me, please?" She felt him oblige and tug slightly as the closure seemed tighter than the last time, accommodating her new and improved bust-line. He turned her around to see the result and they laughed together.

"Well! Are you out to make a statement this evening?" he smiled at her, admiringly.

"Damn right," she said, quoting his usual retort for a question like that.

"That's what I was thinking," he said, watching her dress down the outfit, choosing a pair of flat sandals.

They wandered into the kitchen to collect the flowers they were planning to take to Lynn as a hostess gift. The evening sun slanted through the windows as they started to head out, switching on a small lamp for their return in the dark.

"Is your mom excited about seeing the house?" Kyle asked, closing and locking the door behind them, slipping a camera case over his shoulder.

"Actually, she's seen it before. When I was up there today, talking to her, she said she and Dad had been there after the house was finished."

"I guess Lynn must have thrown a big house warming party in celebration after it was finished," he wondered aloud.

"Actually, she said it was just her and Dad over for coffee. I thought your parents would have been there, but Mom said they weren't."

"Hmm," he said, puzzled, ushering her into the SUV's passenger seat and handing her the bouquet of peonies in various shades of pink from Liz's garden.

Chelsea stood a moment, taking in the most beautiful house she had ever seen. In the sunset, the spectacular home was bathed in a magenta light as they climbed the stairs to the front door, realizing they were the last to arrive. The door opened before they had reached it. Pamela appeared in the porch light, tall and striking, in a pair of black pants and a swingy cowl-neck top. Her almost black hair was pulled back in a tight ponytail and long gold loops swung at her ears. She grinned and greeted them enthusiastically. "Hi, Kyle! Good to see you again!" she said, flashing her amazingly white smile his way and enveloping his hand in a two-handed embrace of sorts. He greeted her and introduced Chelsea, sliding his arm protectively around her.

"Chelsea! It's great to meet you finally! You're as beautiful as I knew you would be!" she said, squeezing Chelsea into her large chest, engulfing her in the Chanel that had been all over Kyle just a couple of weeks before, making Chelsea suddenly understand. Pam took the bouquet of flowers Chelsea offered. "These are lovely! Come on in! Everyone is on the deck. I was just getting ready to bring out the peach cobbler," she said as they followed her, sashaying through the foyer and across the great room to open doors from where a delightful mountain breeze wafted. Chelsea was surprised at her reaction to Pam. She actually liked her and thought she was attractive, though not in a way she would care to emulate, but there was something genuine about her, despite her attempts to discourage the aging process. She watched Kyle with her, acting aloof, but ever-charming, as he smiled indulgently and bowed ever so slightly at her congratulations on landing the project.

"What can I get you to drink? We have beer, a *decadent* zinfandel, a pinot grigio, iced tea, coffee—decaf, for us older folks!" she laughed, winking at Chelsea, her deep-set dark eyes full of humor.

"Chels, what for you?" he deferred to her first. "I'll have a beer," he slipped in as she was thinking.

"No more red wine, I see?" Pam laughed at him heartily. "Chelsea?"

When she said, "Iced tea, please," Pam looked puzzled.

"Will you have a glass of champagne with us later?" Pam queried.

"I guess a couple of sips couldn't hurt," she responded, smiling at Kyle, who squeezed her hand.

He answered Pam's questioning look. "We just found out we're pregnant," he told her; her small eyes got as large as they could.

"No kidding!" she squeaked. "Well, congratulations on that, too! Was this a 'had-to' kind of deal? Or a honeymoon baby?" Pam asked, pointing her finger back and forth between them.

"A honeymoon baby," they said in unison as Chelsea felt his arm tighten around her again. She felt awkward, discussing this intimate subject with a stranger, and felt her face flush. It was as if Pam could see right through her clothes and imagine what they'd been doing. Chelsea took a breath and held her head higher. She caught a flickering supportive look from Kyle.

"Wow! That's just precious!" Pam said, regarding them in astonishment and serving their drinks with colorful napkins from the bar. "Does Lynn know about this?"

"I don't think so. Frank doesn't even know yet."

"Well, this is great news. You should be the one to announce it. We will have an added reason for that champagne!" she said, winking at Kyle and leading them out onto the deck, where Lynn was deep in conversation with Faith and Liz, and the other two men were chatting about the design plans for the condos. Tom's face lit up noticeably when he saw Chelsea, and he extended his arm as she went to kiss him.

"How was the fishing today?" she asked Tom, knowing they'd all had a great time.

"It was relaxing, getting away with the guys, really peaceful." She was glad and knew that Kyle had planned it that way. She waved to her mother who was nodding and talking with Lynn and Faith, Frank's wife. When Kyle wandered toward the men's group, Chelsea felt herself being cornered and separated from them by the large woman beside her. Pam guided her off to the side and whispered conspiratorially in her ear, watching Kyle all the while. He looked back at Chelsea and gave her a subtle wink.

Pam saw the wink and laughed, "Mm-mm...you'll never have to fake it with *him*! You'll never have to close your eyes and pretend he's someone else," she said. Chelsea stared at her, unprepared to respond. Pamela laughed again and shook her head as if she knew something, regarding Chelsea with something like pity. Then her voice took on an encouraging tone, "Maybe getting pregnant so soon was a good move. You'll have to do what you can to hold onto that one. On the other hand, it could work against you. A man like Kyle with a baby is sure to be a chick magnet. It's worse than walking in the park with a puppy!" she laughed, regarding Kyle. Chelsea felt an unpleasant heat begin to creep up her neck and onto her cheeks. It was as if Pamela were talking to another woman about him and not his new bride, much less the mother of his child. Pamela looked at him the way other women did at times, as if he were hers, as if she had some kind of carnal knowledge of him unbeknownst to Chelsea. It was as if she had Chelsea and Kyle's lives all mapped out and she was doing a running commentary after knowing her all of five minutes. She had seen this situation so many times before, the long appraising looks, the posturing and preening, the engaging conversations women held with him. Even her dance colleague, Carmen, had embarrassed them with her comment during the waltz rehearsals, watching them hold each other on the dance floor. "*I can tell you are an excellent lover!*" she'd said unabashedly to Kyle, readjusting his hand to a more appropriate position at Chelsea's waist. Her face had blazed the color it surely was at this moment.

Pam was speaking again, her eyes unmistakably glued to Kyle's buttocks as he talked easily with the men. "It's a good thing you're up here in Podunksville. Those South Beach women would swallow a fine thing like him whole, *absolutely whole!*"

"Yes, I guess that's a good thing," she said, breathing deeply, taking a sip of her tea, hoping it would cool her face. This woman's rudeness was unbelievable!

"He is definitely not cut from the same cloth as most of the men I've seen up here so far," Pam continued as if discussing livestock.

"You should probably be careful who hears you," Chelsea warned her drolly, glancing at her father who was smiling at her, and holding up his beer in greeting.

"Oh, no offense. Your daddy's from here, isn't he?" and after Chelsea nodded she asked, "And Frank, too?" Chelsea nodded again, smiling at stocky and sweet Frank, completely unaware of the insult Pam had just dealt. He was the kind of man Chelsea considered to be the salt of the earth. *And Kyle and I are both from here too*, she thought. This woman had no idea of the *faux-pas* she was committing.

"Like I said, no offense. Kyle's just...*so amazingly hot*. And having a baby might encourage him to stay home and deter some of the women he'll come across," she added thoughtfully, swirling her dark and decadent zinfandel in the large glass absently, imagining something else.

Her words had sickened Chelsea, but it wasn't from the usual malaise that had plagued her already with the pregnancy. "Well, I'm glad we don't have any friends that would do that to us," she said, certainly.

"Don't be so sure...They won't be your *friends* by any stretch, honey," Pam said. She should know, Chelsea thought, wondering about the details of her divorce. Instinctively, she moved away toward Kyle, who looked at her questioningly and drew her to him with his eyes, taking her hand. Her liking of Pam had quickly disintegrated after that brutal conversation, and he appeared to have sensed it. They walked over to the ladies and she hugged her mother. Then he introduced her to Faith, and then to Lynn, who looked elegant and summery in loose, pale blue linen.

She shook Chelsea's hand, smiling at her warmly, with wide eyes crinkling at the corners, the antithesis of Pam completely. "Hello, Chelsea! I'm so very pleased to meet you. Kyle has told me so much about you and your family. I'm really looking forward to working with all of you on this project."

Chelsea took a deep, calming breath and greeted her as well, as Faith and Liz stepped aside.

"I was waiting for you so I could give all of you the tour together," she said pleasantly, catching Kyle's eye as he stepped in to accept her handshake. Suddenly, she looked at him; her face seemed to crumble as her hand left his and grasped his arm, staring, horrified almost, at his sleeve as if it were on fire. He took her arm, attempting to steady her, and Chelsea thought she saw tears spring to Lynn's eyes for just a moment before she struggled to compose herself. Lynn and Kyle exchanged a meaningful look that made Chelsea's heart sink. Hopefully, Lynn wasn't sick, but what was wrong?

"Are you okay?" Kyle said to her softly, concern thickening his voice.

"Yes, yes, I'm fine. I'm sorry," she said as he continued to hold her up. The others had not noticed since Pam had joined them, asking if she could refresh anyone's drinks. Chelsea looked back at Kyle and Lynn. He shot her an apologetic glance and steered Lynn around the corner, still holding her arm as she again grasped onto his. Chelsea could hear them murmuring about it, after a quiet moment, unable to make out their words, but her tone seemed adamant. She didn't want to talk about it. They were back in a moment, he looking distraught, and she, rearranging her hair.

Lynn smiled nervously, avoiding Chelsea's questioning look, and asked the ladies whether they were ready to have a look around. Chelsea tried to put their connection out of her mind. Maybe Lynn hadn't been feeling well and he knew something about it. It was mildly disturbing watching them together, the way they looked at each other. Everyone joined the tour, and they walked through the house, sighing and commenting over the deep warm-toned stain of the wood, the bold, angular lines of the design and the immense windows. Chelsea tried to imagine the house in the daylight and then at sunset. The views must be incredible. She remembered to close her mouth a time or two and felt some of the pride in Kyle's father's work that he had expressed to her. He seemed to relish every part of the place as if seeing it all for the first time. Lynn had done an excellent job of decorating it, Faith had commented. She worked with Frank and Kyle as the interior designer on their projects. Chelsea imagined they would spend lots of time with Lynn making the condos just as special as this place was. Even though she wondered what was going on with Lynn, she was so thrilled for Kyle and this new opportunity that bumps rose on her arms, considering what it could do for his career as an architect. Condominiums had been the last thing he'd wanted to design, but with their new plan, he had seemed more inspired than ever.

After the tour, they returned to the deck where Pam helped Lynn serve the peach cobbler. Pam had placed the flowers in a pottery vase on the table and was pouring flutes of champagne. Candles flickered around the deck as it was now fully dark. They raised their glasses to the impending success of their new project. When Pam prompted Kyle to make his announcement, he caught Lynn's eye, saying, "I'd like to propose a toast to my beautiful bride." He smiled at Chelsea and took her hand. "Chelsea and I are going to be parents!" His voice was still full of the wonder they both felt. Tom and Liz beamed at them from across the deck.

The others "oohed" and "aahed" appropriately and seemed genuinely delighted for them both. After they finished their dessert, he excused himself to walk down to the yard to take the photographs he'd wanted of the landscaping lighting. "You'll be all right?" he asked Chelsea uneasily, stroking her back. She nodded and he added, "You can walk down there with me if you'd like…."

"Go! I'll be fine. I'll come down there if I see Pam coming after you."

"On second thought, I insist that you come with me! Besides, I need you to hold my champagne glass while I take pictures!" he laughed, pulling her along, retrieving the camera he'd left at the door.

She stepped gingerly down the stairs behind him and picked her way along the stepping stones, suddenly aware that she needed to be careful. The protective feeling she had for her unborn child overwhelmed her at times as she realized she had placed her hand on her stomach. Kyle was busy now, focusing the camera on this shot and that, and she felt a pang of longing for him. It was silly; he was right there! But she wondered whether right now she were the one more in love. She knew what she had seen with the other women in the house had something to do with the way she felt, but she wanted nothing more than to plunge her fingers into his thick soft hair and remind him that he was hers. She wiped a tear from her eye with the back of her hand, trying to compose herself before he noticed. Had he no idea the effect he had on women, even his own wife?

She realized he had just snapped her picture. He was staring at her in the darkness, that familiar bore of his eyes, like looking into deep water, penetrating into hers. She knew he had caught her in her little emotional tailspin, making her feel ashamed. This was ridiculous! Maybe it was the hormones playing with her head. Whatever it was, she didn't like it, especially getting busted.

Consumed with feeling for him, she continued to walk toward him until he took her hand, eyes sparkling at her.

"You're so beautiful out here," he said, low in her ear as she came close so he could embrace her. She closed her eyes and felt his kiss, tender and sweet, becoming passionate as she kissed him hard in the moonlight. She didn't want him to see her crying.

He held her face and slid his fingers back into her hair. "I guess you got a little taste of hell in there?"

"I understand what you were talking about now. I thought you were exaggerating that night but now I don't believe you were."

"Pam is…twisted. Don't worry about her. She needs to stay in South Beach. I doubt she'll be up here much. It's not exciting enough for her."

"Well, she couldn't take her eyes off of you all night! Whenever you're done here, I'll be ready to go," she said as they heard laughter at the front door. The others were preparing to leave, so Kyle hurried to take his last photos before they were all out in the drive together.

"This was absolutely lovely!" exclaimed Liz, giving Lynn a hug, and then taking Pam by the hand. The men looked warily at Pam; each shook her hand stiffly and said their goodnights. Liz and Faith promised to have lunch together soon in town, and Frank clapped Tom firmly on the back, wishing him a continued recovery. Then there were handshakes and hugs for Kyle and Chelsea, and more congratulations on the baby news, as everyone dispersed to their respective cars.

They drove back home without speaking, listening to music on the radio, with the windows halfway down. Chelsea was tired and unsettled as they climbed the stairs to the cabin in their own moonlight. Kyle hung his keys on the iron hook by the door, pulling his shirttail out of his jeans.

Finally he spoke to her. "Is something bothering you?"

She sighed, reluctant to bring it up, but it came tumbling out. "So, what was that with you and Lynn?"

He looked apprehensive and ran a hand through his hair. "What do you mean?" he asked looking truly confused.

"She practically melted down right in front of us when you shook her hand tonight. You looked at each other with…something; what's between you two?"

He had no words for a moment and shook his head. "I don't know. I asked her what was wrong, but all she said is that she didn't want to talk about it."

Chelsea looked at him, trying to decide whether she believed him. She remembered the way he'd questioned her about Conner back in college, and how she hadn't liked it. How it had looked to Kyle had been clear. Still, as uncomfortable as it felt, she needed to open this can of worms or it would gnaw at her until she had her answers.

"Look, if I've done something wrong, then I apologize. I hope you'll forgive me."

She thought back to Stacie's words to Kyle years ago as they stood now in the dim kitchen; *"Forgiveness is easy. Trust is harder."*

"It's never you," Chelsea said, frustrated, and turned away from him. She felt him grab her wrist and spin her back around to face him, his jaw working the way it did when he got angry.

"Don't...don't doubt me. I can't believe you think I'm keeping something from you."

"I don't know what to think. If it's not you, then what has her so... *distraught?*"

He looked at her indulgently. "I don't know. It's things she says sometimes. She throws stuff out there and then she won't tell me more, like... she thinks I look like my dad. I don't know why that's a big deal unless she was in love with him. I kind of get that feeling, but she cuts it off when I ask more."

"Do you think she feels the same way about you?" she asked boldly. Suddenly she had to know.

He wiped his hand across his face and looked at the ceiling. "I don't know. God, no! I mean, she's close to sixty years old!"

"Kyle, it doesn't matter! Look at Pam! She practically salivates when you walk into the room! I can just imagine what this would be like if these women were younger!"

"Are you kidding me; *what if?* No. We're not doing this!" he said firmly, walking in the bedroom and unbuttoning his shirt. He turned and faced her as she leaned against the doorway. She felt sick, regretting bringing it up at all, not wanting to argue with him about these women.

"I took vows just a few weeks ago," he said passionately, pulling off his shirt and throwing it across the bed. She had seen him angry before, but never at her. It scared her. "We both took vows to love and cherish each other. I'm trying to do that. I've been trying to do that with you for the last six years, Chels. It's been easy so far. But don't make this hard now," he said, taking her in his arms. She stared at him as he pressed himself into her in the darkness, with every obvious intention of showing her he loved her. "Don't ever tell me you don't trust me again," he said, kissing her hard. And then he showed her that every part of him was hers.

Chapter 9

ROUTINES

Every morning over the last few weeks, Chelsea had taken to kicking Kyle out of bed, not wanting to be responsible for the demise of his physical fitness regimen. He ran up and down the road for thirty or forty minutes most days in the early morning, finishing at sunrise, often coming face-to-face with large deer. Traffic at that hour was not a problem but he stayed alert, wondering whether he would ever encounter a bear. Whatever the cost to him, she had been impressed and commented that anyone who could run up and down a mountain must be in pretty good shape. It was by far the better way to make it through the day, as their previous dalliances in morning sex had left him spent and worthless by lunch time. Also, his morning runs gave her the opportunity to endure her morning-sickness in private.

He spent part of every day at work at the inn, with Frank, supervising the renovations. The roofing was complete and the kitchen and gathering rooms were under way. The two men had become as close as brothers. Frank preferred banging away on the refurbished beams to dickering with the owners about the design, which Kyle didn't mind. Details like that annoyed Frank, but Kyle enjoyed the people and was able to use whatever expertise and diplomacy he seemed to have to work through the details.

The project was generally on track, with the subcontractors missing a day here or there for whatever reason. He and Frank were on their second team of framers, but from what he'd been told about the way things went, they were doing great at staying on schedule and moving along at warp speed. This momentum gave him cause to be enthusiastic about the impending condominium project, so he spent his morning runs mentally planning the day and how to allot his time to accommodate both projects. Chelsea had helped him set up an office in the loft above their bedroom, complete with his drafting table and computer set atop his father's old oak desk. She had arranged family photographs and landscape photos he'd taken around the knotty pine siding, and he felt comfortable working there most evenings after dinner while she worked on her grant, read books, or choreographed dance pieces to fill her time.

As he rounded the curve leading back to his drive that particular morning, he breathed rhythmically and comfortably, grateful to his wife for urging him back into this routine he craved. He felt badly for her, watching her attempt to connect with Abby, who seemed suddenly so busy she did not have time for her best friend. It was wedding season at the Mast Farm Inn, after all. But he suspected that it had more to do with Chelsea being pregnant before Abby, and as hurtful as he knew it must be, it seemed petty to him. Glen played it down, but was embarrassed, having to make excuses for why they couldn't make it for dinner, or a Sunday afternoon hike. It had been three weeks and the four of them had not been together.

Chelsea was in the shower when he returned so he filled a glass of water, cold from the tap, and headed upstairs to the loft to assemble his tube of renderings for the day and his laptop with his CAD designs. He rubbed at the stiffness in his knee, searching around the desk for his flash drive, taking a sip of water, and wiping sweat from his forehead with the back of his hand. Surely, he had placed it in a drawer, he thought, pulling out the left hand drawer of the desk, rummaging through the contents. Suddenly he realized he had spilled his water into the drawer, soaking the brown paper that had long ago been placed in its bottom. He cursed and pulled out the drawer's contents and the wet paper, folding it and carrying it, dripping, to the wastebasket. When he looked back in the drawer, he saw a small rectangle that had been left behind, just under the paper. It was dry, thankfully, he thought, lifting it out and examining it. His breath left him as he recognized the familiar face of Lynn Schiffman, smiling intimately at him, her arms wrapped around herself in a plum-colored sweater from the porch of her house. He blinked and stared. She was obviously a few years younger. Her windswept hair was longer and her face seemed relaxed and radiant, as he had never seen her. This photo must have been taken when she and his dad were building her house some eight years ago. This was obviously a picture his mother was never meant to have seen. He remembered when she'd had to endure the painful task of cleaning out the cabin after his father's death. It took him back to the conversation he'd had with her just weeks ago, telling her about landing the condo project. He had felt the sharp but brief silence on the other end of the phone when he'd mentioned Lynn's name. There was something there, but his mother did not elaborate. He didn't want to imagine his mother being hurt so he had left it alone. This picture was meant to be a secret, and perhaps a forgotten one at that. Surely, knowing it could have been discovered, his father should have had the foresight to destroy it. He drew in a sickening breath and sat down heavily in the desk chair, hearing Chelsea padding around downstairs, calling his name.

"Hey, babe! I'm up here," he called down to her, hurriedly slipping the photo in an envelope and placing it, facedown at the back of the drawer. As he replaced the drawer's contents on top of it, he saw the flash drive on the floor near his right foot. Breathing evenly, he made his way downstairs and tried to avoid her hug as she laughed and planted a kiss onto his throat and he rolled his eyes.

"Ugh! I'm disgusting. At least let me get clean and then you can have me," he said into her ear, kissing her there; she laughed again, her smiling face aglow with the life she carried.

He smiled at her eagerness. They seemed to be perpetually hungry for each other, despite her malaise. "How are you feeling this morning?" he inquired, placing his hand gently across her belly, which had only recently showed the first hint of roundness.

"Not so bad this morning. It might hit me later, but I'll be armed with my oyster crackers just in case. They just laugh at me and shake their heads at work." She had just recently broken the news to the dance faculty that she and Kyle were expecting, and the response had been favorable so far. They weren't sure whether it was because she would be expected to squat, give birth, and move on, or because the faculty really wasn't worried about how to fill her shoes during her maternity leave. Nonetheless, she had worried about their reaction to her status. Whatever the case, Chelsea and he had another week; they would visit the doctor again to hear the baby's heartbeat for the first time, and then it would seem real. They had already tossed around names. Hearing the heartbeat would be the best birthday present Chelsea could have, as the appointment fell on her twenty-fifth birthday. July and August were turning out to be busy months, with Lauren's birthday on Saturday, and Tom's just following Chelsea's at the beginning of August. Their own little miracle would be inserted into the mix, like one more twig in the family nest. His mother and Stacie were dying for them to make a trip to the Outer Banks for a visit before the fall semester started for Chelsea. He could hardly keep all the information in his head. His family had grown exponentially since he had reconnected with Chelsea, and it felt good, but dizzying all the same, with the never-ending pressures of work now.

She sat at her desk in the crowded office, surrounded by posters of famous dancers suspended in gravity-defying positions as she munched her oyster crackers, reading over her grant's final draft. She glanced at the clock on her computer screen, realizing Ashley Compton and her daughter, Amelia, were running late. Out of the corner of her eye, Chelsea was aware she was being observed by the custodian's children, who had been hanging around the studio since school had been out for the summer. They had sat stoically on the edge of the stage area, watching her last intermediate ballet class; the boy and girl looked to be around eight and six years old respectively. As she looked up, her eyes connected with the girl's, large, brown, and vacant, although interested in her cracker consumption. Chelsea held up a cracker, as if offering it to the dark, pig-tailed child, who suddenly looked away, embarrassed, a half-smile on her face. Chelsea rose and walked over to the pair, vaguely aware that their father, Hector Romero, was emptying wastebaskets down the hall outside the studio.

"Would you like some?" she asked the girl, who looked sheepish and ashamed that she'd been caught staring.

"Her don't talk much," said the boy without a smile.

"Are you waiting for your father?"

The boy nodded and she asked their names. "Esteban and her Divina," he replied flatly. Chelsea nodded; there was not going to be much more conversation, she thought sadly.

"Do you guys like to dance?" Chelsea asked. A smile suddenly lit Divina's face. Chelsea extended her hands, but Divina pulled her hands inward toward her lap and looked down at the floor, embarrassed once again. At that moment, Hector appeared around the corner and looked chagrined.

"Are they bothering you, Miz Davis?" he asked in a thick Hispanic accent. She had heard he was from Mexico from Carmen, who hailed from Puerto Rico herself. Chelsea had heard them conversing in Spanish from time to time.

"Oh, no, Hector, they're fine. I was asking if they liked to dance."

Hector broke into a grin. "That's all she does at the apartment! She wraps herself in the...curtains." He gestured in the air, thinking of the word in English. "And she dances to the radio," he laughed, swaying back and forth a little to demonstrate, causing his daughter to redden further.

Chelsea thought a moment. "You know…we're starting a dance class in the fall for young students, and I wonder whether you think she would like to participate." Her thoughts raced ahead to the dance program for special students that she was hoping to get approved through the university. Her grant for "Setting the Barre" was complete and would be submitted the next day. Divina just might fit in.

"Oh," Hector began, thoughtfully, wiping his hand across his face, regarding his daughter, who appeared not to be following the conversation. "Their mama works in Tennessee now, so they sit around a lot of the time when I'm working. It might be fun for her to do it, but I couldn't pay…" he said dejectedly.

"You wouldn't have to pay much. We would work on a sliding scale," she offered, and he seemed to understand the term. He looked hopeful, so she wanted to talk to him more about it, but their conversation was interrupted by a small, thin woman and her daughter, swinging awkwardly along on a walker that wrapped around her from behind. The child wore a hot pink bike helmet and a pair of knit shorts and a T-shirt with sturdy sneakers and a very determined look.

Hector spoke dismissively and quietly to his children while Chelsea extended her hand to the mother.

"Hello, I'm Chelsea Davenport…Davis!" she added, still not used to her new name.

"Hi, Chelsea. I'm Ashley Compton and this is Meme."

Meme Compton looked pointedly at Chelsea and then at her mother.

"Hi, Meme! I'm so glad you came to see us. Are you ready to dance?" she asked and a slow, radiant smile began to grow across Meme's face. Chelsea felt herself fall in love immediately with the seven year-old girl.

She squatted down and offered her hand as Meme awkwardly reached out and shook it. They went to the barre and Chelsea helped her stand away from the walker to get an idea of the balancing issues with which Meme was obviously going to struggle. She bravely let go of the walker handles and took Chelsea's hands in an amazingly strong grip. They experimented with some moves and Chelsea swallowed hard, feeling terrified, but buoyed by the valiant determination of the little girl in her grasp. She was also vaguely aware again of Divina's eyes on them throughout the process.

Later in the office, as she sat with Ashley and Meme, Ashley smiled at her reassuringly.

"I know it's a scary thing working with someone with so much going on," Ashley smiled, referring to her daughter, "but I can tell you that you will never meet a person who will try nearly as hard as Meme will," she said calmly.

"Oh, I can already tell that's true, for sure!" Chelsea said, sharing another smile with Meme.

"Besides, she's a *celebrity*," Ashley said, winking at her daughter. "Everywhere we go, people recognize us. How many places do *you* ever go where people point you out with admiration and recognition?" she asked Chelsea, eyes sparkling. "It's like being an Oscar-winning movie star; at least, that's the way we choose to look at it. The committee hasn't called, but it's only a matter of time! We're special, I'll admit it. We just look at it in a positive light. If we didn't, it would be way too depressing," she laughed.

Chelsea bit her lip and fought back tears at this mother's courage, which had certainly translated to her daughter's persona as well. Kyle would definitely have to meet this family! She was suddenly charged with purpose and a sense of protectiveness. She promised to let Ashley know the moment she heard from the grant review panel.

Abby had not answered her cell phone all morning, to Chelsea's disappointment. The plan was for Jay to pick her up, and hopefully, meet Abby at M.C. Adams Clothier to pick out a birthday gift for Lauren. As she stood on Rivers Street near the bus stop waiting for Jay to drive up at the appointed time, she checked her phone again; still nothing. She sighed and wiped perspiration off the back of her neck. It was indeed summer here, and she was hoping to help Jay pick out something summery for Lauren off the clearance rack at the boutique. It appeared that they would be on their own, hopefully not looking like two fish out of water in the dress shop!

His dark blue SUV pulled along the curb and he waved, leaning over to open her door. She noticed the child safety seats in the back and thought happily that she would have one of those in the back of her Subaru very soon. Still, she shuddered with emotion after her meeting with Meme and her mother just an hour ago in the dance studio. Life was so precious, so amazing, and so surprising.

"Hey!" Jay shouted above the noise from the motor of the bus that was pulling in behind him.

She climbed in fast, tucking her skirt around her legs as he pulled quickly away, avoiding a toot on the horn from the oncoming bus. "Thanks for doing this with me today. I suck at birthday shopping. Are we meeting Abby?"

"No, she's not coming I guess. I can't get her on her phone," she said, noticing her brother looking at her questioningly from the driver's seat. She looked ahead, not wanting to get into it with him. "How's Dad today?" she asked, deflecting the attention to something more important.

"He's doing good. He enjoyed tromping around in the woods last week with Kyle and the surveyor, thinking about access roads for the condos.

He and Mom are walking every day after he dispatches the troops, so it's been quiet in the store," he said, referring to the landscaping teams that headed out to work sites every morning. "You know, it gets slow this time of year. It's good that he has this project to work on."

"Yeah, I hope it won't be too much for him," she said absently, thoughts of Abby's avoidance of her still gnawing at her. "So, what's he been so worried about any way?" she asked, pointing him up the hill to the metered parking, poking through her wallet for a few quarters.

Jay sighed and pushed his blonde curls out of his eyes. "He thinks of all kinds of stuff that keeps him awake all night, you know, like, are the Chinese and the Russians getting together to replace us as the next world power? That kind of thing."

She laughed, "Dad thinks this stuff?"

"Yeah, that and who's gonna live in the house after he and Mom are gone."

"What?" she cried, depositing the quarters in the meter and walking companionably with him down the hill toward King Street. "They've got loads of time before that would ever happen."

"He's been worrying about that ever since Kitty died. He's afraid we'll fight over the furniture. I told him we could turn the place into a Bed and Breakfast…."

"Oh, that's lovely," she said sarcastically. "I'm sure that sent him right over the edge!" They were standing at the corner of King Street waiting for the light to change, so she looked down the street to the left, seeing whether she could make out Kyle's office. He should be there, working on the proposal to the bank for the condo project.

"Well, think about it. Lauren and I don't want to live there, and you and Kyle have the cabin. Charley's never going to live here again. It's not a bad solution."

"Not if your family has lived there for what, five generations before you? What if Kyle and I *do* want to live there someday? I don't think your idea went over too well; that, and the fact that you're bailing on him to go to France. Can you even grow grapes in the mountains?"

"Certain kinds. There are hybrids that you can graft to host vines. They do it at the Banner Elk Winery, and some of their wines are really excellent. But not all varieties can take the cold here."

"Well, why can't you just hang out in Banner Elk and learn what you need to know here, without sending Dad into a tailspin? Banner Elk, fifteen minutes from here; France? It's a no-brainer, Jay," she said, holding her hands out as if tipping a scale.

"So am I the only one in the family who doesn't get to live the dream?"

"Dreams change," she warned him. "Sometimes we don't know what's good for us."

Jay laughed, deflecting her guilt-tipped barbs. Her brother had always pushed the envelope when it came to making the right choices, and his sisters had dutifully and delightfully called him out every time. Somehow he seemed to manage to do the right thing, marrying Lauren, and now he was the father of two adorable little boys, but Chelsea would always have to hold his feet to the fire, she thought with a satisfied smirk.

"Hah! Spoken like someone who's getting ready to turn a quarter of a century!"

"I'll always be four years younger than you *and* smarter than you, no matter how old I am!" she laughed. He turned his head toward her and popped his lips, as if he were blowing a bubble at her, something he had not done to her since childhood, as they walked into the pleasant boutique and were greeted by Megan Adams.

"Hi, are you Megan? I'm Chelsea Davis," she said.

Megan smiled immediately. "Yes. Oh right, you're Abby's friend! It's nice meeting you! She said she was trying to get you in here. Is she not with you today?"

"No, not today."

"Oh well, it's wedding season. I guess she's been really busy at the inn."

"I'm sure that's it. This is my brother, Jay Davenport. We're looking for a birthday present for his wife," Chelsea explained, smiling at Jay's ashen face after checking out a price tag on one of the displays. She took him by the elbow, directing him to the sale rack, and began flipping the hangers of clothing so he could inspect each one. He looked overwhelmed. After a few minutes of holding up this dress and that top, they had settled on a lovely green sundress that would look striking with Lauren's blonde hair, and Chelsea found a necklace and earrings to complete the outfit. After Megan gift-wrapped their purchases, they thanked her and left the store, heading back down King Street to a new little shop called Kudzu Creek. It was owned by Leslie and Martha Jane, friends of Liz and Tom.

"Thanks, Chels. That was relatively painless."

"I thought so too. Let's go in here and see if they have Mom's angels," she said, steering him in the door. Their mother had finally taken her ceramic angels to the consignment places in town, so she was turning her old passion into a great success. Anthony English was helping her develop a website and she was going to other locations to begin marketing her product as well.

"So the dinner for Lauren is a surprise?" Chelsea queried.

"Yep. She thinks I'm taking her to dinner at Proper alone. You guys all get there by 6:45 at the latest. I don't think she suspects a thing. Is Kyle coming?"

"Of course; he wouldn't miss it. I'll have to meet him there. He's trying to meet a deadline for Lynn's bank and he is supposed to meet with her most of the day tomorrow."

"He has his hands full, doesn't he?"

"Yes, but it's good. He thrives on being busy. And it's one way to stay employed. Lynn told him she can throw lots of business their way. Her friends from Miami have been coming up to stay with her, and they all want to build summer homes up here now."

"Ah, yes, *North Florida!*"

"Don't knock it. It's good business for you and Dad too."

"Especially when we can offer them local wines as well while they shop for flowers and design their landscapes."

"Maybe you'll be too busy to go to France," she chided and Jay glared at her.

Chapter 10

BIRTHDAY SURPRISES

Chelsea sat between Kyle and her mother at Proper, a quaint little restaurant in the old, two-story brick house on the edge of town that had hosted the surprise party for Lauren. Chelsea yawned, ready to leave, as the men drank yet another beer while discussing the art of tying flies. Another day of fly-fishing was planned for the next day in the river behind the cabin, and Jay and her father were hoping to get out early, before the heat of the day got to be too much for Tom. He had complained about his recent irritating limitations, and Chelsea thought it was time for him to be going home as well. The sky was fading to pink, hinting that it would soon be dark. It had been a long and draining week. She felt this way on most Friday nights, knowing it was motherhood calling. Absently, she laid her head on Kyle's shoulder and her mother smiled knowingly at her.

"You ready to go?" he murmured, sliding his arm around her waist.

"I think so, since I'm driving myself home tonight. You guys stay and continue the manly bonding. I'm tired," she smiled wanly at him.

"Any chance you can wait up?" he whispered.

"We'll see," she laughed, retrieving her purse from the back of her chair and fishing out her keys. She went around the table and hugged Lauren, as Kyle rose to walk her to her car.

"I won't be long, I promise," he said, closing her door and kissing her through the open window as she started the ancient car. "I'll be right behind you. I'm going to drag your father out of here in about two minutes."

"I'm sure my mother will thank you for that. I'll see you shortly then."

⚘⚘⚘⚘⚘

He watched her pull out of the parking lot and head toward Rivers Street, disappearing to the right as he climbed the steps to the restaurant where he downed the rest of his beer. The others were standing to leave and he was glad to be leaving too. Where was that robust and energetic young college man that would just be getting started on his weekend? He thought this with a smile to himself, knowing that guy was back in another world and probably would never be seen again, especially after the baby came. A tug of concern made him more anxious to get in his car and meet Chelsea at home.

He was the first to get in the car after seeing Tom and Liz to the parking lot and bidding Lauren another "Happy Birthday," the first of many twenty-ninths, they'd joked. He followed Chelsea's path out of the lot and turned his music up, putting windows down for the ride home. Now the sky was his favorite deep horizon blue after the dusk had descended as he drove close by the river on the winding road toward home. He was beat! The work of the two projects was catching up with him. He had not seen the inside of a gym since just before the wedding. At least he was running.

The curves in the road grew deeper as he climbed the mountain, then went downhill before the last ascent to his cabin road. As he wove around a tight curve, he saw a deer on the opposite side of the road, sitting, stunned and wide-eyed, as if it had just been hit. A large man with gray hair and a cigarette dangling from his mouth had pulled over and was loping back toward the spot he had just passed. The poor guy had probably hit the doe and was going to help, for whatever good it would do. Kyle's dad would have been itching to pull out his rifle, put the animal out of its misery, and then throw it in the back of his truck for dinner. He shook his head, remembering those days.

In a few minutes, he was pulling into the drive and stopped short as his headlights illuminated the empty parking spot in front of the cabin. Chelsea's car should have been there. Had she stopped off to pick up something at the store? She hadn't mentioned it. A sickening feeling swept over him as he jammed the Range Rover into reverse and gunned it back out onto the road. If she had been the one to hit the deer, then where was her car? Panic slammed against the walls of his stomach and he felt his leg vibrating oddly as he tried to hold it steady in order to drive back to the site of the deer. His phone played on the dash where he had tossed it as usual.

He looked quickly at the screen while tearing around the curves. "Glen?" he shouted urgently into the phone.

"Kyle, where are you? Chelsea's had an accident on Watauga River Road."

"Yeah, I just figured it out. I'm there in two seconds. Is she okay?"

"She's hanging in there. You'll see my patrol car. Bring a flashlight if you have one. She's talking…gotta go."

It was dark as the blue lights and the cars came into view, but the deer was gone. Kyle skidded to a stop and rummaged in the glove compartment for his mag-light. He was out of the car and running to the spot where the blue lights were flashing, sliding, half-falling down the hill, his knees buckling at the sight of all four wheels and the underside of Chelsea's silver Subaru in view. The car, now on its top, had tumbled down the embankment and had mercifully been stopped by a sturdy pair of poplar trees that had grown together, forming a perfect wishbone. At the moment, their purpose had been to save his wife and baby from plunging further down the hill and into the river.

"No! God…Glen! Is she okay?" How could this be happening? Not to her—anyone but her. If she were gone, he would be nothing, again. He should have been with her. He heard himself groan.

The gray-haired man was there, bent over the driver's side door of the car with Glen, both men perched precariously against the roots and rocks. Glen had the door partially opened and talked into the radio at his mouth, relaying information about Chelsea to the EMS dispatcher.

Kyle looked helplessly back and forth at them, Glen holding him away with a straight arm, the old football move they used instinctively.

"We could knock the car down the hill if'n we're not careful," the gray-haired man cautioned him, smelling of cigarette smoke and body odor.

"That's my wife," Kyle stammered and then shouted, "Chels? Can you hear me?" He tried to get closer to the car but could barely see inside. He was still, listening for sounds from her, as Glen listened to the dispatcher on the other end.

Glen put the radio back on his belt and fixed his grip on Kyle's arm. "She keeps passing out," he told Kyle somberly. Also from their football days, they knew the dangers of concussion and head injury. "As far as I can tell, she has pain in her side, her stomach, her shoulder, and her face and hand. She's probably broken several bones, but she was coherent just a few minutes ago. She's gone into shock. I don't know how much blood she may have lost; if I could just see in there and get to her! The ambulance is about three minutes away. We need to keep her talking. Come on down here and sit with her. Just don't touch the car."

"That poor girl hit that deer up 'ere an' her car turned over and landed smack on toppa them two trees. Prob'ly saved her life," the man said gravely, his steely blue eyes filled with concern. "I seen the whole thing happen, and I called nine-one-one just as soon as I could."

"I'm so grateful! I passed right by and didn't know," said Kyle, trying to take it in and slipping closer to the car to get a better look, shining the flashlight in the window. "Chelsea?" he called again as Glen was attempting to position a blanket over her until the EMS could arrive. She appeared to be held in place by her seatbelt; her face was bloody, and turned awkwardly toward them, supported by the airbag. He wiped the blood from her face as best he could with his thumb, realizing there was a small gash on her left cheekbone. The oncoming sirens pealed into the stillness and lights flashed at the top of the hill. Kyle could hear men and women's voices over the radio as the EMTs made their way deftly down the hill, feet thumping on the earth.

And then he heard her voice, faint from within the car. "Kyle!" she called out.

"I'm here, baby! Are you bleeding anywhere else?"

"My face…I think I broke my nose. I feel wet…I think I hit a deer. God, I hurt everywhere!"

"The ambulance just got here, baby. They're gonna get you out real soon," he said, trying to offer her something to hold onto. "The deer was gone, honey. You didn't kill it, but it sure did a number on you," he murmured.

He was instructed to move aside, so he climbed back up the hill a little way with the man who'd saved his wife, realizing that his face was dripping with tears and that he was shaking.

"My name's John Wilson," the man said, extending a grubby hand. Kyle clamped his over it instantly. "I'm sorry about your wife," he remarked sincerely.

"Kyle Davis. I saw you running down here earlier. I didn't know you'd seen this. She's...pregnant," Kyle said, partly to John Wilson and partly for the benefit of the EMTs attending his wife, his voice cracking as he looked away, trying to collect himself. He listened as the paramedics talked to Chelsea encouragingly, getting more information from her and explaining what was going to happen next. She seemed to respond to their questions, but he could hear how she was fighting to stay conscious. One of the medics asked him how far along she was in the pregnancy. "Eight weeks," he responded. When a fire truck arrived, he watched in amazement as two firefighters managed to haul the "jaws of life" down the hill to extract her from the car. Glen climbed the hill and spoke to John Wilson about what had happened for his report, watching Kyle during the process. The generator from the rescue vehicle had started up, and a long hose was being arranged to get the apparatus in place. Another pair of EMTs brought a gurney efficiently down the hill and positioned it near the car while the others worked at the apparatus, spreading the door away from the car floor, where the ceiling should have been. Chelsea was awake and talking with the paramedic who was, at the moment, protecting her face with a shield.

Kyle sank to a sitting position on the bank and closed his eyes, silently begging God to take care of her. Glen had asked him something.

"You should call her parents," he'd said to Kyle firmly, taking charge of his stunned friend. "Or do you want me to do it?"

"Oh, right," he said and pulled the phone out of his pocket, hitting Tom's speed dial number automatically. He moved away from the scene to hear on the phone and prayed that Tom would answer and not Liz. He heard Tom's voice on the phone and explained disjointedly what had happened. As he filled Tom in on the accident, Tom was calling to Liz to get ready to go. "Maybe you guys should hang tight until they can get her to the hospital and you can meet us there," Kyle suggested.

"Not happening, son," Tom told him firmly. "We're getting in the car right now. You call us when they get her out or if...anything changes, and we'll see you in a minute." The connection went dead. Kyle was relieved that her father appeared to be back to normal.

In the few moments that seemed like an hour to Kyle, the rescuers had freed Chelsea from the wreckage of her car and he heard her cry out in agony as they moved her carefully onto the gurney. A woman brought another blanket to cover her, but the wet stain on the skirt of her dress was clearly visible; they all exchanged somber looks. The other paramedic carefully picked glass and debris from her face and wiped off the blood as his partner wrapped the blood pressure cuff around her arm. The first one listened to her heart with his stethoscope, reporting her vital signs to the dispatcher on the radio as Kyle, Glen, and John Wilson looked on. One applied a splint to her right hand while the other attempted to stabilize her left shoulder.

Kyle placed another call to Tom who reported that they were pulling in across from the rescue vehicles as they spoke. They slid carefully down the hill to the scene and the waiting group, and after a moment of shock for Chelsea's parents, they greeted Kyle and Glen. Liz embraced Kyle and offered to drive his car so he could ride in the ambulance with Chelsea.

⤙⤙⤙⤙⤙

The first time Chelsea awoke she made out the voices around her, her parents and Kyle talking frantically as she was being transported from the ambulance to the emergency room. She hurt all over. It got fuzzy again, going to all the different places they'd taken her. She couldn't follow the conversation and fell in and out of consciousness, feeling Kyle's hand in her good one at times, and hearing his voice in her ear, never leaving her. The next time her eyelids fluttered open, her hand felt wet with something warm and heavy on top of it. She made out the top of his head. He had fallen asleep on her hand and he was drooling! They were alone in a larger, quiet room, and she was vaguely aware of the IV drip attached to the arm she saw. Her mouth was dry and her head pounded. She wished for sleep and let it take her again.

Voices permeated the dream she was in; she willed herself out of the darkness again, hearing Kyle and Glen talking in drained voices.

"I almost lost her," she heard Kyle say quietly.

"Nah, she's a beast! She wouldn't leave you that easily. She's a fighter," Glen said, typically upbeat and forever their champion, though tired all the same. "It should be me or you in this bed, not her," he continued.

"Yeah, like that time you fell off the chairlift," Kyle laughed, trying to humor himself, she thought and felt herself smile.

"Or, how about that time you messed up your knee in the North Carolina game and you had surgery in Charlottesville," Glen reminded him.

"Yeah, and you showed up with those yellow roses. That was a nice touch," Kyle said. She could tell they were laughing quietly, trying not to disturb her.

"Okay, I'm awake," she murmured, and they shuffled to attention beside her bed. Glen was still in uniform, but no one else was around. "What time is it? What *day* is it?"

"About three-thirty, early Saturday morning," Kyle replied after checking his watch. Glen must have come back to be with Kyle after he had gotten off duty.

"In the morning? God, Glen, go home!" she said and winced, realizing she was hurt around her shoulder and her chest. It felt as if a knife were slicing into her side. "Abby will be missing you."

She watched them exchange glances. "She's at her cousin's wedding in Raleigh."

"Oh," she said. "That's right. I guess that was this weekend. She's been the busy maid of honor this summer. Well, I'm glad you had to work. You saved my life, Glen. So, what happened?" She was having trouble remembering some of it. And then she panicked. "Is the baby…okay?"

Glen looked at Kyle and excused himself from the room.

She saw the heartbreak on Kyle's face. Instantly, her eyes swam with tears. "I lost it?"

He sat carefully on the bed and held her left hand in both of his. He seemed so big and so sad. "Baby, I'm just glad you're alive! When I saw your car…but about the baby, we would have found out sooner or later. They did an ultra-sound as soon as you got here. I thought I saw blood on your dress, but you were just wet."

"I remember, sort of." What he was saying confused her.

"The ultra-sound showed there was nothing inside the placenta," he said, meeting her eyes, his voice gentle and slow, letting her absorb his words. The morphine she'd been given made him seem surreal.

"I don't understand. There wasn't a baby?" she whispered as her tears rolled down her face, burning the places where she'd been cut and burned from the airbag. He took a tissue and touched it to her face, gently around her wounds.

"They called it an 'empty sack.' It's not very common. The doctor said sometimes conception occurs but the embryo doesn't embed itself in the wall of the uterus. Everything else happens; the hormone levels are high and you feel pregnant. The placenta grows, but there's nothing inside. We would have found out on Monday when Dr. Mueller would have tried to find the heartbeat. We'll need to go and see him again…when you're up to it. You'll have to have a D and C. They have to remove the placenta."

She was dumbfounded. "We never had a baby? All that time, all the plans we were making?"

He shook his head. "I know…it's hard to wrap my head around it, too. I'm so sorry…" his voice drifted off.

"I'm sorry, too. I really wanted this child."

"I did too. Maybe…maybe it just wasn't the right time for us. When it *is* right it will be the best thing that ever happened," he said, bending and kissing her forehead tenderly, letting his lips linger there.

"It will be a gift," she murmured and he nodded. Suddenly, she was overcome with the realization that she could have died in the wreck, and she could tell by the look on Kyle's face that it wasn't lost on him either. She said a silent prayer of thanks and watched his expressions.

"Right now you're the only gift that matters to me," he said softly.

He stroked her hand feverishly and told her the extent of her other injuries: the concussion, a broken collarbone, wrist, and two cracked ribs. Luckily, her lung had not collapsed and her nose was not broken. Her face was cut and bruised from the contact with the broken window and the ground as the car rolled over. There were burns on her face and hands from the airbag. He told her it was a miracle she had survived and probably would not have, except for the wishbone tree upon which she had landed.

He kissed the wounded side of her face; she heard his thick voice in her ear, "Tonight, it's me. After tonight, it's always going to be me."

Unable to speak, she shook her head.

On Sunday morning, Chelsea woke for the second time to the scent of soap and shampoo, the remnants of Kyle's shower lingering in the air. She wanted to smile, but the pain stabbed her again in her side. It happened every time she moved, or breathed deeply, or laughed. It was inadvisable to stretch as she felt herself come awake, propped with several pillows on their bed. How he had slept beside her, she didn't know, the way she had moaned and groaned all night, attempting to get comfortable, forgetting her limitations as she awoke each time.

He was standing beside the bed in her favorite old jeans and a UVA T-shirt, holding a bowl of oatmeal in one hand and a steaming cup of hot tea in the other.

"Good morning, Sunshine," he said softly and groggily, so she knew instantly that he had not slept.

"Hey…You're up early, aren't you?" she asked, unsure of the time. He set her breakfast on the table beside the bed and smiled at her.

"It's about eight-thirty. Do you want to try to use the bathroom?"

"Sure," she replied and swallowed, gearing up for the painful ordeal of sitting up and standing. Everything hurt, even her teeth!

He slid his arm behind her carefully, mindful of the broken ribs and the fractured wrist in a sling on her right side, and her broken collarbone on the left. They had opted for the figure-eight bandage for her clavicle, thinking that two slings would be difficult to manage. She held her breath and closed her eyes, doing everything she could to help him pull her into a sitting position. Then came the turn, and she brought her legs off the side of the bed, creating more of the stabbing pain in her side again. He let her rest a moment and handed her a glass of water and two of her pain pills.

She looked at him gratefully and swallowed the capsules, trying to breathe evenly. His hair was still damp and only fingered in place from the shower and he had yet to shave. She tried to reach for him but was limited by her current range of motion restrictions and the pain the move caused her. "God, you're good-looking," she said.

"Must be the drugs talking," he chuckled, taking her glass.

"Oh, no. This is the part that sucks the most. I can't even touch you," she said, trying to catch her breath with the pain it caused to talk.

Kyle leaned forward and placed his hands on the bed on either side of her. He looked deep into her eyes the way he always did, making tears spring behind her eyelids. His face was inches from hers. He smelled clean and glorious, and she breathed as deeply as she could without causing more pain.

"Then, can I touch you?" he asked, leaning closer, slowly, touching his lips to hers in the softest kiss she had ever felt. He pressed her lips gently apart. She felt herself wanting to melt, knowing that this couldn't happen, and withdrew from him. "Did I hurt you?" he whispered tentatively.

"No," she whispered, looking away. "I just know I smell bad and I could really use a wardrobe change," she continued, looking down at the pale blue, patterned hospital gown the nurses had sent her home in the day before because nothing she owned would accommodate the limited range of motion with which her arms allowed her to contend.

"Well, we'll find you something to wear, and you don't smell," he said, locking his eyes with hers. "Your mom is coming over pretty soon, and she's bringing the tub bench and the handheld shower…you know," he said, helping her stand and walk into the bathroom. She remembered the equipment he was talking about. It was what they had used to bathe her grandmother before she died six years ago. Kyle knew it would make her sad.

In the bathroom, Chelsea avoided looking at herself in the mirror. She couldn't imagine how Kyle could stand to look at her, with all the bruises on her face and chest. After he had helped her use the toilet and brush her teeth, he helped her back into bed, positioning a tray, and helped her eat her oatmeal. She felt beyond helpless. She couldn't even raise her own spoon to her mouth. She couldn't imagine how he could manage her and try to go to work. He worked all day and at night too, to accomplish both of the jobs he was working on. He looked exhausted.

They heard a knock at the door. "That's probably your mom," he said, settling her back on the pillows and taking the tray out of the bedroom with him. She heard him greet the person at the door with a surprised and pleasant voice. It was a woman's voice she heard, but not her mother's.

They were hugging and he was telling her how great it was to see her. Then she heard him murmuring, "It's okay; it's okay."

Abby's voice filtered in from the front door. "Is it too early? I didn't want to disturb you. I got home last night. I felt so bad about not being here."

"No, it's fine! You were in a wedding. She'll like these flowers," Chelsea heard him say. "Glen's sleeping, I hope?"

"Yeah, he's pretty beat. He'll come over later before he goes to work."

"He's the best. He was with us the whole time, all of Friday night and as much as he could be there yesterday. You tell him I said he's the bomb. Let me check on Chelsea. I'll tell her you're here." His voice got closer as he entered the bedroom. He smiled at Chelsea and whispered, "You up for company? Abby's here…."

Why couldn't she smile? Abby had been her best friend since they had met on the school bus the first day of kindergarten. Her absence through this pregnancy had hurt Chelsea deeply. Her reticence at seeing her best friend was palpable. Kyle noticed immediately, but seemed to take it in stride. He seemed to understand everything. He had been through all of this before in some form or another. Carefully, he moved to the bed and sat beside her, so as not to jostle her around. "Do you want me to say you're asleep? She brought you some flowers…."

Chelsea shook her head. "I don't know why I'm being like this. Of course she can come back here," she said, blinking back tears. He gave her a moment to compose herself, not looking at her, which would have surely unraveled her further.

"Okay?"

"Okay," she sighed, wincing as he tried to move carefully off the bed. He stood and kissed her forehead. Crying hurt too. She steeled herself for

Abby's reaction to her. Kyle was the only one so far who could look at her without turning his head.

In a moment, he returned with Abby, and after a nod from Chelsea, he left them alone. Abby set the pottery pitcher of yellow tulips on the dresser. Then she walked slowly over to the bed and stood at the chair opposite Chelsea. She gasped and gaped, wild-eyed, at her friend.

"Chelsea! Oh my God, you look like *shit*!" she cried and Chelsea laughed. Abby began to laugh too, but her laughter quickly dissolved into sobs as she looked at Chelsea's face.

"Stop it! I'm not supposed to laugh! It hurts like hell," she breathed. Abby wiped tears from her face. She stepped close to the bed, trying to reach out for Chelsea, unable to figure out how to hug her in her predicament. She rubbed Chelsea's leg absently.

"Oh, Chels! I'm so sorry! About everything. Glen told me to be prepared, but it's worse than I thought. You have bruises everywhere!"

"You have no idea. You can't see half of them."

Abby looked down at her hands and was quiet a moment. "I'm sure," she said and Chelsea knew the kind of bruises they both understood were there. "You must hurt like crazy. I'm so sorry about the baby. I've been just the worst friend. No, I haven't been your friend at all. You've always been so good to Glen and me, ever since high school, and with us trying to get pregnant, you never said all the stupid and insensitive things other people say: '*Maybe you can adopt,*' or '*Maybe if you'd just relax it would happen!*' That's my mother's favorite. Or they tell me to stand on my head, or I'm putting too much pressure on Glen. It's awful, all of it. And I've said awful things to you. You've been nothing but supportive and kind and fun and non-judgmental, and I just...*dissed* you completely when it happened for you," she continued bitterly, sniffing and wiping more tears with the back of her hand.

"Well...apparently, it didn't really happen."

"Yes. It did happen. You're going to have a D and C, so yes it did happen. Your dream is gone. I understand that," she said quietly.

Chelsea's eyes filled with tears. She let herself imagine what it would feel like to be in the hospital, having the empty sack being scraped from her womb, when sadness overwhelmed her again. "It's like the death of our dream," she wept.

"I know. You and Kyle need to grieve. You've lost something tremendous. *I know*," she said fervently.

"I know why you want a baby so badly now. I thought I knew it before, but I *do* understand it now," Chelsea said, drying her eyes with the back of her good hand, so grateful to have her friend back.

"When are you going to have your procedure?"

"I don't know, maybe Thursday or Friday, or maybe next week. I have to get a cast put on so I might as well get it all done at once. But I can hardly move right now. Kyle's being so good about all this. I know he's exhausted. I can't even go to the bathroom without his help, or feed myself."

Abby leaned forward and placed her hand on Chelsea's leg, not knowing where else to touch her. "He's the perfect husband."

"Not really. He doesn't like the Grateful Dead," she tried for humor.

"Like I said, he's perfect! You must hurt like hell! God, look at you! Do you remember the accident at all?"

"Thankfully, not really…I remember seeing a deer running into the road and it hit me…and I lost control of the car, and that's all I can remember. Then I remember being at the hospital and Glen and Kyle were there, and my parents and Jay maybe. It's all really fuzzy. They had to cut me out of my clothes."

"What were you wearing?"

"That blue dress with the ruffles at the neckline."

"Oh, no! That was my favorite!" Abby moaned in sympathy.

"I know. It was Kyle's too. He said when they pulled me out of the car, I was wet and he thought I'd bled and lost the baby, but I'd just wet myself when I wrecked. I scared him to death."

"And Glen too. We talked on the phone four or five times that night. If I hadn't been Jessie's matron of honor, I would have been right back here."

Chelsea wanted to say, "I know" but until now, she really didn't. "How was the wedding?"

"Not nearly as nice as yours. But it was nice. There was a band, a sit-down dinner, a chocolate fountain, open bar, big country club deal, but whatever. I'm just so glad to be sitting here with you right now."

"Glen was awesome," Chelsea said sincerely.

"I know. He's a rock. I want to be like him someday. I should be that kind of a friend. I *will* be that kind of a friend. I've learned a lot, Chelsea. I'm sorry that I've hurt you. Look, let me make it up to you by bringing you something to wear! What's the problem here?" she asked, gesturing at the gown.

Chelsea explained what they were dealing with as Abby made it her mission to find appropriate clothing. Chelsea's mother arrived while Abby was rifling through her closet. Kyle busied himself with weed-eating the hillside of their backyard while Chelsea got a bath and a nap under Liz's supervision.

❦

The next time Chelsea awoke, she heard Kyle and a woman speaking quietly.

"She looks like Sleeping Beauty, lying here," the woman said, and she heard Kyle laugh quietly.

"I know she does. Be sure you tell her that, although she'll never believe you."

"I only see her, not the bruises," the woman said. Chelsea's eyelids fluttered open to see Stacie's face smiling above hers. She was curled beside her on the bed, her head propped on her right hand above Chelsea's pillow and her other hand rested on Chelsea's left arm. Her pale blonde hair hung loosely around her shoulders and the blazing blue eyes that were so like Kyle's smiled down at her. Chelsea gasped, causing another stabbing pain.

"Oh, my God, Stacie?" Chelsea thought she must be dreaming. Stacie looked like the angels Chelsea had always imagined, and she smelled just as heavenly. Suddenly, everything was right with her world, as Kyle sat, grinning at the two of them at the end of the bed.

"Well, I couldn't very well miss your birthday, could I?" she asked in her throaty voice.

Chelsea swallowed and tried to compose herself. "When did you get here?"

"Shelly and I got here about ten minutes ago. Tyson wanted to come too, but it's crazy busy there, and I didn't think you'd be up to having our Abby bouncing around like the wild child she is. Maybe they can get up here another time when the tourists leave and you're feeling better," she said, referring to their restaurant, The Sound Side in Kill Devil Hills on the Outer Banks. Kyle had spent many summers there, working as a waiter. Chelsea had visited as well on summer breaks after Kyle and Shelly had moved there before he entered college.

"Did you do this for me?" Chelsea asked Kyle, who was still grinning and rubbing her feet at the foot of the bed.

"I'd like to say yeah, but it was their idea, and your mom was in on it too. It was a conspiracy."

At that point, Chelsea realized there were others in the house, and their voices made their way into the bedroom from the porch. Stacie was looking at Kyle and nodding to him. "Do you mind giving us just a minute?" she asked and he indulgently removed himself from the room, giving Chelsea's foot one last stroke.

"Just don't make her laugh. Seriously, it hurts a lot when she laughs... or cries. God, please don't make her cry," he warned.

"Just go, okay?" Stacie did the laughing and then he was gone to join the others.

She settled herself around Chelsea's shoulders as best she could. "I'm trying to hug you without hurting you," she explained to Chelsea. Chelsea looked into her lovely face, clean and tan without makeup, small lines just now appearing around her eyes. Her expression was mixed with joy and sadness all at once, deepened by the kind of wisdom Chelsea had always gleaned from her.

"I'm so sorry for the loss of your baby," she began. "I had to come here and tell you this face-to-face because I know how much it hurts." Chelsea nodded, wordlessly, knowing that Stacie had lost a baby at one time in her life too. "And I'm so glad you're okay. I know you don't *feel okay*, but you're going to be as good as new again, and then I can give you a proper hug in a few more weeks. And I have to tell you also that your husband was so devastated by your accident. I know he's been putting on a grand show for you because that's the kind of good guy he is, but if he had lost you, Chelsea, it would have destroyed him."

Tears streamed down Chelsea's face while Stacie stroked her hair. Stacie kissed the top of her head. "I'm sorry; I'm not supposed to make you cry. Y'all are going to need some major help around here, and so we came to assist you for the next few days until you can start to cope with it all."

"I can't thank you enough. I'm not usually this much trouble!"

"Oh, honey! We're so glad to do it!" They sat a moment and Stacie stroked her arm. "About the baby…I know it hurts, but you and Kyle will have another chance."

"I know. I'm so confused. I was ready to be a mom and we were both so excited. I guess it just wasn't the right time."

"Sometimes the timing is everything," Stacie said with a sigh and stroked Chelsea's hair absently. "It took me forever to have a child, and it was the best thing that ever could have happened to me. I was forty, you know. But Tyson and I had just found each other, and I had fought the idea of loving him so hard…I was sure he needed to be with someone younger. And then I thought I couldn't have kids…and then it was like a miracle for us that Abigail happened. It's been so good since I stopped trying to be in charge of things, you know? Sometimes we have no idea what's best for us. This will all work out for you and Kyle too. This will bring you even closer together, if that's at all possible."

"Hey! Happy Birthday! Mind if we come in?" Shelly's smiling face appeared in the doorway, followed by Liz, and the three women circled the bed in one large smile. Shelly's brave smile began to crumble as she took in Chelsea's bruises and the sling, imagining the other bandages, most likely.

Stacie rescued her and said to Chelsea, "See, here we are, the three good fairies, Flora," she said, gesturing to Liz, "Fauna," to Shelly, and then to herself, "and Merriweather!"

Chelsea beamed at them all while trying not to laugh.

"Your mother will have her hands full taking care of you, while Shelly does the cleaning and the laundry, and I'll be cooking for everyone while this lasts! You'll get to see your daddy every day, too, because he'll be here for dinner."

"What do I get to do?" asked Kyle, coming in on the tail-end of Stacie's announcement.

"Go to work," said Shelly.

"Bring home the bacon, read the paper, pay the bills, entertain your wife with all the exciting architectural highlights of the day, and stand around looking sexy for her," quipped Stacie.

"Don't look sexy, please. It's killing me," muttered Chelsea. They laughed. "I don't know if I can stand being laid up like this for six weeks. I can't even touch him without it hurting!" She thought of their honeymoon just a few weeks ago; this was a far cry from the way they'd been. Still Kyle didn't seem to mind.

"Well," he started, "we really appreciate all this help from you ladies. I know I can't do it all, and I have to say I was a little worried about how I was going to pull this off. But I just have one favor to ask," said Kyle awkwardly.

"What's that, sweetheart?" asked Shelly.

"We'll need some private time...you know? We're so used to being by ourselves...and you guys are going to be a houseful," Kyle said tenuously, not wanting to offend them. "It could be really overwhelming for Chels since she doesn't feel good," he added for good measure.

"Oh, of course! That goes without saying! You're still on your honeymoon, but you'll have to be careful!" exclaimed Stacie. "I mean, don't even think about touching her!"

"Of course! And you just have to say the word and we'll leave you alone," Shelly agreed. Liz smiled and squeezed Chelsea's hand. If it were possible to blush beneath her bruises, Chelsea was sure she was doing it now. Kyle grinned at all the women in the room and stroked Chelsea's feet again.

Chapter 11

WELCOME TO CHICKVILLE

Another knock at the door announced Abby, back from her successful clothes-finding mission, followed a few minutes later by Sonya McIntyre and Carmen De Silva, bearing flowers. As Kyle let them in, he wondered whether this should just be the birthday party he had wanted to throw for Chelsea on Monday night. So much for even the intimate plans he had made for her instead! They had managed to prop her up on the sofa with multiple pillows, and she seemed delighted with her company. Still, he worried that when she hit the wall with all the stimulation, it wouldn't be pretty. It was almost too much for him, all these females in his dad's fishing cabin! The dance colleagues were huddled around Chelsea, stroking her hand, and reassuring her that all would be well for the remainder of the summer session. Sonya would be taking her place instructing her ballet classes for the next three weeks. There would be a week off and then Chelsea hoped to be returning to work for the fall semester, in a wrist cast at least.

He contemplated the idea of buying her another car, knowing that her little Subaru had become a total loss in the accident, and he wondered how comfortable she would be resuming driving again. Their lives would be a work in progress for the next several weeks, but what else was new?

Since they'd been married, there had only been one surprise after another. Stacie, winking at him, busied herself in the little kitchen, displaying the flowers and preparing to put out an appetizer for the visitors, the sweet chocolate aroma of a birthday cake filling the air. He spotted his mother alone on the porch. Shelly and Liz had been exclaiming over the bottle tree, but now Liz had come inside to welcome the group around the sofa. Hands in his pockets, he wandered out to speak with his mother, watching as she gazed out over the porch to the river that was just visible through the leafy green canopy around them. She reached behind her neck and pulled, as if working out a stiff spot.

"Hey!" he said, circling his arm around her shoulder and giving her a little squeeze.

"Hey!" she returned his greeting and wrapped her hand around his arm. "Is this all too much for you two? After tonight, we promise there won't be all this traffic."

"No! Chelsea seems to be enjoying the company, for now at least. Maybe it'll take her mind off things if other people are around."

"Well, I hope so. We were worried that all this might be too much of an imposition. If you want, Stacie and I can stay up at Tom and Liz's place. You just say the word. You're in charge."

"Let's play it by ear, okay?"

She smiled up at him. "How are you doing? This has got to be hard on you, too."

Kyle sighed and gazed out where she had been looking moments before. He was quiet a moment. "You know, when I saw her car..." his voice caught unexpectedly. "All I could think was, *not her...not the baby, not one more person in my life gone!*" Tears deep in his throat made his voice thick, making him stop talking.

"Oh, honey! I'm so sorry. We're just a wreck still, aren't we? It never goes away does it? I can hardly walk out here and look out at the river and not think of this cabin as '*the other woman.*' That's the way it seemed that last year or two of Stu's life. I felt so shut out. There was nothing I could do but give your father his space, but in the long run, it was the wrong thing to do," she said; the familiar troubled look was in her eyes as she rubbed her hand up and down his arm absently.

"You didn't know that," he whispered, encouragingly.

"No, I didn't. I have so many regrets, honey. But you don't ever get over it, do you? You move on, but it's always there. Anyway," she said, dismissively, "I meant to comfort you, not depress you. I know you were both so disappointed about losing the baby."

He was glad she did not remind him that they were young and had their whole lives ahead of them. He was grateful she did not tell him that they'd rushed into it too soon. She knew he needed to grieve and she was allowing him that opportunity. Shelly pulled her son's head to her shoulder and rubbed his back. They had finally come to an understanding, the two of them, after so much hurt and deception over the years. She was so open, so different now, and he hoped Mark Hargett was the cause for some of that.

"I love you," she murmured in his ear, and he whispered the same words back to her. It was the first time in his life that he remembered saying those words to her. It did not feel awkward, but solidifying in some new way, as if a new door had been opened for the two of them.

He glanced at the people inside and noticed a new member, a slight figure clad in beige linen; instantly, he recognized Lynn Schiffman holding his wife's hand at the moment. He breathed in deeply, realizing this moment might not go well, especially in light of the conversation that he and his mother had just had.

"Who is that?" Shelly asked him curiously.

"That's Lynn Schiffman, the woman I told you about who's developing the condos at Sugar Ridge."

He felt his mother draw in a breath, but she said nothing further. Lynn turned then and noticed them, walking toward the door. He suddenly thought of the picture he'd found in the desk drawer. With all the excitement over the past few days, he had forgotten all about it.

"Hi, Kyle! I'm so sorry. I didn't realize you were having a party. I just heard about Chelsea, and I thought I'd stop by with some breakfast things to help out a bit," she said, glancing at Shelly and smiling at her pleasantly. "I'll just stay a minute."

"Hi, Lynn. Thank you for coming over. It's really not a party, just lots of people here helping out. Have you met my mother, Shelly Davis?" he asked, trying to keep the wariness out of his voice, and feeling his mother stiffen beside him.

Lynn extended her hand for the exquisite handshake he knew would follow and Shelly mechanically held hers out as well.

"Of course, I remember you! We met when your husband was building my house in Blowing Rock. He did a wonderful job. You saw it, didn't you?"

"Yes, I do remember that. He did his best work on your home. I saw it just before it was finished, I think."

Kyle remembered Chelsea's story about Tom and Liz going there to have coffee when the house was finished, but his parents had not been there. What had that been about? Lynn didn't seem to miss a beat and her eyes showed nothing.

"I'm so pleased that now Kyle has taken on the new project with the condominiums. I'm looking forward to something special with that project as well."

"I'll look forward to seeing what he does for you, too," Shelly said, her voice vacant, but not unfriendly. At that moment, Liz and Stacie were coming to join them, Liz with a concerned look on her face.

"Did you know that Tom is working with us on the project too, Mom?" Kyle asked Shelly.

"Yes, you told me that. I think it's great."

Liz greeted Lynn, and Shelly introduced Stacie. The conversation shifted to the accident and Chelsea's condition as Glen's head peeked out the door. Kyle glanced at his mother, who seemed over her initial shock, and went to greet Glen.

Glen held a twelve pack of bottled beer in one hand and shook Kyle's with the other.

"Damn, buddy, you've got a whole houseful of women! Only you, right? What is this, *Chickville*?"

"Looks that way. It's been okay so far, but I don't know how much more I can stand," Kyle laughed quietly. "You saved the day. Let me have one of those," he said, referring to the Mexican beer Glen had brought.

"Can't forget my friend," Glen said, winking. When they went back into the kitchen, Stacie intercepted them.

"Here, put those in the cooler. It's empty now, but the fridge is full of the food I brought," she said, retrieving ice from the freezer and covering the beers Glen had deposited.

"You remember my Aunt Stacie," Kyle said, and Glen gave her a hug.

"Sure, of course I do, the party girl from your wedding!" he said, making Kyle remember how much fun they'd all had before he and Chelsea had departed for their honeymoon.

"So when are you coming to visit us at the beach, Glen? You and Abby need to come with Kyle and Chelsea the next time they can get down there…which I was hoping would be soon, but I guess we'll have to see about that. You should plan on Chelsea's fall break. That's when it really gets nice; all the tourists are gone, and she should be healed up by then," she offered, bumping Kyle's shoulder affectionately.

"Sounds like a plan." Kyle grinned at her and Glen nodded enthusiastically. Stacie opened beers for the three of them. They clinked their bottles together in a toast.

"Well, speaking of chicks, I'd better go check on mine," Glen said as they watched Abby holding up the purchases she'd made for Chelsea while the other ladies were cooing their approval.

"I'm two steps behind you," he said, peering out the door to the porch, watching Liz, Lynn, and his mother ensconced in conversation. He bounded up the stairs to the loft and opened the desk drawer, retrieving the envelope with the photo of Lynn, slipping it in the zipper pocket of his laptop case. If his mother were going to be doing the cleaning around here, he didn't want her finding it. With the haunted feelings she'd described, he could imagine her looking through his father's desk, searching for some semblance of peace. This would not be it.

When he returned downstairs, he saw the line of ladies leaving. They each hugged him and offered their help whenever he needed it while wishing him encouragement as they headed out the door. Abby and Glen sat by Chelsea on the sofa, but they made room for him to sit beside her and take her hand. It was time for another pain pill so Liz had gone into the bedroom to get it.

"Are you ready for a rest back in your bed?" Kyle asked her.

"It might be a good idea in a few minutes. No matter where I am, it hurts, and I am getting tired."

"That's the thing about broken ribs. They get worse before they get better," said Glen, remembering his own experience from a high school football injury.

Liz joined them. "Why don't you try to sleep for an hour or so? Stacie has a nice jambalaya dinner planned for your birthday. Dad will be coming down by the time you wake up. You two are welcome to stay and join us if you can," she said to Glen and Abby.

When Abby looked apprehensively at Glen, Chelsea made an encouraging face.

"I really don't want to wear you out, Chels. I think we'd better let you rest and have this time with your family. But I'm just a phone call away. Do you mind if I come back with your birthday present tomorrow?"

"Of course not! But Mom and I will be gone after lunch. I have to go back to the doctor and get a soft cast to replace my splint…right, Mom?" she still seemed fuzzy on the details. Kyle winced, knowing the doctor would probably have to reset her wrist, but he kept it to himself.

"That's right, sweetie. Why don't we call you when we get back here?" suggested Liz as Abby and Glen stood to leave.

Later, as Kyle settled her into the bed again, Chelsea sighed deeply. "It's good that you made me get in bed. It really does feel better."

He sat carefully beside her on the bed and touched her hand. "You've had a big day. You need to take care of yourself or your pain will get out of hand. So that's my job now, taking care of you, okay? Between your mom and me, we should be able to keep tabs on you well enough."

"I'll try to be a good patient. Thank you for taking care of me. Will you do me a favor?"

"Anything."

"Kiss me again…like you did before. I miss holding you, and being with you."

"I miss it too," he murmured, touching the unaffected side of her face, leaning in close to her and taking her lips in a tender kiss.

"Kissing is the only thing I can do that doesn't hurt. I love you so much," she whispered next to his mouth, so he kissed her again, smoothed her hair, and held her hand until she fell asleep just moments later.

As he looked for a safe place to pull over, Kyle looked at her beside him in the passenger seat of the Range Rover. Her face was pale and her eyelids were heavy with the sedatives she had been given. "Are you sure you want to do this?" he asked her warily. They had come from the hospital where she'd had her D and C procedure, and it had been an ordeal for both of them, mentally and emotionally for him, and in every way for her. Besides that, she had started to remember more and more about the accident. It would come back to her in pieces as she awoke some mornings, and she wanted to see the tree that had saved her life.

She turned her head slowly, making him question whether it was worth it even to be here. Would she even remember this trip? Or would her drug-induced state help her to deal with it? Her face was still so bruised, reddish today. Every day, the bruises were a different color, black to blue to purple. It hurt him to see it, making it difficult to look at her, but he never turned away. "Baby...are you sure?" he asked her again.

"Yes," she said, her voice surprisingly lucid. "I want to get it over with... today."

The car ground to a stop on the shoulder where he remembered Glen's patrol car being parked that night. "We'll have a little bit of a walk. Do you think you're up to it?"

"Yes," she said, leveling her gaze at him. She was trying not to get irritated with him, he thought, reading the tone of her voice. Even with all the drugs she had taken over the course of this ordeal, she had not gotten out of control. A few tears shed had been the worst of it for her. He remembered how to pull inside himself and wondered whether she was doing the same. Would she ever just let it all out? He had wanted her to cry, to sob, to let him comfort her, and to cry with her. But they had each held themselves together for the sake of the other, he supposed. Yet again, she surprised him, not knowing how strong she seemed. He sighed and walked around to her door to help her slowly out of the car. She made the little gasping sounds she tried to squelch whenever she had to twist sideways. It had been almost a week, but the pain of her broken ribs was still as intense for her as it had been in the beginning.

Gently, he wrapped his arm around her, holding her left side and giving her his arm to hold with her left hand. He looked out for traffic, and they walked slowly to the scene. She would have to look down from the road, as there was no way she could step down the bank for a better view. She stopped when she saw the twin poplar, the only tree within a several foot radius, forming the perfect wishbone shape, with most of the bark from six feet down to the bottom of the trunk scraped away by the assault from her car, revealing its raw white insides. She drew in a ragged breath and held his arm tighter, looking slowly up at him. They watched a moment longer and then she asked, "Did you ever find my cell phone?"

He shook his head. "No, I've looked around down there a couple of times, and they've gone through your car pretty thoroughly. We'll get you a new one." He expected some kind of reaction, tears, angst, something, but this was it. She looked a minute longer and then turned to go.

"Thank you," she said and nestled her face into his shirt, holding his arm and stroking it. He held her for a moment before they headed back to the car. She stared blankly out the window until they pulled into the drive in front of the cabin. She finally spoke again, "I guess that was horrible for you, driving up on that scene that night. I can imagine what you must have thought." When she turned to him, he saw the tears welling in her eyes. They were tears for him, not for herself, he realized, amazed again at the amount of love she felt for him. He swallowed.

"Glen told me you were talking and I was so relieved. Losing you would have been beyond...."

"I know," she whispered, placing her hand over the one he'd laid on her leg.

⚘

They made it inside and he seated her on the bed, arranging the pillows before going to her dresser and taking out clothes. She watched him intently, shuddering slightly, realizing how worn out she was and how glad she was to be back here with him, by themselves again. Stacie and Shelly had gone to town for lunch and some shopping. He had been so ready for them to go away for a while and give them back their privacy, but like it or not, they still needed the help for a couple of more days. He returned to the bed and removed the sling from her right arm; then, he maneuvered the blousy knit top off of her. When he removed the figure-eight bandage, she sighed gratefully, feeling free, if only for a few moments. He helped her stand and helped her out of the skirt she'd worn. He held her gently and kissed her, then seated her again, this time taking his softest T-shirt and pushing his fists inside it, stretching it to accommodate her limits. He slid it over her head, helping her work her arms into the sleeves and pulling her hair free. She loved the feel of his touch, and she closed her eyes, letting him take care of her. He replaced the sling, this time to her left arm, and helped her step into a pair of soft shorts. His kindness moved her so deeply that she found she could not speak. He kissed her again, helping her under the covers, and sat beside her, running his fingers gently along the wounded side of her face. Her stitches had been removed and the pink smile of a scar crested her cheekbone. He kissed the scar and laid his hand on her other cheek.

She was overwhelmed with exhaustion. Determined not to fall asleep just yet, she looked deep into his eyes and murmured, "Today...it's me."

Chapter 12

BEING THE CLAY

Chelsea sat on the sofa surrounded by Kyle, her mother, and her father. She wiped the flood of uncontrollable tears away from her cheeks with the tissues her mother had handed her.

"Some birthdays we've had, right, Dad?"

"I know it. I'm sorry, sugar. Maybe next year will be our year," Tom said, patting her hand from his perch on the coffee table. "I thought when I saw him under the oak tree that he was just sleeping in the shade like he always did," Tom said heavily, describing how he had found Fella, their old yellow lab, that morning. "I never thought he was that close to leaving us."

Kyle rubbed his hand up and down Chelsea's back. "How old was he?"

"Fourteen. That's pretty old for a dog," Tom replied. Kyle nodded.

Chelsea pressed the wad of tissues to her eyelids and exhaled roughly. This was not just about Fella, she realized as the sobs wracked her sides, strangely not causing her the pain she had expected. At least her body was healing. She knew their hovering was a response to her latent grief, and she was glad to be embraced by the three people she loved most in the world. Everyone should be so lucky to have souls like this among them.

"I'm sorry I'm being such a baby about this," she said.

"No, sweetie, it's okay. Let it out. We cried too this morning," said Liz, stroking her hair.

What was supposed to have been a celebration of Tom's fifty-sixth birthday had quickly plummeted to a somber occasion. Jay and Lauren with their boys were outside taking care of the grill and setting up the picnic tables for the party later. Tom's brother, Wayne, his wife Becky, and their two children home from college, would soon be arriving, bearing side dishes and condolences.

"Ah! My face probably looks like a blowfish by now. I hope I don't scare Thomas and Ethan when they see me."

"Not a chance," Kyle reassured her. "Your face looks way better than the last time they saw you!" he joked with her to elevate her mood.

"You do look so much more like yourself without the bruises and the sling," her mother said encouragingly.

"Let's go get a beer, son," Tom suggested to Kyle as they discreetly left the women alone.

After a moment, Liz asked, "How are you doing, sweetheart?" Concern was tight in her voice.

"Oh, Mom, I guess I feel like…the clay, you know? I'm just muddling through right now, not really knowing what all of this is about. I don't know why there wasn't a baby and we thought there was. I'm glad Abby and I are friends again, but I don't understand why it got so weird there for a while…and my colleagues in the dance department must think I'm trouble and wonder why in the world they hired me…and now Fella is *gone*! Why?" she blubbered and blew her nose.

"Oh, sweetie, I know you and Kyle have had a lot on you. And you've had one ordeal after the next. Things just come in waves, it seems. I think maybe your trouble is coming to an end. I have to say I think you've dealt with all of this really well. Shelly and Stacie were so impressed with both of you when they were here."

"Well, Kyle and I couldn't have managed without all of you, and what you did for us. He's working so hard and the last thing he needed was me laid up like I've been," she said, lifting her hand, covered in a black cast halfway up her right arm. A dozen signatures in ASU gold lettering decorated the contraption and she couldn't wait to be free of it in two more weeks. "I guess God has a purpose for all of this, but heck if I know what it is."

"It may be a long time before you know, but I think it will become clear one day. And strangely enough, this may not even be about you. All of what you're going through might affect someone else in a profound way. People say God doesn't give you things you can't handle. I don't believe that. I think He gives us things that test our strength, certainly, and these challenges build our faith…or not. It's up to us the way we handle it. Dad and I are just so glad you're back here and that we have you and Kyle again. The best thing will be when Charley and Steve and Kitty pull up in the driveway and we're finally all here together again. There's nothing more important than family."

Chelsea nodded and smiled. "I guess I'd better go try and make myself presentable," she said, then went upstairs to her old familiar bathroom to place a cool washcloth over her swollen face. After a few moments, she allowed herself to take a look at her face. In the mirror, she saw Kyle standing in the doorway.

"Much better," he said, smiling.

She sighed. "I guess it took Fella's dying to let out all this emotion," she said, folding the cloth over the side of the old sink and pressing it down carefully. She turned and looked directly at him. He offered her his beer and she took a long pull off of it gratefully. It was satisfying and cold, washing the last of her tears away.

"I don't think I was ready to be a mom after all," she said. He looked at her in amazement.

"You fooled me," he said softly, coming close and wrapping his arm around her right side, always careful of her left shoulder.

"Now I realize how relieved I am that we're just us again, the way we wanted it. I'm sad still, but I know it wasn't the right time for us," she said gravely, searching his face.

"This whole thing, the accident, thinking that I'd lost you, all of it has just made me appreciate you so much more. The baby part was hard to deal with, but it wasn't first in my mind. Life is so fragile, you know? But for me, it's all about *you*, Chelsea. I've waited so long finally to have you in my life for good. I know I couldn't live without you if things had been different..." he said, and she wondered what he must have thought, seeing her car and thinking she was dead. Their eyes were locked together in the familiar way they related to each other.

"You wouldn't have..." she ventured, thinking about the despair his father must have felt and how he could have come to such an end. "No. How could your mother have dealt with one more thing, Kyle?"

He shook his head imperceptibly. "I honestly don't know," he said quietly. "I don't know how I would have handled myself. I would have had to find a way to keep you in this world with me. We're not going to talk about 'what if' again, okay?" he murmured, his lips pressing into her forehead. After a quiet moment, he added, "Wayne and Becky are here, and Bri is asking about you. Your dad just got a call from Charley and they're about thirty minutes out."

She took a deep breath and squeezed him around the waist. "Okay, then, let's go party."

There was cause to celebrate again the next week. Kyle brought Chelsea a cold beer on the porch as they sat under the trees late on a Wednesday afternoon, the sun searing through the green leaves on the trees to create jewels overhead. She drank deeply of the icy froth, enjoying the taste without having to worry about any more drugs in her system. It was a wonderful feeling, being without pain, without bruises and with little left than her wrist cast and the dark scar on her cheek; she was almost herself again. He tapped the base of his bottle to hers and sat down opposite her, relaxed in shorts and his shirt open at the collar.

"Here's to the woman with a *grant*!" he exclaimed, raising his bottle to her and grinning.

"I know! I can't believe it's actually going to happen. When I read the letter, I was speechless. We're going to set up a meeting with Sonya and some of our students to go over the names we have so far for our participants. I called Meme's mother immediately and they are so thrilled. Both of Hector's kids are going to do it. Divina was scared to participate without Esteban, so both of them will be dancing with us. There are two more girls that are on the list. Then there's another little boy who has an obsession with power tools!" she laughed and met his curious eyes with her own, shaking her head. "They're not sure if he will actually go through with it, but if he does, that's six kids right there!"

Kyle nodded, smiling encouragingly. "It sounds really exciting. Will you publicize it some more, now that it's a go?"

"Yes, we'll advertise it through the newspaper, the library, with the school system, and with all the area dance studios. We should be able to start by late October if it all goes according to plan."

"That's excellent. Will Sonya's students be helping out too?"

"Yes. It will all happen at her studio on Saturdays. Hopefully, we'll be able to handle ten to twelve kids."

"I can't believe you'll be back at work in less than two weeks."

She looked at him and nodded.

He cleared his throat. "Which means we need to do some car shopping," he threw out tentatively, seeming to gauge her reaction.

She smiled slowly. "I guess I could be ready to try a little driving. At least it's summer, so we don't have to worry about the bad weather and messy roads for now," she said, pondering the act of driving around the bend in the road that had almost taken her life. Thankfully, her tree was still there, but there would not be a saving tree at every hazard so she would have to buck up and work through her nerves. She would have to if she intended to live normally again.

He was looking at her and nodding. "One thing at a time," he said quietly. He had been her friend again, the way he had been in high school, supporting her, looking out for her, and practicing the same sexual restraint as then, too. At first it had been almost unbearable for them both, but she remembered why she loved him so much. It had more to do with kindness and a kind of telepathic connection they had than the physical part of their relationship, making it comfortable just being with him. She'd been able to do so much more around the house, laundry and cooking; she could even bathe herself! Her new independence took the load off of him so he could work in the loft again in the evenings, relieving her boredom and helplessness in the process. Her strength was coming back, so she felt ready to be in the world again, and soon with him in their bed again the way it once was.

The plans for the inn were coming along steadily, and he stayed busy with the condo project at night, preparing permits and planning strategy meetings for the bank and the zoning board. Lynn kept in touch but had never been overbearing. They met at his office in town, and Chelsea wondered what it was like for him to be around her since he had so many unanswered questions, but that topic had not been discussed since the night at her house when Chelsea's suspicions had made him so angry. As far as she knew, the relationship was nothing more than professional, and she did not inquire any further about it.

She had prepared a cold chicken salad and Gazpacho from her mother's tomatoes for their dinner, and in time, he went in with her to help her serve it. They ate companionably at the table on the porch, with the fire-pot creating its ambience in the warm August evening. There was little breeze and just the soft lulling sounds of the river, mixed with the music of summer insects and a few birds calling through the trees.

"Is tomorrow a good time for you to go kick some tires?" Kyle asked, relaxing in his chair. She knew he was expecting her driving debut to be a major issue and seemed to be treading carefully around her feelings.

"I have nothing going on...except the bathroom I should be cleaning."

"You can't do that yet, and this would be a whole lot more fun anyway, don't you think?" he replied and took a sip of the cold soup out of his spoon.

"I can too clean the bathroom if I'm careful. I can get those big rubber gloves over my cast and scrub away! I think you're more excited about getting a new car than I am," she said, smiling at him.

"Guys and cars," he murmured; then decided to bring it out into the open: "How are you feeling about driving again?"

"I think I'll be okay, but we'll see. This is all new to me. What are they calling it?"

"Post-traumatic stress disorder," he said casually, sipping his soup, referring to the condition her doctor had warned her about.

"I really don't think it's going to be like that. I've been trying to imagine driving around that bend, and it doesn't seem to be that strange. It will feel odd buckling a seatbelt on my left side, though. I still feel so vulnerable."

"The doctor said it would take six weeks for all your bones to heal."

She nodded. "I don't want to take a chance on having to go through this again, hurting myself, and having to wait for the healing to take place again," she said, pushing a strand of hair behind her ear. She was glad occasionally to be rid of the figure-eight bandage, but at the same time, she had been taking it very easy. He nodded too. She knew he was thinking about not being able to touch her and hold her the way she wanted him to. At times it was all she could do to restrain herself from engulfing herself into his arms and pressing her mouth into the supple flesh of his shoulder....

"So, yeah, let's go kick some tires!" she said, grinning at him, looking purposefully away from the wide plane of his shoulders. She wondered whether he would ever look at her the same way he had on their honeymoon, since the accident and resulting injuries had left her pale and pathetic. Often he looked away, doubtlessly because she was not the same as she was. Was there a change in the works here, or was she just imagining it in her insecurity? She would have to buck up in this part of her life too if she wanted to hold on to him. Words that Pamela Van Dervere had said to her at the party came springing back to her memory like unwelcome bats returning to the attic: "*You'll have to do what you can to hold on to that one!*"

She squared her shoulders—painlessly—and watched him grinning at her, offering to take her plate.

"Hell, yeah!" he said, catching her mood. "That's my girl. It'll be fun to do a little car shopping together," he said, bending down to kiss her on the forehead before walking to the kitchen with her dishes.

"I'm getting there!" she declared more to herself than to him, but it appeared to be working. "So, are we heading down to the Subaru dealership?" she asked, smiling, knowing that would be his pick.

"Great place to start. They have some beautiful new body styles, and you'll definitely need an all-wheel drive vehicle."

"Do I get to pick the color?" she asked wryly.

"I was hoping I'd get to do that," he joked. "You can check out the engine and all the safety features; after all, this is going to be your car, and a family car at some point, right?"

"Well…I guess so if I keep this one as long as I had the last one. One thing at a time, okay?"

"Okay. I'm getting your drift. We're not rushing into anything, but I like to keep the long-range goals in mind when you're looking at something like a car."

"Oh, absolutely! It helps to put everything into perspective. It feels normal, talking like this again, about the future and all." She realized what he was doing, distracting her with their dreams for the future again, getting her mind off the more immediate problem of not wanting to drive. Maybe it wouldn't be as bad as she thought. Maybe with him beside her in the car the first few times, she could do it without her palms sweating, as they were at this moment, just imagining it.

***

Driving had not been bad, and she loved the feel of the nice new seats that surrounded her in her new white SUV. She drove them to the music in the park on Friday evening, where they met Abby and Glen. Anthony was there too with a new woman they had not met before. She was dark and lovely, walking with her arm wrapped around Anthony's elbow, but from Chelsea's practiced eye, Anthony did not look as attached.

"Nice ride!" Anthony had commented upon seeing them drive up. "And I'm proud of you for getting back in the saddle!" he'd said, gingerly touching her on the elbow, then slapping Kyle on the back, greeting him as well with a handshake and an introduction to his date, Joelle. She worked in the advertising department at the university where they had met over a project they'd worked on together.

They spread a blanket on the ground and opened baskets filled with fruit, pasta salad, and bread and cheese for a light picnic supper and bottles of wine. Glen took a look at the offerings and shot Kyle a glance that said, 'Meet you at Wendy's later!' It was hard for Chelsea to get up and down off the ground so Kyle helped to lower her in place, promising himself that he would remember to throw some chairs in the back for next time.

Abby talked excitedly about plans for them to get pedicures and do some shopping the next day. Chelsea was due for some fun, she insisted; then she asked whether Chelsea would drive her, wanting to ride in the new car.

"Did Kyle put you up to this?" Chelsea asked suspiciously.

"Uh, *no!* This is what happens when you get a new car. You have to drive your friends everywhere so they can try it out! Besides, my house is on the way! How's driving going?" Abby asked, making Chelsea glance at Kyle, who was waiting to hear her candid response.

"It's not so bad. I haven't been past the 'scene' you know, but so far I haven't broken out in a cold sweat yet!" she laughed.

"I'll give you a police escort if you like," Glen said, grinning at her. "Anyway, you should go. Kyle here needs to get his butt back in the gym. I'm leaving him in the dust. If you're out with my wife, he has no excuse!"

Kyle shot him a warning look, while at the same time, nodding his approval at Chelsea.

"Sure! Sounds like a plan, but I think I'll be able to swing this by myself."

"You look all back to normal," Abby commented, tossing her hair, handing Chelsea a plate of food and then a plastic cup of white wine.

"Thanks. I feel so much better!" This outing was turning into her social debut, Chelsea realized as many people they knew stopped by to welcome her back to the land of the living, inquiring about her progress.

Anthony was at her side then, refilling her wine after a nod from Kyle. She thanked him, complimenting on the way he had designed her mother's website, which left him beaming proudly.

"It *does* look good," he laughed. "It's nice that I get to help her out for a change, after all she taught me back in high school. You know, she gave me an angel that she made. It kinda looks like me!" he said in mock bewilderment, making her laugh.

"That's because she thinks of you as an angel for doing it for her."

"Well, I hope she does really well with her business. She's got a good thing going. Did she tell you I'm going out to Colorado next week?" he asked her quietly.

Chelsea's eyes moved to Joelle and back to his face quickly. Joelle had said next to nothing so far this evening. He smiled a little guiltily, she thought. "No. Are you visiting our high school chum?" she asked quietly, referring to Meredith with whom he'd reconnected at their wedding.

"Yep. I have some time off before classes start back so I'm going to Colorado Springs. I was invited," he explained to her still questioning face. "We're still just friends, you know."

"Oh, I know," she laughed, unable to continue the conversation under Joelle's interested gaze looking their way. "Well, have fun, and say hello for me." It was all she could do to refrain from saying, "*Behave yourself!*"

"I was thinking of whisking Chelsea away somewhere before school starts for her too; now that we have a car that needs breaking in," Kyle said, winking at Chelsea. "How 'bout the Outer Banks for a few days? Mom wants us to come, and you know Stacie's having a fit to get us down there. I'll drive...if you don't mind."

Chelsea smiled awkwardly, knowing that Glen and Abby had been invited as well. Kyle remembered, looking at them, nodding, including them. "We'll have to see. We just had our honeymoon," she reminded him. "It *would* be fun," she said while applause broke out around them as the bluegrass band finished its number.

"That would be nice, but we just had our vacation," said Glen, throwing a questioning glance at Abby, who nodded in response.

"It would sure be fun if we could all swing it," Kyle said. "Oh, well. It's wishful thinking at this point."

"We said October when Stacie was here. Maybe we can all make it work then," Chelsea said.

Chelsea felt bad that Joelle was being excluded in all the plans, but she had looked away, shifting her attention to folks nearby playing a friendly game of corn hole. Chelsea glared at Anthony, but he did not seem to get it. Some guys never got a clue, she thought.

It was nice being out without being the major focus of attention and pity for a change. She leaned into Kyle's shoulder for support, not even tired, although it had been a long day, she thought, sipping her wine, letting herself slip into a languid mood. Her husband was smiling at her again. That was *desire* in his eyes, this time, she thought for a fleeting moment, but then he turned his head abruptly, making her ache inside. It was her tonight, the one more in love, she thought sadly. He didn't look at her the same way he had before the accident. It was too bad she still wasn't ready for what they both wanted; but it wouldn't be long. Right now it was enough to sit here with their friends and just enjoy being together.

This is what it was supposed to be all about. She felt grateful, but sad just the same.

✦✦✦✦✦

After stopping at their mailbox, he stuffed the small stack of letters into the front pocket of his computer case as they drove up the driveway. She languished comfortably in the seat, apparently enjoying the effects of the wine and the new car essence. He extended his hand, helping her slowly out of the car, then shouldered his bag and carried the picnic basket up the steps behind her. After opening the door and setting his bag in a kitchen chair, he slipped the basket onto the surface above the cabinets. He took her gently in his arms, keenly aware of her tender collarbone and the ribs that didn't seem to hurt her much anymore. Stroking her hair from her face, he kissed her mouth, pushing his fingers into her hair; she returned the kiss with equal passion. It could be tonight maybe, if he were tender with her, if she felt trusting enough of her own body. Since the accident and her miscarriage, she had been so tentative that he hadn't wanted to push her. Trying to imagine how she would feel with the weight of his body on hers, he felt her stiffen slightly, and realized it wasn't the right time. He released her after another kiss. She reached in the bag, retrieving the mail. Normally, he went through the mail first. It was a task she didn't like, unless there was a letter or a card from someone. Bills and junk mail held no interest for her. The phone rang as he watched her glance curiously at a small envelope with no address, slipping her finger inside the flap. He answered the phone, turning, greeting his mother on the other end.

"Hey! We were just talking about you tonight! Yeah, Chels and I met some friends at Music in the Park," he continued as he watched her pull a photograph out of the envelope. She stared at what she saw in surprise and bemusement. It was that kind of look you didn't want the ones you loved to have on their faces. He had forgotten about the picture once again. She blinked. Her puzzled eyes met his swiftly, then returned to the picture she held. "Mom, do you mind if I call you right back? Yeah, we just walked in. Okay, bye."

"What's this?" she asked, her tone calm, as if she were trying to control her reaction. He remembered the night they'd argued about Lynn; he knew this didn't look good.

"It's a picture of Lynn I found in Dad's desk upstairs. I meant to show you, but then the accident...and I just...forgot about it."

She nodded, going to the window, but he saw her frowning as she held the photo to the evening light. "When was this taken? It doesn't look like a recent shot."

"I think it must have been back when he built her house. I guess he took it and had it in the drawer up there all this time. I found it under some brown paper lining the drawer after I spilled water in it," he explained, stepping slowly toward her. "It was supposed to have been hidden."

She looked questioningly at him, not speaking, but he knew what she was thinking.

"It just makes for more questions I'll probably never have answered," he shrugged. He touched her arm, inviting her to sit with him on the sofa.

"It makes you wonder, doesn't it? The expression on her face is so...."

"Intimate?" he asked. She nodded. He sighed in agreement. "I kinda wish I'd never found it."

"Will you give it to her?"

"I should. It's not mine."

"Maybe it will start the talk you need to have with her."

He sat back and raked his fingers through his hair. "I guess so, when the time is right. We haven't talked about Dad in a long time, and our professional relationship is great. I haven't wanted to mess it up." He took her hand, feeling her relax into the sofa with him. "I thought you'd be mad, seeing it."

"Were you afraid I'd think you took this picture? I can tell by looking at it that it was years ago. Lynn looks great, but you can tell she's aged since this was taken."

She studied the picture, then his face. "You know I trust you, right? I *did* learn that lesson. I'd never think you were doing something with her."

"Then, what is it? I can tell something's bothering you still," he said.

She shook her head; suddenly, her face became vulnerable and soft. "I just…you don't look at me the way you used to. I want you to want me, like you did before the accident. I feel something slipping away from us," she said, her voice breaking. He saw tears form in her eyes as she tried to divert her look.

He stopped breathing for a moment. He couldn't believe she thought that. His fingers touched her hand gently, and he locked his eyes on hers. Inwardly, he vowed he would never look away from her again if it caused this misunderstanding, the kind of hurt she must have felt.

"Oh, no, Chelsea….I want you so bad right now that it hurts," he said, shaking his head. "Sometimes when I look at you…I have to look away because I can't let myself hold you and love you the way I want it to be. I'm trying to be good, but believe me, it's more of a struggle than you obviously know. And just so you know, it's not just about sex. Having to hold back the way we have makes me realize how much I really love you. I can wait as long as you need."

Her face broke into an expression of relief, making her sigh heavily. "Then, it's nice to know we're both on the same page. I want to feel better. I've never been so impatient about anything before. It won't be long before I'm ready."

"And I thought *driving* was going to be the toughest part of all of this!" he said, shaking his head.

Chapter 13

....

NORMALCY

....

Chelsea did not anticipate the butterflies that accompanied her to the dance studio the day of the meeting. After talking with Sonya and Carmen, they had all agreed to meet at the university first, then have lunch together later as a way of welcoming Chelsea back to work. She smiled, smoothing her favorite blue dress, her birthday present from Abby, an exact replica of the dress that had been cut from her body following the accident. The sweater she wore hid the figure-eight bandage. It was not only solidifying to have her best friend back in her life, but to have her life at all resounded more and more significantly with her each day.

Her mentors greeted her with careful hugs, each concerned with how she felt and how she did driving over to campus by herself. She thanked Sonya profusely for taking over her classes when she had to take her leave. The musty smell of the studio along with the hubbub of dancers heading here and there, talking, laughing, preparing for class, comforted her. The noise, the smell, the feel of it all recalled the familiarity of discipline, of creativity, bringing back the core of who she was. It was a hopeful feeling, and she sank gratefully into its arms, dispelling the butterflies instantly.

As the students who would be assisting with her Setting the Barre project arrived, they helped arrange chairs in a circle on the studio floor, chatting excitedly over the possibility of a new challenge with new people, while greeting each other after a long summer break. After introducing her to the students, Carmen gestured to Chelsea to take over the meeting. She began by introducing Sonya as her mentor and teacher, describing the project in more depth, and finally going through the folder she carried, discussing each of the participants, their backgrounds, and special needs.

Meme Compton was easy to describe, with her quiet determination and surprising smile. She told them about Hector's children, Divina and Esteban, the two girls with cerebral palsy, and finally, the little boy whom she had yet to meet, so Sonya filled them in.

"As Chelsea has told you, he has an obsession with power tools and talks about them non-stop. I hope he will give this program a go because he really is precious, but I'm afraid the talking may be a problem, unlike with our other folks!"

"We may need to try some special interventions with him if that's the case," said Chelsea.

A physical therapy graduate student across from her spoke up. "What about giving him *talking tickets*? We could get a police officer's cap and write him tickets when he's over the limit?"

Chelsea laughed, nodding, "Great idea! Maybe he can have a power tool intervention for when he behaves…."

"Like Weed Whacker Day or something," De Silva said, chuckling.

"I can get Kyle to come over here with his weed-eater, or the leaf blower, and let him try it out behind the gym," Chelsea offered, being met with grins and nods.

"Maybe the number we should do is 'She Thinks My Tractor's Sexy'!" another girl said.

"You're getting the idea. We'll have a lot of fun with this. If the kids don't buy into it, the program will never work. They've got to have fun and learn to trust us. Then it's a win-win for everybody."

They finished with other details and assignments for publicizing the project further, adjourning in time for lunch.

After quizzing Chelsea about her walking stamina, the three women passed up the nearby dining hall for a short walk down Rivers Street, coming upon Café Portofino for lunch. The warm sun felt good on Chelsea's face, but she enjoyed the walk even more. They laughed and caught up over salads and iced tea, with only the fun topics for discussion. No one brought up the baby or the crash; the healing had already been covered, so all that was left was normal girl talk. They admired Chelsea's new pedicure, and she told them the story of the dress.

"I didn't see Hector today. Where's he, on vacation?"

Carmen looked somber, "No, actually, I need to tell you what's happening with him. There's a possibility we might lose Esteban and Divina from Setting the Barre."

"Why?" asked Chelsea.

"Hector's wife works in Tennessee. She was there on business and took a bad fall down some stairs. She's in the hospital now with a brain injury. Hector took the children to see her. Some of us in the department pitched in and sent some money and books along for them. I'm not sure where they're staying, but it's not a good situation. He had to borrow a friend's car. I never knew he didn't have a car, but he's been walking to work since he's been with us."

"That's terrible!" said Chelsea, swapping concerned looks with Sonya. "How long do they expect to be gone?"

"We don't know. No one has heard from him in a couple of days. We got him a cell phone to take, but lots of times he doesn't answer. He has some leave built up, but we really don't know what's happening."

"I'm sure he needs to work to support the kids, especially if his wife is going to be out of commission for a while," said Sonya.

"Can they bring her here for her care?" Chelsea asked.

"There's some kind of problem with that, but he wasn't very clear. It's up in the air right now. Well, on to happier subjects," Carmen continued. "I guess you saw that you're teaching an improvisation class in addition to the ballet you say that you loathe!" Carmen said, winking at Sonya, who had taught Chelsea ballet.

"I don't *loathe* ballet! I just want something different, and yes, thank you for giving me that class. I can't wait for classes to start next week. I've been thinking about it all this week and how much fun improv is going to be."

"You'll choose a student to choreograph a piece for the freshman show-case, and you can do one yourself if you're up to it."

Chelsea drew in a breath. She had not expected this. She had not danced at all since the wreck, but she smiled and drew up her shoulders. "I'd love the challenge," she said. "Can you give me someone who's intuitive since I can't move around the way I'd like?"

"Of course. I'm sure we can match you up with the right person. I already have someone in mind. She's very creative and has a nice energy about her."

⁂

Kyle poured his coffee to the accompaniment of guitar and piano music this morning, wondering where Chelsea was. He'd finished getting dressed when the music started, thinking it odd to hear something other than the low voices of doves on the porch where he and Chelsea usually ate their breakfast. For a moment he stood at the kitchen counter, sipping the hot, bold coffee, waking up and getting his head ready for the day. He had a meeting with Lynn starting at ten o'clock that would probably last most of the day. After Lynn's tennis game with her daughter who was in town, they would get down to business. Sustainable materials would be the topic for the day, so he prepared himself for the typical battle he knew would ensue—holding down the price without sacrificing the integrity of his design. Lynn usually drove a hard bargain, but he knew she trusted his opinion; still he had to bring his A-game. He hoped Frank would make an appearance, but talking details was never his preference. It was a good feeling, knowing that Frank was comfortable enough with his work to leave them alone.

He wandered to the sunroom and found the door open to the deck. He stopped short; Chelsea was there, in her nightgown, moving across the deck. Since the accident, he had not seen her dance. He observed her for several moments. Watching her dance had always entranced him because he realized how she used her art to transcend to another world; she was doing it now, possibly for the first time since the wreck. Her movements were filled with tenderness and passion. He saw the way she lifted her arm, half-covered by the cast, gracefully above her head, as she stretched, tentatively, seemingly testing her limits. Then both hands caressed her stomach, reaching out and up as she turned slowly on the ball of her foot. In the morning light, he thought he saw a tear at the corner of her eye. Caught in her reverie, she paused, looking at him, smiling at his surprised face.

Slowly, he lowered the coffee mug, stepping out onto the deck to join her. Her look of embarrassment made him smile. He knew to keep it light. "Is this a...*fertility ritual* of some sort?" he ventured, eyebrows raised in amusement.

She covered her face then, possibly embarrassed, or was she hiding tears? "Maybe it is...but it's not for me," she said, walking slowly into his arm, accepting his kiss.

He thought otherwise. Maybe it was her way of dealing with her loss. They had not discussed it much, but he knew that losing the baby had to be on her mind. It was certainly on his mind, but each was practiced at keeping his or her feelings in. They could only talk about it so much until the discussions became counterproductive and a bit depressing. He had realized that many times. Thankfully, Abby and Glen had stopped talking about their quest for parenthood as well, so the four of them were able to coexist; although, sometimes he felt they were walking on eggshells, at least for now.

"Abby then?"

"Possibly. The music makes me feel...*maternal*, in a way."

"Well, I hope it works, whatever you're trying to do," he said, the double entendre hanging between them, needing no comment. "It's beautiful. Don't change it," he said, referring to the choreography she'd just put together.

"Thank you," she whispered, taking his mug, sipping his coffee. She gave him another kiss, on the cheek this time, pushing him gently inside for his breakfast.

⚜

Lynn was late, clad in tennis attire, apologies floating in the door ahead of her. She greeted Frank's wife, Faith, who was sitting in the gathering room at her computer; Kyle was observing over her shoulder as she designed the new kitchen for the inn in Blowing Rock. Kyle inquired about Lynn's tennis game, then screwed the top back on his water bottle as he led her into his small office. He opened his laptop, producing his own new designs for her to view.

After she declined any refreshments, he began his presentations, comparing the differences in the units he'd offered her, comparing his cost analysis with her budget. It was no wonder that his father had not taken advantage of her the way he had done with some of his other clients; she scrutinized every penny that would be going in and out between them. So far, she seemed pleased with the way the project was heading, though quite different from her original concept. Hours passed. Frank showed up at last, joining them for lunch—sandwiches Faith had ordered in. She had decided to eat in as well, so the four of them had a companionable but short meal together. The conversation shifted from business to Chelsea, to Lynn's daughter, who was staying a few days at her home, on a vacation from her job in New York.

When they resumed their work, Frank left, returning to supervise the work at the inn. Lynn regarded Kyle shrewdly, catching him veering off into his own thoughts about her and his father. "You seem distracted today," she ventured, but Kyle was unwilling to address any of his concerns about Lynn and his father now. Faith had gone back to her office, but he refused to let himself be distracted any further. He was sorry she had noticed.

"I'm sorry; just tired, I guess," he said, rubbing his hand across the back of his neck. It wasn't a false statement.

"Well, I can imagine you have your hands full," she said, referring to their previous conversation about Chelsea's progress with her recovery.

Rather than give her the idea that anything else was on his mind, he nodded. He realized he wanted Lynn to tell him her innermost thoughts, but he was unwilling to share his own. "Yeah. It's getting better, though. Chelsea's almost back to normal." Diverting the attention further, he commented, "I've even been back in the gym a little since we got married."

"Oh, yes, things change when you get married, don't they?"

"For the better, of course," he said, smiling at her until she looked convinced. "It's all about time management, really. Being married is great," he said, lightly. The last thing he wanted to talk about with her was his personal life. But how would he ever get his answers if he were so unwilling to take the plunge himself? "So, when is Rachel going back to New York?" he asked, a much safer thread of conversation, as it appeared she wanted to wrap things up.

"She'll stay a few more days and then fly back. Being here is a real change of pace she definitely needed. She needs to slow down. I took her to the Gamekeeper last night, by the way."

"Oh?" he said, suddenly curious. "Did she like it?"

"Yes, she did. That was a different experience for her, too! I heard some people talking, and it seems your friend, Belle, was it?"

"No, Elle," he said guardedly.

"Right, Elle. Anyway she apparently quit or something, so it would be safe now if you ever wanted to go back in there!"

He laughed loudly. She remembered all the awkwardness of that evening! He shook his head. "Actually, I felt like I needed a do-over with that place! I liked it so much I was thinking of taking Chelsea there, but I was wondering how to find out if Elle had a night off!"

"Oh, it was pretty obvious that night you had a bone to pick with her."

He raised his eyebrows, dragging a hand across his chin. "Well, without boring you with all the sordid details, let's suffice it to say she's no friend of mine."

"Well, good. Since she's gone, you should take Chelsea there for something special. Recovery is *really special*," she said, wrinkling her nose in a smile. "For both of you."

"Yeah, it is." He could tell she knew how relieved he was that Chelsea was all right, that Chelsea was *alive*. "Thanks for looking out for me."

"I remember what it feels like when the one you love is hurting, Kyle. You and Chelsea should go and enjoy yourselves. You deserve it after all you've been through." She stood, lifting her bag to her shoulder, reaching out to shake his hand. He felt a little guilty wanting to probe into her past when she was being so nice to him. How could anyone treat her badly? He felt sorry for her, losing her husband, and knowing how it must feel. Maybe he was totally wrong about his ideas about her and his father. Quite possibly, his father had felt something for her but she hadn't returned the feelings. If that were the case, he would probably never know, now.

"Thanks, Lynn. I think we made good progress today."

"Well, of course! I let you win all the arguments!" she said, grinning, her hazel eyes crinkling at the corners. "Seriously, I'm very happy with the way Sugar Ridge is coming along. You and Frank and Tom are doing a fantastic job. And I'll look forward to getting into the good stuff with Faith when we're ready to start on the inside of the units," she said, loudly enough for Faith to hear, as she headed to the front door. "Bye, you guys! Give Chelsea my best!" She waved to them both, disappearing out the door.

⚜

"Do you have it?" Kyle asked as Chelsea arranged herself in the Range Rover's passenger seat, shaking raindrops out of her hair. He had picked her up at the sidewalk in front of the varsity gym.

"Yeah, it's right here in my bag," she said, patting the bag she'd set on the floor next to her feet.

He merged out into traffic as rain pelted the windshield. "Man, it's really coming down!"

"I know! I'm glad you picked me up here; otherwise, I'd be swimming to my car right now!"

"No problem," he said, grinning at her. He headed north on the highway a few miles, both of them looking for the sign they thought would be on the left side of the road for Boone Body and Paint. In a few more moments, they realized they'd passed it, so Kyle turned around and eventually pulled into the lot. He held her hand as she nervously followed him in the door of the small office that smelled of cigarette smoke and paint. A bell rang, announcing their arrival. A medium-sized brindle bull dog looked up at them uninterestedly from the floor under the television, twitching his stump of a tale, woofing once in greeting. After a moment, a gray-haired man emerged through the door, wiping his hands on a rag, and asking whether he could help them. Chelsea peered into his steely blue eyes and recognized him instantly.

"Well, hello!" the man said, extending his hand to Kyle, then glancing at Chelsea curiously.

"Hi, John. Do you remember us?" Kyle asked. "I'm Kyle Davis and this is my wife, Chelsea."

"Law, son, I sure do!" he said, pumping Kyle's hand. "And ma'am, I have to say you look a mite differ'nt than the last time I saw you!" he said to Chelsea smiling, exposing teeth stained from years of tobacco use.

"Hi," Chelsea said, smiling back, extending her hand as well. He shook it gingerly, holding her cast. "I'm feeling better than the last time I saw you, too, sir!" They laughed.

"That was a night I'll never forget," said John, meeting her eyes directly. "I guess for a while there each of us thought you were gone. I'm so glad it wadn't that way!" he said, shaking his head, remembering.

"Well, Mr. Wilson, you saved my life that night. If you hadn't seen my car go off the road, I might not have made it."

"She's right," Kyle added. "I drove right by her and never saw the car. I saw the deer and then I saw you, but it still took me a minute to put it all together. You did, sir; you saved her life."

"Words can't thank you enough," Chelsea said, reaching into her bag. She handed John a package, wrapped in brown paper, tied with raffia. He looked stunned. "Open it," she coaxed. "My mother makes these. We give them to people when special things happen. She made this one for you."

He untied the raffia, slowly unrolling the paper until a creamy white ceramic angel settled in the palm of his hand. The angel looked to be about eight inches tall, with longish gray hair that looked just like his. He looked up at her with moist eyes, cradling the angel carefully. "Law, honey! This is the nicest thing you've just gone and done! I really appreciate this."

"We wanted you to have something to remember us by, and to remind you how we think of you. You were my angel that night, John," said Chelsea.

"Ohhh my!" he said, gazing at the pottery creature. "This looks like me! You tell your momma she did good. This is somethin' I'll surely treasure, don't cha know? Wait'll I show my wife!" he said, in the same twang her father used, setting the angel down carefully in the wrapping, looking at it again.

"I'm glad you came by," he said. "I wondered how you did after they took you off that night. I felt real bad for you and your family. But I'm so glad you're okay. You look like you're gone be just fine."

"Yes, sir, I am. Thank you for what you did. We'll always remember you," Chelsea said, extending her hand again. He took it, mindful of the cast again, shaking it ever so gently.

"Looks like you have a lot of admirers," John said, smiling, referring to all the faded gold names scrawled here and there on the cast.

"Yes, she does," said Kyle. "We're blessed that way," he said shaking John's hand, too.

❧❧❧❧❧

On a chilly Saturday night, they climbed the rustic stairs of the Gamekeeper as twilight settled around them, holding hands and feeling like a couple again. Finally the birthday celebration Chelsea had missed would happen, and in a special way at that. Kyle was pleased that she wore the bracelet he'd bought her on the sly during their honeymoon in Punta Cana. She looked pretty in the replaced blue dress and a little makeup she'd figured out how to apply with the cumbersome cast on her hand. He was impressed with how adept she had become with her cast at doing the small things, and the rigid posture the figure-eight bandage required seemed almost natural to her now. Her courage and resolve to be unaffected endeared her to him even more, knowing it couldn't be easy, trying to work at a new job, driving now, managing the household, and keeping him happy. Of course, he'd tried his best to help with the chores, and keeping him happy was easy; all she had to do was breathe and he felt whole again.

The hostess appeared to recognize him, as well as the bartender, making him smirk inwardly, knowing the last time he'd visited his party had doubtlessly been memorable! He was sure he would leave a better impression this time. His date was already registering approval from the male staff.

"Ah, yes, the birthday celebration!" the hostess said, smiling at the two of them. "Happy birthday!" she said to Chelsea.

"Yes, it's a birthday, and more," Kyle said, winking at Chelsea, taking her hand again and following the hostess to their table. They were fortunate it was a cool night; the low crackling fire in the fireplace added to the ambience in the woodsy dining room. They ordered a bottle of wine— only one, he promised her, making her laugh. He loved hearing her laugh; it was happening more and more lately.

"So what exactly are we celebrating, besides my birthday?" she asked, happily, tossing her hair over her shoulder.

He raised his glass of pinot noir to hers. "To you, to your recovery," he said.

"And yours?" she asked, surprising him, touching her glass to his and sipping her wine. "I know I'm not the only one who's gone through this. It's been equally painful for you, Kyle," she said. "Maybe you didn't have the broken bones, but all the other pain goes with it. You're a part of me; how could it not hurt you, too?" She didn't mention the baby as she gazed at him earnestly, reaching for his hand across the table, fingering the wedding ring he wore, turning it on his finger. The warmth from her touch and her words seared deep into his hands and into his head, making him look longingly into her eyes. Everything she did made him realize how much she loved him, even when she didn't feel good. He didn't know how she did it. He didn't know how much longer he could stand not taking her in his arms and holding her tightly.

He would have to think about food to keep from jumping out of his skin tonight. That would be easy in this place. It had been interesting, creating the myriad of diversions over the past few weeks. Work had been an easy distraction as it was always there, always calling, but he felt guilty, after tucking her in bed most nights, creeping back up the stairs for another hour or two of rendering the plans for Sugar Ridge on his computer, until he was exhausted and spent.

The server was at their table, describing the delicacies available to them for the evening as they followed along in their menus.

"Maybe we should split something, and get an appetizer so we can try more things," he suggested.

"That's a good idea. I don't want to eat so much that I'm miserable," Chelsea agreed.

"Yes," said Laurel, the server. "You want to be able to enjoy your...*dinner.*" Laurel smiled sheepishly, possibly thinking they would be celebrating alone later, making Chelsea smile demurely from under her eyelashes at Kyle, worsening his condition from the sensual thoughts arousing him.

He tore his eyes away from her and laughed, shaking his head. They ordered. After the salad and the *delicata* squash, stuffed with rattlesnake sausage, rabbit, fresh herbs, and goat cheese, Chelsea moaned with pleasure. "I can see why you wanted to come back here. This food is amazing!" Of course, he thought, it wouldn't be too much out of the ordinary for her. She had talked about eating rabbit stew and plenty of venison at her grandparents' table in her youth, but this was something out of the ordinary even for mountain folk.

"The memories I'm making with you are definitely an improvement over the last time too." He had tried to redeem himself over and over after that night. Maybe after tonight, in his own mind, he would be done with it and things would finally be back to normal again. Lynn was right; this night together was exactly what they needed. He wanted Chelsea to feel happy. Seeing the glow on her face reassured him that he had done the right thing, bringing her here.

Over dinner, she asked about his work. In turn, she told him about her progress with the Setting the Barre project, about her new classes, about the challenge of teaching her improvisation class. A new vitality radiated from her that he hadn't seen in awhile. It had done her good to be back at work, even though it exhausted her for now. She would get her stamina back. He rested his chin on his hand and watched her speak, sultry in the firelight and from the wine. Still he knew tonight would not be the right time for them. He wouldn't push her. She was so afraid of hurting herself again; he didn't want to be responsible for re-injuring her.

She talked about driving. She glanced up at him hesitantly. "Today I went by the place where the accident happened," she began.

This revelation surprised him, knowing she had to pass it on her way to and from town each day, but so far she hadn't mentioned it. "Do you mean for the first time?"

"Yeah, I've been taking the back way to town, just to avoid it." She looked apologetic.

His hand came out from under his chin. "Are you kidding? You've probably spent hours going out of your way....I could have gone with you again. Why didn't you say something?"

"No, not hours, really. I mean, I didn't want to trouble you with it. It's my problem. With you there beside me, it didn't bother me the first time. Nothing bothers me when you're there. I just had to do it myself, and I'd get really shaky every time I'd get thinking about it, so I'd take the back way."

"So, how was it?" he asked, riveted to her eyes.

"Well," she started, "it wasn't that bad once I drove by and nothing happened. My heart was pounding out of my chest, waiting for another deer to run out and crash into me, but that didn't happen so I was okay. But isn't that stupid, Kyle? A deer could run out into the road anywhere, and I only worried about it right there in that one spot! Then I thought, this could happen again, anytime, anywhere, and it could be all over. But I had only thought about it in that one place."

"Don't..." he hesitated, knowing he was judging her.

"I can't just *not* think about it, Kyle. I almost died that night." She didn't have to remind him of that awful fact. "I had to pull over in the church parking lot past the curve just so I could pull myself together. Like you said, *life is so fragile,* you know? It could be over in a minute for any of us, for you too! I can't imagine losing you," she whispered. "I thought the same thing when my dad was in the hospital after his heart attack. I just feel so...vulnerable! And I think of you that way too. We all are. It's all I can do to leave you every morning."

And here he had thought she was holding it together so well! Again, he thought he knew her and again she surprised him. He realized he was kneading her hands in his, struggling to find the words to put her at ease. Her fingers felt small protruding from the hard cast. His eyes wandered, thinking how to tell her the way he felt. "Chelsea, I don't know if this helps, but I feel the same way. Every time you walk out the door, or I leave first, I pray that it's not the last time I'll see you. It's as if we're both hanging by a thread, but I guess we have to keep going. I know I should have faith, but that night, thinking you were gone, makes me crazy. I've told you I love you even more now. I didn't think that could be possible."

Her eyes were wide and shining. She clasped his hands harder. "The lucky people stay married for years and years. Do you think they all worry about these things all the time?"

"I think after you go through a crisis like this, the worry eventually fades. Maybe we have to learn to put it behind us and concentrate on right now. We used to talk about living in the moment. Why not do it now?"

She smiled at him, gazing into the fire. "We should do it. Thank you for bringing me here tonight. You've made this night the perfect birthday. It was probably hard for you to walk back in here."

"Nah. It's *perfect now.*"

"Well, in a weird way, this has been my best birthday ever," she said, smiling, and sipping the last of her wine.

"I'm just glad you *had* a birthday," he said, winking at her, unable to release her hand.

Chapter 14

SOLID GROUND

The dance department was beginning to feel like Chelsea's home away from home. She had enough to do to keep her head busy all day, making her sleep like a baby at night. The ballet classes she had initially resented had grounded her, giving her a sense of authority over the other faculty members who were not as well-versed in the discipline. Her class this afternoon was intense; she had not seen a group as yet who were so vested in their training, even at this novice level. Well, except for Brittany, who looked as if she had her head in the upcoming weekend already, and it was only Thursday.

As she led the class in the second combination, she noticed a familiar figure, leaning at the doorway of the studio. She had not seen Hector in the three weeks the two of them had been gone. She had hoped the university would allow him to keep his job, in the wake of his family's hardship, but like anything, there was work to be done and someone had to do it. The studio was noticeably dustier and more neglected with his replacement temporaries filling in.

Hector waved at her as the class filed out, finished for the day. She greeted him with an enthusiastic handshake and a smile.

"Hello, Hector! It's so good to see you!"

"Hola! How are you, Miz Davis? What happened to you?" he asked, regarding her scar, her cast, and the figure-eight bandage visible at the neckline of her blouse, searching her face for answers.

"Oh, Hector, I'm so much better! I was in a car accident, but I'm definitely on the mend. You and I have both been away. How is your wife? I heard she had been in an accident too. You and the children were visiting her in Tennessee?" she asked, noticing the troubled look that immediately clouded his eyes.

He wiped his fingers across the stubble of his face before answering. "She is still in the hospital," he said, casting his eyes around the studio. "Is Ms. De Silva here today?"

"She was, but right now she's in a staff meeting. Is there something I can help you with?"

"I think I need to talk to her, but I can tell you also; I don't know if Divina and Esteban will get to be in your dancing group…."

"Oh, no! Why not? Are there complications with Deb?" she asked, referring to his American-born wife.

"She doesn't want to come home," he said.

Chelsea felt the breath leave her momentarily. "Why? What's happened, Hector?"

"She went there to work and to be with another man. I thought it was happening, but she thought she was fooling me. She met him when she took this new job and started going to Tennessee. I could read over her shoulder on the computer, but she didn't think I could read so good. I knew enough, you know? He is married and cannot help her up there. Her sister is there, trying to help her, but my wife has nowhere to go and her sister is fed up with her. Deb doesn't want to come home, but I can't stay there for long. I have to work here and the babies need to go to school now."

"Oh, Hector, I'm so sorry! Do you think she is just not rational because of her brain injury?"

"I asked the doctors, and they said that could be a part of it, but I know my wife. Deb does not want to be with us. She wants to stay there. But soon, when her sister leaves, there will be no one to take care of her. I don't know what to do."

"She would leave her children?" Chelsea asked under her breath. "Surely she's not herself."

The look that passed between them spoke volumes of the hurt he must feel, the degradation.

"I am just a janitor," he said. "Now with her job, in that place, she thinks she is someone new, and a new man will love her, but he is married and will not leave his wife."

"She sounds very confused, Hector. Maybe in time she'll come to her senses."

"I don't know what to do. The doctors want to keep her there until she can come here to the hospital and get the help she needs. Her sister will be there another day, and then she must return to her family and to her work. I cannot go back there for a while."

"Maybe the time alone will do her some good. Maybe she will understand that what she thinks she wants is not going to happen," Chelsea suggested, her hand going instinctively to his arm.

"I guess what I'm trying to tell you is the children might not be dancing with you this time."

"I certainly understand, Hector. You have to do what you need to do." Her heart went out to this kind, hardworking man, who was *just a janitor*. "Will you stay with her?" she dared herself to ask.

"She is the mother of my children. She is my wife. I must take care of her..." he said, his voice halting in mid-sentence.

For better or for worse, Chelsea thought. She remembered her own wedding vows that she recently thought had been challenged, but she had experienced nothing compared to what this man must feel! How could one cleave to a person who did not want him? How could a person deal with such humility and hardship and hold his head up ever again? What he felt was surely love—love that she knew nothing about. Her face burned with humiliation.

"I'll tell Carmen that you were here, and what's happening. Will you be here tomorrow?" she asked.

"Yes," he said, looking around the studio. "I will. This place looks terrible," he said, breaking into a large smile.

Kyle drank deeply from the glass of ice water he had filled at the sink, relaxing into the rocking chair on the front porch. Sweat dripped down his sideburns and down the back of his shirt. He untied his shoes, releasing his hot feet to the faint breeze stirring in the trees. Chelsea would be home late this afternoon, after her doctor's appointment. He had had an early day for a change, promising to make her dinner followed by a casual evening at home for the two of them. They'd begged off from a Friday night out with Abby and Glen, since the two of them were not working. Chelsea's cast would be coming off today and there would be no more bandages, only the tiny scar on her face to remind them of the accident.

He breathed in the musky fragrance of the summer woods, feeling fine after the day of tromping around the Sugar Ridge site with Tom and Frank. The site was going to be cleared next week, and they had met with the company who was on hand to start the process. No foreseeable problems loomed, to their relief, so the project was a go at the day's end. Spending time with his father-in-law was always something Kyle enjoyed;

today was no exception. He ran a hand through his hair, a twinge of guilt tugging at him.

The troubled cry of a hawk pierced his thoughts, reminding him sharply of a time years ago when he and his father had cleaned fish at the sink under the deck of the cabin. They'd heard a hawk just like that over and over, and they had commented on the sound. "A bird of prey," he recalled, feeling frustrated at the memory of his father's remark that day. Something, an arrogance maybe, in his father's tone had made the statement sound like more, but why? His eyes grew wide at the haunting remembrance. Memories of his father had come to him this way many times now that he was back here, making it almost unbearable to be alone. He had wondered how he could have stayed on here if Chelsea had died in the wreck. It was his *thin place* with her, but his hell without her. He had thought maybe the best thing for him to do would be to try to get his old job back at the firm in Alexandria and leave this place after these two projects were over. But that would have been running away, and he didn't do that.

Surely there was a reason he had to think about all this. The guilt he felt after his friendly conversations with Tom that day left him confused if not satisfied. He had not had conversations with his own father that were nearly as satisfying. His own father had been larger than life to young Kyle. When his dad had made time for him, they had played golf, hunted, and fished in the river together, but there was little talk between the two of them, other than how he was doing in sports, or how his grades were in school. Life was a competition at best to his father; unless he were the smartest or the best, things weren't worth doing. Kyle had tried to keep up, to excel, always trying to make the bar. Whatever he did, it never seemed to be enough for his old man, he thought bitterly. His father never expressed displeasure, but there was rarely more than a pat on the back, either. Never the words, "*I love you, son,*" as Tom had told him at the wedding. After his older sister, Desiree, had died in a spring break accident and his parents had sent him away to prep school, Kyle was sure the reason was the result of failing to please his father.

As Kyle grew older he realized how competitive his father was, wheeling and dealing, outdoing his friends with having the nicest cars, traveling, taking vacations and ski trips because he could afford it. He and Shelly had remodeled the house. She had enjoyed indulging herself and her children with the latest fashions. The business appeared to be booming although the reasons for its success were not apparent to the family. Stuart Davis had wanted it all and nothing seemed to stand in his way. What does it take to corrupt a man, Kyle wondered miserably. What kind of mess had his father invented, putting himself up for sale at such a large price, like so many ostentatious mountain properties no one really needed? Kyle remembered Tom saying he thought Stuart had tried to come clean after meeting Lynn and building her house. He could only hope that were the case.

He tried to remember the last time he saw his father. There had been a moderate snowfall before Kyle had returned to school—the last Christmas break he'd had at Christ School. The two of them had spent the morning shoveling snow from the walkway, the steps, and the long driveway. There had not been much conversation between them, as the labor was heavy and tiring. His father had been more somber than usual, Kyle remembered, and before he'd left, his father had clapped him on the shoulder, saying, "Do it right, son. Make your mama proud of you." At the time, Kyle had had no idea of the implications his father had intended.

Kyle bent forward in the chair, feeling himself sigh, hands thrust into his hair, sensing the wind picking up. He would never be like his father, would he? Kyle knew firsthand the money was good in the architectural field; how long it would last in this economy was another question. He would never allow himself to be caught up in such greed, would he? Lately, Kyle often wondered whether his father's desires had gone beyond his marriage to other women, particularly to Lynn Schiffman. He racked his brain, trying to recall any signs of infidelity. His parents had never been particularly physical in his presence, and they'd had their share of arguments like most parents, but Kyle had never doubted that his father loved his mother. How could he have betrayed Shelly's trust that way if he had had a relationship with Lynn? But it was a possibility. Kyle would never do that to Chelsea. That fact was certain. He would never hurt her the way Stuart had hurt Shelly. Chelsea was the reason he lived, so he could never destroy his ties to her. Thunder rumbled vaguely in the distance. Shaking himself out of his funk, he thought about fixing the meatballs he had planned for dinner before taking a shower. He felt suddenly cooled, shivering slightly as he picked up his shoes before going inside.

⤟⤟⤟⤟⤟

Chelsea walked into the house as the first raindrops began to fall, delighted by the aroma of meatballs and garlic. She smiled at the sight of him, barefoot, in a T-shirt and shorts, as he stirred marinara sauce at the stove. Low blues played on the sound system. An edgy piano accompaniment played to Joe Cocker's "Feelin' Alright." A bottle of red wine stood uncorked beside two waiting glasses on the table. Kyle tossed the kitchen towel over his shoulder, going to her, and taking her cast-less hand gently in his. They grinned at each other. Without speaking, she circled her arms around his waist and kissed him, long and slow, the kind of kiss she knew he had wanted for so long. She felt him respond, hearing him moan softly.

"Look at you," he whispered, eyes shining, touching her shoulders, probably noticing the figure-eight bandage was no longer protruding from her tank top.

"I know. I'm free!" she said, laughing. She hadn't felt as well in a long time. He felt good in her arms, huge and strong, hands sliding across her back, drawing her closer into his chest and holding her carefully but tightly. She nestled her face into the warmth of his neck, kissing him there, feeling him sigh contentedly. She pulled away just enough to show him her wrist, clad only in a removable brace; he touched it gingerly.

"Does it hurt?"

"It's a little tender without the brace, but it feels wonderful having the cast off for good. It's like being naked!" she laughed.

"I like *naked*," he said, grinning at her again. This was what she wanted, this easy, sexy banter with her husband, without having to hold back because of her injuries.

He released her after a moment and went to pour their glasses of wine. After handing her a glass, they toasted to her new freedom and tasted the merlot, rich and chocolaty. Then he kissed her again, making her dizzy, abandoned, the way she liked to feel with him when they were alone.

"Why don't we sit for a minute? Dinner's almost ready. Are you hungry?" he asked, glancing at her short skirt appreciatively.

"Famished," she said, only to go along with the effort he'd clearly put in. He had lit candles and set the table for their dinner. All she could think about was taking off her clothes and finally feeling his skin next to hers, her hand caressing the hollow of his hip….

"So, what did the doctor say?"

"I'm completely healed. He says I can do anything I want, within reason. No heavy lifting with this hand," she said, holding up her right hand in its brace. "And I probably won't be able to sleep on my left side for a while, still. The ribs are fine," she said, sitting across the table from him. He sat, hand propped under his chin, watching her, eyes bright with desire. She knew this was the night they'd waited for, wondering whether they would actually eat dinner. She wondered whether he'd thought the same thing, playing it safe with spaghetti and meatballs, knowing it would save easily if they became otherwise entangled.

✦✦✦✦✦

He watched her pull her hair around to the right side as she had done a million times in the past, always making his heart pound. The curve of her creamy shoulder and her neck were so alluring to him right now that he wanted to reach out and touch her, but not yet. He still wasn't sure. But damn, the way she was looking at him had him going! She was talking to him.

"It will be nice to wash my own hair for a change," she said, peeling the brace away from her wrist and offering her hand to him. Her wrist looked pale and pitiful, but it offered so much promise for later, he hoped, gently stroking her arm, smiling in spite of himself. He swallowed, hoping she was not aware of how much he was struggling. Carefully, he raised her hand to his lips, kissing her palm.

"I'll miss washing your hair," he said, thinking about her in the shower that morning, in her usual pose with her right hand at the shower curtain rod, trying to keep her cast dry, and so vulnerable!

"There's something really humbling about having someone else bathe you," she said absently.

"You didn't seem so humble about it this morning!" he chuckled, remembering his hands on her, and not just washing her hair, either.

She giggled, remembering too. "No, I meant, when my mother had to come up here and bathe me on the tub bench when I could hardly move. I'm sure she was glad when you felt confident enough to take over. I know she had plenty of practice taking care of Kitty, but it just kind of sucks, being so helpless."

"I know. I'm glad you're not helpless anymore either. I'm just giving you a hard time. What are husbands for?" he asked, feeling her slender fingers moving up and down his forearms, then to his biceps, making the hair stand up on his arms.

"Your kindness through all of this has been especially humbling. I never expected to be loved this much," she said. He looked at the small pink scar, the tiny smile on the side of her left cheekbone. Aside from that, no other marks were on her; the shadows of her bruises were long gone. He touched the side of her face carefully, watching her close her eyes. "The doctor said I could have my scar revised in a couple of months if I wanted to," she said.

"I don't think you should do anything else to it," he said, watching her reaction, feeling the small dent in the softness of her cheek beneath his thumb. "It gives you character. I like kissing it. I like it, but you do what you want."

Her eyes flashed at him. They served their plates and devoured the spaghetti in no time. The salad wasn't touched until they covered it with plastic wrap and tossed it into the refrigerator. Dishes were rinsed and placed inside the dishwasher as the light faded early due to the rain that pounded on the tin roof. There would be no drinking on the deck this evening. Wine glasses were left on the counter after he drained the last of his. It was all he could do to wait to get her into the bedroom. He knew that if they did not make love tonight, he would go insane!

They undressed each other eagerly in the twilight, but he tried to take his time, helping her lift the tank top carefully over her head. He held her, naked in his arms, and whispered in her ear, "I'll be gentle. I promise."

"I know you will," she murmured back, kissing his open mouth, letting him ease her into their bed beside him.

He stared at her, so beautiful in the fading light. It was like holding an angel in his arms. The rain poured soothingly over the roof, lulling them into the thin place once again.

Tonight it was him.

⁂

They rarely had the opportunity to meet for lunch, so Kyle was unprepared for the crowd at Macado's that Thursday. He took a seat at the bar, hoping Chelsea wouldn't mind sitting there. He checked his watch. Faith had promised to be finished with Lynn by one-thirty when he had planned to return, allowing them a few hours to go over the last plans, complete with Faith's interior designs to finish their package for Sugar Ridge. He sighed, relieved, feeling as if he were coming down the home stretch.

October was chilly already, and the woman who brushed by him in the crowd knocked him with her jacket that she'd draped over her arm. *Oh brother, here we go again*, he thought to himself as she smiled coyly at him, sliding into the seat beside him. Should he play along this time? When she stood up again to rearrange her purse, he distinctly felt the press of her breast on his arm, making him close his eyes and hold back a smile. He took a sip of his tea, pretending not to notice her, avoiding any eye contact, lest she get the wrong idea.

Her breath was in his ear, forcing him to turn toward her. "Excuse me," she said. "Is this seat taken?"

"Actually, I was expecting my wife, but you'll do nicely," he said, low and suggestively in her ear, flicking his eyes over her and looking around to see whether anyone was watching them.

Laughter bubbled from her lips and she swept her auburn hair around to her other shoulder, then wrapped her hand around his arm. "You're *so bad*! Sometimes I wonder about you. You play this game far too well!" Chelsea laughed and he chuckled along with her. It was a game they had played often, usually when he had gone to Raleigh to meet her or when she had escaped to Alexandria for a weekend during their two-year long distance relationship that had been both frustrating and erratic. They would plan to rendezvous in a bar or at a restaurant and play out their scintillating scene. Now, he leaned over to kiss her, and she returned the sentiment in a passionate way that seemed to entertain the bartender at least.

"Do you mind sitting here?" he asked, as she settled herself at the bar.

"No, this is fine," she said, smiling at him as he motioned to the bartender for a glass of iced tea for her.

They looked at their menus as he glanced at her. She seemed excited, as he was, in anticipation of their upcoming trip to the Outer Banks starting on Saturday morning, the first day of her fall break. It would also be the first break he had been able to score with both of the architectural projects underway so he was glad for a respite, and a change of scenery. They would be departing just in time to avoid the onslaught of leaf-lookers heading to the Blue Ridges for the breathtaking views of autumn at the season's peak. She had been packed for several days, he thought with a smile. He was just restless and ready to go. It would take him all of two minutes to throw his things in a bag and hit the road.

"How's your day going?" he inquired over his menu.

She closed hers, placing it back on the bar, and rubbed her temples, taking a long drink of her tea.

"I'll tell you, I'm learning so much more from my students and the other people around me than I could possibly be teaching them," she said, shaking her head.

"Anything wrong?"

"Not for me, but I just feel so bad for some of them. Hector was telling me today about Divina and Esteban. They seem so dismal and withdrawn, but I would be too if my mother were a mess the way theirs is," she started. He waited for more, but she appeared to be thinking about them.

"Isn't she back here?" he asked.

"She was. She was here at our hospital in rehab for a few weeks, and then she moved home. Hector took a few days off to help her get settled, and do you know what she did?"

He shook his head.

"*She left them.* As soon as she was back to normal, she left and went back to Tennessee, and not just to return to work, but to live there!" She shook her head, disbelieving, and he did the same.

"Did she go back to the guy she was seeing?"

"Apparently so, but he's still married. How does somebody do that? Hector's given up so much to help her and take care of her and the children at the same time. The poor man has his hands full. The children can hardly talk. You know they must have trouble in school. And here she goes, leaving them all. How does a mother leave her *children?*"

"I don't know," he said, feeling her indignation.

"Hector doesn't even have a car. He applied for citizenship before he got the job at the university, but if he weren't an American citizen, the children could be taken away from him! Can you imagine?" she cried, and he shook his head again, rubbing her arm, attempting to sooth her. The bartender was ready to take their order so she began to simmer down a bit.

"Well, on to brighter topics, are you getting excited about our trip?"

"Of course," she said, breaking into a large smile. "I can't wait to see your mom and Stacie and Tyson—and Abigail. It's too bad that Abby and Glen couldn't get away and come with us."

"Yeah, but it will be great to see everyone and to get away. I'm beat from this pace," he said, rubbing the back of his neck. "You won't mind if we just vegetate while we're there?"

"That's exactly what I have in mind: that and eating some really good seafood. Stacie has the Margarita machine primed and ready, and the menu planned for each day we'll be there," she laughed.

"Does that include the night we cook for them?"

"I don't know, but I'm sure they'd love a break as well. And I'm looking forward to spending some more time being around Mark and getting to know him."

Kyle nodded as their sandwiches arrived. "You'll really like him. He's certainly opened up my mother. He has to be something special to have pulled that off!"

"I've never seen your mother happier."

"I know. She deserves it after all this time," he said. They fell silent. Kyle was thinking about all the sadness and the loneliness Shelly had felt, especially when he had not been equipped to help her through it. He had wasted so much time when he could have been forming a relationship with his mother; he had to remind himself that it wasn't totally his fault, but still, it didn't help. After losing half of her family, she had withdrawn, oddly shutting him out. As a teenager, he had not understood and had angrily treated her the same way. During college, he hadn't been around much. Summers at the beach with her had been better, and somehow with the help of Chelsea, Stacie and Tyson, and now Mark to guide them along, they were beginning to heal their wounds and develop some closeness.

After lunch, Chelsea and Kyle clung to each other for a moment, stealing a kiss on the sidewalk before they each headed off to their separate destinations for the afternoon. Kyle met the two women in the conference room of the Mountaineer Builders' office, as they chatted amicably, the remnants of their lunch in wadded paper on the table. Faith showed him the latest interior design renderings that Lynn had approved, and he seemed pleased that they had made good progress in his absence. Lynn Schiffman was a dream client; they could only hope to be so lucky with their next people.

Faith left them for the day in the conference room, laughing with Lynn, promising to do lunch next time she was up from Miami. Lynn's visits were becoming less frequent as the busy season with her hotels was approaching. They could most likely handle the remainder of their business through emails and faxes, making him feel a bit sad that he would not see her for a while. She would surface again next summer when the building would hopefully be in full swing. Building often came to an abrupt halt here in the mountains due to the harsh winter weather with which they had to contend.

The meeting did not last as long as Kyle had anticipated. Frank made his usual reticent appearance, approving the final plans, congratulating them both on a job well done, and thanking Lynn for her trust in their team. After his departure, they seemed at odds in the room, now dim in the afternoon light.

"I could use a drink; how about you?" asked Lynn, laughing.

Kyle looked around, knowing there was nothing in his desk drawer, so he went to Frank's office. After a brief and somewhat guilty bit of rooting around in Frank's desk, he produced a bottle of Jack Daniels whiskey and held it out for her approval.

"That'll do!" she said, smiling. "It's not my brand, but it works for me."

Kyle knew her brand ironically had been his father's, as he retrieved a couple of glasses from their small kitchen. They seated themselves in the gathering room that served as the lobby, as Kyle poured two fingers for each of them. He felt uneasy, wanting to relax but needing to ask her things at the same time. He wasn't sure he wanted to know, but it would be now or never, probably.

They raised their glasses. "To Sugar Ridge," Lynn said, grinning.

"To Sugar Ridge," Kyle replied, as they downed their drinks.

Lynn leaned forward, resting her elbows on her knees. "This has been a great experience for me, working with you and Frank and Faith—and your father-in-law. It's been even better than when your dad and I worked together," she said, and he held his breath, watching her unreadable expression. Okay, she was bringing it up for him. He waited. She studied him, making him sweat, but then she looked away.

"You're not like him," she said wistfully.

This surprised and relieved him at the same time. "How do you mean?"

"Oh, you look like him, and you have that same confidence and determination about you that he had. But you're different. He was so *arrogant!*" she said, smiling, as if it had been an endearing quality. "You're not that way. You work a lot harder than he did too," she said with a twinkle in her eye.

He poured them another shot. This was it. He might as well get into it, but she picked up where she had left off.

"I knew there was something going on with him. Something was bothering him all the time. I thought it was that he wasn't getting along with your mother. He had that guilty feeling about him. I mistook it for depression, and maybe it was. After losing both of his parents at a young age, and then losing Desiree, it was understandable. But after the things you've told me he was doing, it makes total sense now. He obviously would never have told me what was going on with the business, but I swear to you, he seemed to be trying so hard to be good! Thinking back on it, it was like he was trying to prove himself to me."

Kyle watched her for a moment. She wrapped her sweater around her; then she looked up at him. "How do you do it?"

"What?" he wasn't following her.

"How do you hold it together? You're the most disciplined young person I've ever met, and you just seem to have it all together, in spite of losing your sister and then your dad." Her statement hung in the air like a question.

He shook his head, rubbing the back of his neck. If she only knew! "I don't have it together. If I do at all, it's because of Chelsea. She's my lifeline to this world. Before I met her, I was so angry and depressed. When I thought she was gone...I didn't know what I'd have done," his statement hung too, reminding them both of the desperate measures his father had taken.

"How did it happen with your dad?" she asked softly. "If you don't want to talk about it, just say so."

He sighed, a ragged breath, and began, "I found him at the cabin one Saturday morning when I'd shown up from school unannounced. He'd taken a bunch of pain pills and drained a bottle of Maker's Mark." She winced at the mention of the brand. "I guess he'd been gone several hours by the time I got there. I called the police, then my mother. I found a note he'd left."

"Really? What did it say?" she looked decidedly worried. She must have thought it had something to do with her, he guessed.

"It was a letter to my mother. He apologized to her about being so dishonest in his business and causing all the problems she was about to take on. He asked her to forgive him and to make sure I did the right things. He warned her not to let me turn out like him," he said, looking down at the floor.

He heard Lynn sigh; relief maybe, or just sadness. When he looked up, she was staring at him with an expression of heartbreak. She seemed to have no words to tell him how she felt. But he knew her thoughts by the look in her eyes.

He stood and carried his glass to the conference room, reaching into the pocket of his computer case. Finishing his drink, he returned, handing her the envelope. "This should be yours. I found it in his desk at home."

Hesitantly, she regarded him and took the photo out of the envelope, her face breaking at the memory the photo must have conjured for her. She stared at it for several moments and tapped it against the palm of her hand. She sighed and stood, walking to the window as he poured two more hefty shots. A hand went to her hair, and she gazed out the window as she spoke.

"I'm sorry about all of this, Kyle. I guess you deserve some answers."

"It was no accident that you picked me for this project, was it?" he began for her, emboldened by the whiskey that had warmed his face and his brain.

"No, it wasn't. I knew who you were. But even so, it was such a co-incidence when I started researching the firm. That was when I saw your name...and your picture. I looked up your work in Virginia as well. I talked to your former employers and a couple of your clients. Of course, you had excellent references. I expected as much."

He was starting to get angry, feeling used. He wondered how much Pam knew about all of this. Surely Frank had been in the dark about her scheme, and a bigger pawn than he'd been. She saw the reaction on his face and held out her hand as if to calm him. He could feel his jaw working, tightening uncontrollably, and he had to look away from her troubled face.

He swore under his breath, not believing this was happening. "How many times did you go to the cabin? My mother told me that my dad used to go there all the time without her. Were you having an affair with him?"

She shook her head sadly. "No. It wasn't like that, Kyle." She looked him in the eyes again. "He took me there once when he was showing me properties that he'd built. I don't think he ever cheated on your mom. Not with me anyway." She walked toward the window, continuing. "I wanted him to, though," she said, tapping the photo again, absently on her hand.

"It had been a while since I'd had a man pay attention to me; a man I liked, anyway. I wanted to feel young and in love again after Ben died. Your dad was devilish and funny, and we had so much fun together working on the house. You could say we flirted. One weekend, your mom had gone to visit her sister and you'd been injured in a football game, so he was hanging around without a game to see." She laughed ruefully. "I thought he was inviting me to the cabin. He had made it pretty obvious that he was going to be there alone, so I went. I got so lost, trying to find it again, but I got there eventually. He was there, and so surprised to see me. It kind of hurt my feelings because I thought it was the plan. Anyway, he was wearing that shirt you had on, that night at my house, when you brought your family and I lost it?" she said, wondering whether he remembered. "We had drinks and he cooked fish he'd caught that day in the river. It was fall and getting cold. He built a fire in the fireplace. We were getting drunk. I thought he'd ask me to stay, but then, he started talking about you and Shelly, and how he was planning a big trip for her on their anniversary. He was going to surprise her and take her on a cruise to the Greek islands."

Kyle thought back, not remembering a trip like that. She saw his confusion and laughed again.

"I thought as much. He was making it up to get rid of me. It was his way of letting me down easy I guess. So…I left. It was the last time I ever saw him. I was so shocked to hear a few months later that he had died, but I never knew he took his life. I think I've grieved the loss of him even more than I've grieved for my own husband. And here I had the audacity to think I might have been responsible in some way….I was never that important."

Kyle sat back, not knowing what to say. They stared at each other for a moment.

"I'm sure this has been hurtful to you, Kyle. Things were so good with you and me. I never wanted any of this to get in our way."

"Me neither. I've wanted to ask for a long time, but I was afraid to hear about it."

"Well, it seems I was the one to let you down, Kyle, not your dad. He was a *good guy*. He told me how much he loved your mother. For whatever reason, he lost sight of what he was supposed to be doing, but he never let it get in the way of his family."

"Yes, he did," he said, and she nodded sadly, pressing her lips together.

"I hope this isn't the last time I see you, Kyle. I'd like to consider you my friend," she said awkwardly. "We certainly have worked well together."

He nodded. "I guess I'm glad to have heard your story. But I'm sorry it was hard on you, too. Knowing how it really was is helpful, though."

It was almost dark in the room now, but he had failed to turn on a lamp in the intensity of their conversation.

"You'll never make the same mistakes he made. You have the best of him in you. It's wonderful for me to see that. You should know it. Your mother should know it. Don't ever doubt yourself, Kyle. You should know he would have been so proud of you. I don't know if he ever told you, but he told me a lot of times how special you were…you are."

"No, I never heard that from him."

"I'm sorry about that. I'm glad I at least got to tell you that much."

"Okay, then. Friends?" he asked as they stood. She hoisted her designer handbag onto her shoulder.

"Yes, thank you. Friends," she said, smiling, giving him her incredible handshake. "I'll see you in June then, if not before," she said over her shoulder, as if none of the intimacies they'd shared had been uttered. The ultimate businesswoman then walked out the door.

Chapter 15

DUCK

They left at dawn, and by mid-afternoon, crossed the last bridge to the coast. For Kyle, the normal feeling of exhilaration crossing the bridge was magnified exponentially this time, due in part to the freedom he felt not only from getting out of town, but from his cathartic conversation with Lynn two days before. He had recounted it all for Chelsea that evening by the fireplace in the cabin over glasses of wine. The emotion that poured out of him surprised them both as she held his trembling hands, sharing his relief at learning that his father had remained true to his mother. He wondered to himself whether, when finally left alone in the cabin again, the troubling thoughts would return, or he would at last have peace. At least for now, he could forget his worries, look forward to seeing his family again, and enjoy a new sense of lightheartedness. It was "the great exhale," as Chelsea called that trip over the bridge, and they put down the windows, letting their cares blow away through the ends of their hair.

The reunion with his family that night at The Sound Side was loud and filled with laughter. Kyle had not seen the place in over a year. Aside from the new metal roof and some kitchen upgrades that were sorely needed, the place looked virtually the same, rustic and alluring, but strangely emptier than usual, since the tourist season was over. Kyle and Chelsea drove

Shelly there for dinner after settling in at the house, meeting Stacie, Abigail, and Mark who arrived straight from work. The sporting goods business was slow as well, with the local little league and high school football teams, and the fall fishermen keeping him afloat through the winter.

Tyson visited their table from time to time, checking on their reaction to the shrimp and grits, everyone's favorite.

"I've been *dreaming* about this stuff!" Kyle moaned, forking more shrimp into his mouth and savoring the taste. "There's nothing like this at home."

"Well, if that's what it takes to get you back here, then I'm glad you've missed it," Stacie said, leaning across Chelsea to speak to him, giving a sleepy Abigail a squeeze on her lap. "And you, missy," she said to Chelsea, "look fantastic! You look two hundred percent better than the last time I saw you."

"Thanks," said Chelsea. "I feel two hundred percent better. Sometimes I even forget that it all happened. It feels so good to be back here. We can't tell you how much we appreciate your coming and helping us out this summer. We never could have managed without you."

"We couldn't possibly have stayed away," Stacie said, sharing a look with Shelly, who nodded and winked at them as she savored a bite of her dinner.

Stacie tapped her cheek, the same spot where Chelsea's scar was on her own face. "Your scar is healing nicely."

"I might just leave it alone. It's a reminder for me to stay humble," Chelsea said, making them look at her more carefully.

"How do you mean?" asked Shelly.

"Just remembering that when I needed help, everyone was there, helping me. It's what love is all about. It makes me want to return the favor, especially with my young students who have more special needs than I'll ever have to deal with."

The women wanted to know about Chelsea's Setting the Barre undertaking. She filled them in about the children's progress and her current job. The conversation shifted to Kyle's architectural projects, then to business on the beach. Before long, several of them were yawning so the party broke up just as the guitar player was preparing to take the stage. It had been a long day for everyone.

Back at Shelly's, Chelsea had discreetly excused herself to the bathroom, while Shelly and Kyle continued their conversation about his work in the kitchen. Scooping coffee into the basket of her coffeemaker, Shelly looked hesitantly at Kyle.

"What's Lynn like?" she asked, a puzzled expression on her face.

Kyle ran a hand across his face as he leaned against the sink. "She's a very nice person. She's a good businesswoman; she trusts me completely in the design of her condos. I think it's going to turn out really well when it's all finished."

"That's not really what I mean. I guess what I want to know is, did she ever talk about Dad?"

Kyle met her troubled eyes, knowing exactly what she was getting at. He sighed. "She apparently didn't know what he'd been up to with some of his other Florida clients." He watched her, going on carefully. "She liked him and she hired us because she knew I was his son. At first, I think she was just curious to see what I was like." He laughed, continuing, "It could have been really disastrous if I hadn't been any good, but I think I surprised everyone, including myself."

"Not everyone," his mother said, shaking her head. He smiled, appreciating her vote of confidence.

"Well, it made me pretty angry when she told me about it, and that she'd checked my references. That's something anybody would do, but it was because of me that she even picked Frank's firm."

Shelly nodded, "That is pretty strange. Then she must have been…?" She couldn't finish her question, looking away from him. The intimacy of this conversation with her son had to be difficult for her, he thought.

"Mom, there was nothing between them. She told me about this just the other day before she left. Or if there was, they never acted on it." Shelly looked unconvinced. "I *asked*."

She was quiet a moment. "That's what he told me. I never even asked him about her. Still, he knew I was worried about it. Stu said nothing was going on with her, but I didn't know if I should believe him."

"Why would he have even brought it up if it weren't true, especially if you hadn't asked?" Kyle asked, eyes narrowing.

"Men *always* deny those things," she replied as if he were naïve. "He knew I thought she would have been the obvious diversion for him. I figured he was doing it because he said he *wasn't* doing it. I guess when he told me he wasn't carrying on with her I should have believed him because he sure didn't tell me about the business fiasco. Still, I didn't know…."

They were quiet a moment, gazing at one another. Nothing like trust in a marriage, he thought, keeping it to himself. What was the point in driving in that nail? No wonder his mother had been so miserable. Had she ever felt loved? Never the way he had, he was sure. He looked away for a moment. Chelsea could be heard in the bedroom, putting clothes into drawers, filling a glass with water from the adjoining bathroom. Anger flared within him at his father one more time. He wanted desperately to make his mother feel better.

"She said he was a good guy, Mom. That says a lot."

"I know." The hurt was thick in her voice. "He *was* a good guy. And *I'm* telling you that, Kyle. You remember, don't you, the good times?" She squinted at him in the dim light of the kitchen.

"Yeah, Mom. He always came to my games. He did stuff with me when other guys' dads never showed up. Yeah, he was a good father. He just got off-track somehow."

"And he couldn't make it right after a time. I sensed it, but I didn't know what was making him withdraw from me like he did. I always thought it was because of losing Desiree. I had no idea what he was keeping from me. He was so depressed." She sighed, running her fingers through her short, windblown hair. "None of it made any sense. I hope you never have to live your life with all the confusion I've had in mine."

"I know, Mom. Maybe all that's over for you," he said as a question, making her smile.

"You mean Mark? Yeah, he's a good guy, too. He's a better guy."

She finished with the coffee, wiped her hands on the sides of her slacks, and smiled. "Just so you know, your father thought you hung the moon," she said wanly.

He thought it best to keep his next comment to himself as well. *So I've heard.* "Thanks, Mom; that means a lot," he said instead, and hugged his mother.

Sunday was chilly, but bright and breezeless, so Mark had invited Kyle on a golf outing. Tyson didn't play golf to Kyle's relief. It had been years since he'd held a club, so he was apprehensive about anybody seeing his game. Mark was an affable and forgiving kind of fellow, so Kyle didn't think his lack of practice would matter all that much to him. Thankfully, Mark had brought him a pair of golf shoes from the store, and he was able to rent a set of clubs from the pro shop at the course. After a rocky start,

Kyle was able to get back into the swing of the game and made a decent showing on the back nine at least.

As they sat on the patio enjoying a beer and changing shoes, Mark looked contemplative.

"How's married life treating you?" he asked, a devilish grin beginning.

"Couldn't be better," Kyle answered, returning the smile and making Mark nod, knowingly.

"So are you getting used to being back in the mountains?" Mark asked.

Kyle shrugged. "Yeah, it's great," he said, wondering what had brought on the question.

Mark continued, "I just thought it might be hard readjusting after you'd lived in Alexandria those couple of years. That would be a pretty fun place to live, I would think."

Kyle shook his head. "I guess it would be. All I did was work."

"No diversions?"

"Not really. Sometimes I'd go out with some of the guys after work for a beer, but usually I just hit the gym or went sightseeing in D.C. when I had time."

"No dating?"

"There were a few opportunities, but I was trying to keep things going with Chelsea. It was pretty damn hard with her schedule and mine, and being so far apart."

"I can imagine that would be tough," Mark said, smiling, the thoughtful look returning to his ruddy face. "I need to ask you a couple of important questions," he said, eyes intent on Kyle under his incredibly blonde eyelashes.

"Shoot," said Kyle, taking a long pull off his beer.

"I felt that this was really important to ask your opinion about, or just to…ask for your blessing," Mark began as a slow grin started to spread across Kyle's face. "I'm getting tired of waiting too. I'd like to marry your mother; and I'd like to have your blessing," Mark said, assuredly, smiling at his young friend.

"Absolutely!" Kyle said, the grin in full force now. "This will make her so happy. And I haven't seen my mother happy in a really long time, so… absolutely. You have my blessing! Thanks for asking me."

"Oh, I wouldn't have done it any other way. You're protective of her. I think that's a fine quality in a man. I feel the same way about her. She deserves to be happy, and you're right—I hope I'm making her happy."

"She is…you are. I haven't seen her this…*relaxed* in ages. Have you guys talked about this?" Kyle asked, inclining his head a little, wondering.

"Yeah, we have. I have no doubt she'll say, 'Yes,' but like I said, I wanted to run it by you first."

"Wow! This is awesome news. Do you have any idea when this might happen?"

"Ah," he said, tapping the table and considering his answer. "Possibly in February. It should be before the summer season hits. I was thinking about Valentine's Day. It's actually on Saturday this year. But it'll be up to her. It's got to be what she wants." He shrugged; the perfect husband answer, Kyle thought.

Kyle grinned again, nodding and peeling the label from his beer bottle. "Women love that kind of stuff. That's a great idea. So, what's the other question?"

Mark looked concerned. "Well, I know your mother's traveled a lot. For the honeymoon, I wanted to take her somewhere she's never been. I want to do something big, too, really romantic. You got any ideas?"

The breeze blew suddenly. Kyle felt that eerie sensation he got sometimes when his father started crowding him. His smile built slowly. Then he shook his head, laughing out loud. "Oh, wow!" he muttered. "What would you think about a nice cruise to the Greek Islands?"

Chapter 16

....

FIVE YEARS LATER

....

The snowfall that day was magical, descending in flakes as large as goose down. It was promising to be a white Christmas, which would just about make things perfect, Chelsea thought with a contented yawn, as she sipped her coffee. She took a moment and gazed out the "Christmas card window" at the captivating flakes, letting herself drift along. Kyle had told her about it the night he had proposed to her when he'd brought her to the cabin and they'd gotten snowed in, two days before Christmas six years ago. She enjoyed the memory of him telling her that when she woke up in the morning, looking out that window would be like looking into a Christmas card; he had been right, she thought with a slow smile. Lately, there were seldom opportunities for this kind of reverie. Kyle was so good at giving her a break like this, especially on Saturdays when he was home.

The festive little tree at the window caught her eye, decorated with ornaments they had made, set protectively in an old-fashioned wooden playpen to ward off Foscoe and the others. Today would be a big day, culminating in a party at Abby and Glen's house. Still without children, the Dunhams usually offered their place as the venue for whatever loud and late activities their crowd undertook. Everyone was looking forward to the get-together. Anthony and Joelle were always part of the fun, and tonight Meredith would be in town for the holidays. Anthony had given up trying to follow her around the country as her career as a journalist kept her on the move. But it had ceased to be awkward and he had eventually married Joelle. Chelsea turned her attention from the snow to the kitchen counter. Two bottles of Davenport Winery wines were wrapped and ready for the party. She would prepare her appetizer later in the afternoon. Planning in increments was becoming her specialty these days.

The thud of footsteps on the deck called her back to the window, where she could see Kyle and the twins bundled up, filling the birdfeeders before the snow covered the ground. He caught her eye and grinned at her, winking, and pointing to her so the boys could wave. Her heart swelled just at the sight of them, the spitting images of their father at three years old, blonde hair and blue eyes with pensive little faces so full of trust and innocence. Kyle lifted Stu to pour in a scoop of the seeds while Ty held the lid, watching every move.

She'd better get a move on if they were to eat their lunch and visit Santa Claus. The boys would need their naps before spending the night with her parents, so they would be on their best form and be invited back! After stirring the soup on the stove, she darted downstairs to the laundry room, feeling her hair, almost dry from her shower.

She hummed a Christmas carol as she folded the socks, still warm from the dryer. Foscoe, their yellow lab mix, had followed her downstairs and now sat at her feet, waiting for one to drop. Socks were his favorite—the dirtier and smellier, the better. His tail twitched from east to west as he watched another tempting pair being folded into each other and rolled into a ball, finally landing soundlessly in the laundry basket. He often found a way to snag a pair, a glove, or best yet, *underwear*, as the laundry room doubled as his room. Kyle had cut a door with a high window into the back wall of the room, years ago, when they'd found him, abandoned on the side of the road in the neighboring community of Foscoe. After all their searching and advertising for his owner, he had been destined to end up with them.

"Here, buddy," she said, tossing him a plastic toy squirrel as she hoisted one of the baskets on her hip, heading for the stairs. The aromas of lunch, tomato soup, and grilled cheese sandwiches wafted down the stairs toward her. The boys were back inside where Kyle was commandeering the kitchen, having them wash their hands as he held each of them up at the kitchen sink. She was glad he enjoyed entertaining the boys while she took a shower or did a chore or two. Foscoe bounded up the stairs ahead of her, trotting around the corner and into the kitchen.

"Whose glove?" she asked warily, letting them know that Foscoe had procured one that should have been put away in the storage bench by the door.

Kyle eyed the twins suspiciously. "Stu? Ty? Whose glove does Foscoe have? Somebody forgot to put their gloves away," he said, sliding a sandwich out of the pan onto a plate.

"It's yours, Daddy," Tyson said from his perch on his booster seat beside his brother.

Kyle looked over at Foscoe, as still as a statue, pretending to be invisible, no doubt, with Kyle's glove clearly inserted between his teeth.

"Damn!" he muttered.

"Mommy says don't say, 'Damn,'" said Stu, taking a bite of his grilled cheese and fanning his mouth.

"Yeah, Daddy," Chelsea giggled, returning from the bedroom where she'd left the laundry protected by closing the door soundly. She removed the glove from Foscoe's mouth as the three-year-olds continued their discussion with Kyle that she'd heard from downstairs. This was an important day, so they were planning accordingly.

"Is Santa Claus nice?" asked Tyson, biting off the middle of his grilled cheese, the best part.

"Yeah, he's very nice. Chew with your mouth closed, please," Kyle reminded Tyson. Chelsea slipped behind him, giving him a brief hug around the waist and a kiss on the shoulder. She served the soup into four mugs, adding ice to the boys' and giving it a stir.

"Do you know what you're going to say to Santa?" she asked her twins. Their large blue eyes looked up at her, so earnestly it melted her heart for a moment. It seemed only yesterday that she'd discovered another surprise pregnancy on her part; how things always changed around here! She would need to brush their hair before they went over to the Mast General Store to visit Santa, far superior to the loud confusion at the mall's set up. That was another trait they'd inherited from their father, the eternally messy blonde hair. It would probably darken over the years as his had, but his penchant for being outside had kept streaks of gold in it most of the year.

"Clammaw said we 'pose to tell him what we want for Christmas," said Stu. Kyle shrugged defensively, knowing Shelly had coached them over the phone for their first visit to Santa Claus. The way the twins had tried to pronounce "Grandma" had sounded more like "Clammaw," which Mark thought wildly entertaining, especially since Shelly absolutely did not want to be called *Grandma*. Since they lived at the beach, he thought it would be appropriate to be known as "Clammaw and Clampaw." He had even painted it on a sign for their mailbox at their new house in Duck.

"Well, yes. He'll ask if you've been good, and what you do to help around the house, things like that," Chelsea said, winking at Kyle.

"What do we do?" Tyson asked, puzzled.

"Tell him you pick up your toys and your clothes…usually," said Kyle. "And you can tell him you eat your vegetables."

"Sometimes," Chelsea added. "You can say that you go to bed when you're supposed to."

"Sometimes," laughed Kyle. "And that you're always nice to Foscoe," he said, taking a sip of his soup straight from the cup. He glanced at Chelsea, as if this were a good time for bringing up what they'd discussed last night. "You can ask Santa for three things," he said.

"Free?" asked Stu.

"Yep, three," Kyle said, nodding and holding up three fingers.

Stu looked at Tyson, then back at Kyle. "Only free?"

"Free's a lot," said Tyson, raising his eyebrows and giving Stu that wise look that always made Chelsea laugh. Stu did not look convinced, glancing questioningly at his parents, so jaded at such a young age.

Kyle explained. "Santa has a lot of children to see, so we can't waste his time being greedy."

Chelsea smiled into her own mug of soup, knowing he would always fight his father's ghostly mistakes, whether knowingly or not, greed being one of them, but she had never called him on it. It seemed he would spend his life working it all out with his dad.

"Besides," Kyle continued, "Jesus got three gifts at Christmas and that was all he needed."

Both boys pondered this seriously, regarding each other as if the gauntlet had been thrown.

"Then I want a train...and Spiderman, and a fishing rod!" said Stu.

Tyson was quiet, still thinking. Finally he looked at Chelsea, saying softly, "What do you want, Mommy?"

She closed her eyes for a moment, burning tears forming at the backs of her eyelids. They were all looking at her for her response. Ty's question reminded her of a sermon she'd heard in church after Christmas one year, about the wise men's search for Jesus, and finding him much later and not at all where they expected him to be. *One never knew where one would find God*, the priest had said. But she knew now. It was all here, God, Kyle, and her family; her trinity, all she had ever wanted.

"I have my three gifts, right here," she said quietly, and Kyle winked at her, rubbing her shoulder, then took his dishes to the sink, running a little water over them before placing them in the dishwasher. She was so emotional at Christmastime, he thought, smiling to himself, remembering the first Christmas back in high school when she'd cried in the barn upon hearing "Away in a Manger" during the annual celebration they had at her father's tree lot. Kyle had been so crazy about her then, but she had never seemed to get it, always thinking she would somehow lose him to another girl, as if that would have ever happened. Other times, she became emotional like this when she was pregnant. Suddenly, he felt his stomach lurch and he glanced at her apprehensively. Surely, she wasn't pregnant again! They'd always been careful, but somehow they had messed up twice—the second time around being a double whammy for their whole family with the birth of the twins. No one on either side of the family had managed to produce twins. But they had been the chosen ones, her mother had said, so they'd had to step out of the way and let things happen as they would. "Being the clay," as Liz said, was interesting business!

It was fortunate for his growing family that he and Frank had enjoyed so much business over the years. Frank had allowed him to buy into the business as a full partner after the restoration on the inn in Blowing Rock, the Sugar Ridge project, and a house Lynn Schiffman's friend had sent their way. His work with Tom and Jay on the French-inspired Davenport Winery had been the crowning project that had sealed Frank's opinion of him as an architect, so he had finally come on board as an official partner. The boys' birth had rocked their world for a year or more, but Chelsea was eventually able to go back to work at the university, where she could take Stu and Ty for childcare while she taught. It wasn't easy but they made it work. Life could be a blur if they'd allow it, so they made a concerted effort to enjoy it as much as possible, living in the moment whenever they could.

She poured trail mix into a container for later in case the boys got hungry on their outing, while Kyle repacked the little guys into their jackets, hats, and boots, as Foscoe sniffed each one of them curiously. "You have to stay here, buddy," he said, stroking the dog's head, coaxing him down the stairs to his laundry room. "We'll be back soon, and then you and I can run around in the snow." He produced a treat from his pocket, seeming to satisfy his friend for the moment.

Just before they walked out the door, Chelsea was detaching her cell phone from the charger when it rang in her hand. The caller ID displayed Abby Dunham's name. She must need more wine for tonight, Chelsea thought with a smile. The Davenport Red was everyone's favorite, especially at Christmas. "Yes, ma'am, let me guess; you'll be needing more wine for this evening?" she laughed into her phone.

Abby's bubbly voice laughed back. "Nope, I won't be drinking a drop tonight! I have the most *wonderful news!*"

Chelsea sank down into the nearest chair, running her other hand through her hair, and catching Kyle's eye. He looked at her inquisitively. A large smile took over Chelsea's face as she regarded her husband, confirming the news with her happy face. "Oh, Abby! You're pregnant! I'm so thrilled for you! Merry Christmas!"

"Thanks, lovey. I feel the same way you did, Chels. It's a gift."

"Yes, it is, Abby. It absolutely *is!*"

The End

BE SURE TO READ ALL OF MARY FLINN'S NOVELS

THE ONE (2010)

Is following your heart worth having it broken?

The first in the trilogy, and set in the mountains and the Outer Banks of North Carolina, *The One* is a tale of first love. Seventeen year old Chelsea Davenport is looking forward to a normal senior year, returning to ballet and fun—without the boys. Chelsea is sick of boys. Then Kyle Davis shows up at her sister's engagement party and turns her world upside down. Football player Kyle and Chelsea go way back as family friends but Kyle has been away at prep school following the tragic death of his sister and more recently the suicide of his father. Kyle is a much-changed young man now, no longer arrogant, but adrift in a sea of anger and depression, making Chelsea want to help, opening up his soul once again. They quickly become a couple but Chelsea isn't the only girl who wants Kyle. Local mean-girl, Elle McClarin will do whatever is necessary to win Kyle for herself. So, who will win his heart? Is the heartache over for Kyle or just beginning? Must Chelsea sell herself short to have what she wants? Is Kyle worth loving? *The One* is a poignant story about family, loss, self-discovery, and coming of age.

SECOND TIME'S A CHARM (2011)

Forgiveness is easy. Trust is harder.

Stacie Edmonds, fiercely independent and too much fun for her own good, is about to turn forty, although she looks twenty-five. The Sound Side, her marina-turned restaurant, a diamond in the rough on the backside of the island known as Kill Devil Hills, has been her place for three years. Ever since Rick, Stacie's ex-husband, had driven them apart by his errant lifestyle, culminating in an affair, Stacie has been making it the kind of place where everyone wants to be in the summer on the Outer Banks of North Carolina. While Stacie has been focusing on running her restaurant, Tyson Garrett, her chef and ten years her junior, has been focusing on her, biding his time until the right moment to make his move. One problem looms large: Tyson wants a family and Stacie is unsure whether she can bear the child they both want. Is it fair to let him love her? Can she trust again?

Second Time's a Charm is a story of rediscovering love and trust, of mastering destiny, of taking second chances, of forgiveness and redemption. Stacie and Tyson's story is hardly a new twist on an old problem, but readers may empathize with them as they encounter the realistic struggles of dealing with disillusionment, waning hope, and floundering in the doldrums of life without purpose or joy. While a stand-alone novel, *Second Time's a Charm* also reintroduces Kyle, Stacie's nephew, and his girlfriend Chelsea and other familiar characters from Mary Flinn's previous novel, *The One*. Readers of *The One* will be thrilled to learn more about Stacie and Tyson, while new readers will discover new friends in these pages.

Second Time's a Charm is best read in the shade on a warm beach with a chilled beverage at hand, if one is so lucky, but if necessary, a couch indoors on a rainy day will certainly suffice!

Coming in 2012...

THE PRODIGAL'S PAGES

Chapter One: Cat

We were the invisible girls, Laney and I. Friends since we were in diapers, when our mothers met in the park down the street, pushing us in the swings. We were the B average students—our parents said what was special about us couldn't be put on paper. At least, that's the way my mom always made me feel. Laney's dad, J.J., had spent his life trying to make her feel special. We were the good girls; didn't drink, do drugs, or get in trouble. Maybe we were not the prettiest girls in school, but we were cute enough to have a date sometimes for whatever dance came up. Besides that, we were spinsters in training. Seventeen and never been kissed, if you didn't count my moment with Art Caviness behind the garage when we were five. My family was known as The Tall Family. Mom thought boys were afraid of me because of my height, so I slumped as much as possible, which she didn't like. I was too tall and Laney was too short, so people were always calling us Mutt and Jeff. I knew I was Mutt. We were the invisible girls, until Laney got a brain tumor.

www.TheOneNovel.com